MEN
MURDER

An absolutely gripping cozy mystery novel

JEAN G. GOODHIND

A Honey Driver Murder Mystery Book 2

Originally published as
A Taste to Die For

JOFFE BOOKS

Revised edition 2022
Joffe Books, London
www.joffebooks.com

First world edition published by Severn House
Publishers Ltd in Great Britain and the USA
as *A Taste to Die For* in 2007

Cover art by Dee Dee Book Covers

ISBN: 978-1-80405-242-6

CHAPTER ONE

A cooking competition between top chefs was bound to be murder. Honey Driver was sure of it.

The event was part of the Bath International Taste Extravaganza — BITE for short. Following a process of elimination, the six finalists were coming together in one place to compete for a £5,000 prize. The money was just reward, but chefs are like stags during mating season. But then, stags don't have knives.

The day had started in the quirky kind of way that days in the hospitality industry sometimes did.

Despite the hammering of the chambermaid on the bedroom door, the occupant of room twenty had failed to rise and shine, appear at breakfast or pay his bill.

'Perhaps he's dead,' said Honey's daughter, Lindsey.

Honey was pragmatic. 'No worries, as long as it's not food poisoning. It's bad for business.'

She punched in the night porter's number on her instant dial facility. He answered groggily, not surprising for a man who hadn't long clambered into bed.

'Reg, did you see Mr Slade in number twenty come in late last night?'

'Yes. Him and his wife came back at about one in the morning.'

'I guessed that.' Honey snapped the phone shut. 'Give me your keys,' she said to the housekeeper.

'Did he come in late?' asked Lindsey, matching her mother's marching pace up the stairs and along the landing.

'Yes. With his wife.'

Lindsey giggled. The housekeeper looked puzzled until the penny dropped. Mr Slade, a sales manager for an IT software company, had booked into a single room. He had not brought his wife.

'What's the betting he's severely indisposed,' remarked Lindsey.

Her mother smiled wryly. 'Where did I get such a worldly-wise child?'

Lindsey, just a shade closer to nineteen than eighteen, grinned wryly back. 'Under the gooseberry bush?'

'Poor Mr Slade. If my instinct serves me correctly, we'll have to do a check of the left luggage in the storeroom and find him something to wear,' said Honey as she opened the door.

Just as expected, the overnight occupant of room twenty was laid out on the bed stark naked. He was also bound and gagged and wearing a leather harness with little bells that jingled between his legs.

Following a swift assessment of the circumstances — what was in the room and what was not — she turned to Lindsey. 'How's the petty cash?' The sales manager's clothes were gone. So were his briefcase and whatever else he was carrying. The high-class tart he'd picked up had pickled him right and proper.

'I refreshed it yesterday afternoon. I've only bought postage stamps and a bunch of wildflowers for Mary Jane.'

Her mother raised her eyebrows questioningly.

'Sir Cedric likes wildflowers. The scent helps him to materialise.'

Mary Jane was their resident professor of parapsychology, having retired to the hotel from her little house straddling the

San Andreas fault in La Jolla, California. Sir Cedric was one of Mary Jane's antecedents and the hotel's resident ghost.

The maid threw a crumpled towel over the poor man's credentials.

Honey checked the state of his bill from the dossier Lindsey had brought with her before peering down at the bondage addict.

'We've got your name and address, Mr Slade, and we've taken an imprint of your credit card. We'll give you enough petty cash to get home and we'll find you some clothes.'

He looked up at her bug eyed.

'Do you understand?' she asked.

He nodded and mumbled.

'That's good. So, you won't be offended when we charge you the price of a double room instead of a single.'

More mumbling came from behind his gag, accompanied by a frenzied jerking of his bound hands. In consequence the towel covering his meat and two veg slipped.

Honey readjusted it. 'Not this early in the morning, please.' She glanced at her watch. 'Things to do, places to go and an impatient chef waiting. Lindsey will take care of you.'

Lindsey pulled a face. 'Thanks a bundle.'

Honey checked the storeroom halfway along the landing, a place of forgotten candlewick dressing gowns and left-behind toys and garments. Unfortunately for Mr Slade, most of the adult garments were women's clothes except for a few old chefs outfits of varying sizes. The choice was obvious: pink candlewick dressing gown or chef's white jacket, blue-checked trousers and tired white clogs.

She lay the chef's outfit outside the door. Lindsey would deal with the rest.

Smudger Smith, her head chef, was waiting for her at the bottom of the stairs, hopping impatiently from one foot to the other. She explained what had happened. He was less than sympathetic.

'Silly sod! Can we get going? The kitchen's taken care of . . .'

He listed all that had been done to ensure a smoothly running kitchen in his absence. Not that it could run as well as when he was there. No chef would countenance otherwise. Like a lord of the manor, they ruled over all they surveyed. It was the cooking that counted — always the cooking.

The final cook-off was being held at an afternoon 'do' in the Pump Rooms, that epitome of Regency elegance. Everything they needed had been transported in the hotel van and installed in fridges adjacent to the competition area. Things were buzzing by the time they got there. The atmosphere was electric.

Stainless-steel worktables had been set up on either side of the room for the six chefs that had reached the finals. Those already there looked daggers at Smudger, eyeing the new arrival with barely veiled hostility.

Honey's ample chest expanded further with pride that her own chef—Mark 'Smudger' Smith, bless his cotton socks — was one of them. And he was keen. Keen as mustard. Especially when he'd heard there'd been a change of judges.

He'd arrived at the hotel early that morning. By the time everyone else was up and about he was already whizzing around the kitchen like lightening, gathering pots, pans and ingredients. He whipped one straight out of the kitchen porter's hand, hot and straight from the dishwasher.

'Have you heard the news?' His voice, his demeanour — everything crackled with excitement.

Honey had made a wild stab at an answer. 'All the other chefs have withdrawn because they heard you were entering.'

He grinned at Honey, his eyes shining. 'That's possible. OK, so what's the second-best thing?'

'You've bribed the judges.'

'Getting warm.' He'd paused, enjoying the moment of keeping her in suspense. 'Neville phoned while you were upstairs. Casper has been asked to step in as chair of the judges. Now, there's a man who knows a classic when he tastes it.'

Her dear, slightly volatile — well, very volatile — chef wasn't far wrong. When it came to fastidious taste, Casper

St John Gervais came top of the tree. He adored quality, and no amount of money or persuasion was likely to colour his judgement.

However, it wasn't likely to be *that* easy. 'You're up against stiff competition.'

Smudger Smith jerked his head in a *so-so* fashion. 'At least there's a chance the judging will be fair.' For no apparent reason, his expression suddenly darkened. 'As long as everyone plays fair,' he added.

That was the point when she began to get *really* apprehensive.

Her misgivings were swiftly justified the moment she saw Smudger's reaction to Oliver Stafford, head chef at the Beau Brummell Hotel. There were some people Smudger liked, some he tolerated and some he hated on sight. Most chefs and catering suppliers fitted into the second bracket; Oliver Stafford fitted into the third.

She might have been able to keep the lid on things if it hadn't been for the chicken breasts.

'Someone's been in my fridge,' said Smudger, his evil look swivelling in Oliver Stafford's direction. 'These aren't my breasts. See? They're not properly defrosted. Mine were totally defrosted. And anyway, I looked in his fridge. He had boxed stuff. Already ground-up chicken. No need to pinch mine!'

Honey grabbed his arm before he had chance to swing around and get himself in position to slug Stafford on the chin.

'Don't! Do you want to be disqualified or do you want to win?' Swallowing her misgivings, she kept her voice even and appealed with her eyes.

She felt his arm relax. The anger remained, boiling in the pinkness of his face. He began cracking eggs.

'I could kill 'im,' he said, clutching his egg whisk with a murderous look in his eyes.

'With an egg whisk?' The mind boggled.

'There are ways,' he muttered, his eyes narrowing to needle-fine slits.

Unfortunately, the object of his criminal intent was working alongside them at the next table.

'The dish, Smudger. Concentrate on the dish.'

'He pinched my breasts.'

Honey blushed, but luckily no one else heard.

'He just took yours by mistake.'

Smudger scowled. 'I don't believe that.'

'Lucky we brought some spare,' she said gaily in an effort to jolly him along.

The sound of meat being minced came from Oliver Stafford's station. Smudger glared. Oliver smirked. He also had the effrontery to wink at Honey. She had no problem with that. She liked having youngish men wink at her. Cheeky. Sweet really. But the look in his eyes was bolder. My, but he was sexy. And knew it! That much was obvious.

A bell sounded.

'Let the contest commence,' proclaimed the master of ceremonies, a professional man of ample proportion, his face as red as his jacket.

The judges swept forward. There were four of them: a food writer, a television chef, an official from the tourist board and Casper, chair of the Bath Hotels Association.

Resplendent in a lavender jacket and crisp white cravat, Casper St John Gervais was the most recognisable judge the contest had ever had. He looked absolutely wonderful. But that was Casper — always rising far above the occasion. He slid past Honey smelling of lavender, and she wondered if his aftershave had been chosen to match his jacket.

'*Wonderful* attendance,' he murmured with a sideways shift of his mouth. 'People from all over the world.'

'They must have heard you'd be here.'

'Sweet,' he said, and glided on.

Judging that the worst part of the crisis was over and Smudger was as self-controlled as he was capable of being, she joined the gathering who'd come to watch. En route she bumped into Stella Broadbent, owner of the Beau Brummell Hotel. Oliver Stafford was her head chef.

When they spotted each other, the smiles froze on each of their faces.

'Hannah!'

She spoke Honey's real name sharply and quickly as though she wanted it out of the way.

Honey reciprocated. 'Stella!'

Friends would have air kissed. They didn't. Instead, their teeth remained bared like vampires competing to take the first bite.

As usual Stella Broadbent was wearing enough gold jewellery to sink the *Titanic*. It gleamed, dazzled and was over the top for the outfit she was wearing. The gold was the reason for her nickname 'Bling'.

Stella's smile was red and hard. 'Everything going well with your chef?'

You mean you hope he drops dead.

Honey's sweet smile camouflaged the sour thought. 'There was a mix-up with the chicken breasts. I think your chef picked ours up by mistake.'

The wide mouth stalled into a rictus smile. 'If he did, I'm sure it was a genuine mistake. But I doubt it. We only use the highest-quality ingredients.'

'Frozen ingredients?'

Stella was one of the early birds who'd already navigated their way to the drinks table. Judging by the colour of her cheeks, she'd found it long before anyone else. Rumour had it that Mr Broadbent had been much older than her. On his death he'd left her a small fortune. Rumour also had it that she'd been celebrating ever since.

'Such accusations! I assume this means you're going to be a bad loser!' Her manner was haughty, her tone belligerent.

'I'll send you the bill.'

Stella burst out laughing. 'You'll . . . do . . . what?'

Honey waited for her to stop laughing. 'Unless you can't afford to pay for a few measly chicken breasts?'

Stella's mouth froze open. The liquid in her wine glass slopped from side to side.

Honey turned her back abruptly. 'I'll send it to you.'

She could do with a drink herself after that. She was no coward, but Stella made her toes curl. There was something about that yellow-and-black outfit with the seventies shoulder pads that made her want to whack her with a fly swat. And all that bloody gold — courtesy of her dead husband, presumably.

What was even worse, the Beau Brummell was one of the few privately owned hotels in Bath with its own car park. Nothing could diminish the beauty of the compactly designed city that had its finest flowering in the days of sedan chairs and carriages pulled by matching bays. But this was the age of convenience travellers. Despite all the council's efforts to promote public transport, people did not easily give up their cars. To be able to park them and wander off into the city centre was a rarity in Bath. Honey told herself she wasn't jealous but seethed all the way to the drinks table.

Liquid refreshments to suit most tastes were on offer. Those in the audience of a health-conscious nature could sip the iron-rich water distilled from a Georgian fountain. The Celts had worshipped the hot spring, the Romans had splashed about in it naked, the Georgians had 'taken the waters' fully clothed and modern-day tourists drank little glasses of it. Some swore by its health-giving properties. Some of those gathered just spat it out and sought more palatable alternatives.

Wine could be purchased by the glass or the bottle. The bottles went very quickly. Honey restricted herself to one glass. This was going to be a long day. Tonight, stalls would be set out all around Abbey Square, where the public would be invited to sample food cooked by chefs from the city's top-class hotels. The money collected would go to charity.

Honey had promised herself that she'd keep a clear head. If Smudger won this competition he'd want to get drunk, and if he lost he'd want to get really drunk. She was there to channel his energies to the outdoor event, impressing upon him that it was the good causes that would win the day — regardless of who won the competition. Either way he'd be unbearable to live with. With that thought uppermost in her mind, she reached for a second glass, had second thoughts and resolved to remain sober.

Just as the final judging was about to commence, her phone rang. It was her mother.

'Has he won?'

'They're just doing the final judging now.'

'Have you told Casper he should win?' Honey closed her eyes and counted to ten. Her mother had no scruples when it came to success, a reason why she'd accumulated only rich husbands.

'Of course not.'

'You should. Tell him you won't do that police liaison thingy anymore if he doesn't give him top marks.'

'Bye, Mother.'

She ended the call. Her mother believed you could achieve anything if you bullied hard enough. She was like a good dog you couldn't put down. Well, not without feeling guilty about it.

Casper St John Gervais was hobnobbing with the other judges. Heads together, pens poised over clipboards, they muttered to each other, eyes sliding sidelong, rechecking their notes, everything and anything to make it look as though they really knew what they were doing. This competition was a shop window for the high-class cuisine on offer. Bath depended heavily on foreign tourists visiting the Roman Baths, the Georgian Pump Rooms and the elegant crescents and squares. Businesses, especially those in the hospitality trade, knew the power of bad press on visitor numbers.

If a show had to be put on, Casper was the one to do it. It was Casper who instigated the police 'thingy' her mother referred to, which had turned out to be more than just liaison. She'd actually got involved in a criminal case and been instrumental in solving it. Most of the liaising happened between her and Detective Inspector Steve Doherty, and it wasn't entirely professional. There was something potentially explosive between them. It was just a matter of time before they lit the fuse.

Running a hotel was not the glamorous job it was cracked up to be, all grateful clients with huge tips, celebrity guests and champagne parties. *Routine* was the best way to describe it. Order meat on a Monday, vegetables on a Tuesday, see the wine rep on a Wednesday, and in between lay tables, fold napkins and deal with guests who'd sampled too much Highland malt.

She'd been hankering after a secondary career for a while, and her duties as crime liaison officer helped alleviate her humdrum existence. So did Steve Doherty.

The three judges stopped at each table, tasted, tittered among themselves and nodded like donkeys dining from the same manger. Coming to an agreement, they then jotted their deliberations onto their clipboards.

Not once did their gaze drift from the food, their clipboards or each other to the chefs. All the dishes were based on chicken; the rest of the ingredients were up to each individual chef. All that mattered to the judges was taste and presentation. Eyes, nose and mouth; sight, smell and taste. The judges nibbled, deliberated, poked and prodded the meat, dismembered the display, and sipped at the sauces using nothing bigger than a teaspoon.

At last the decision was made. Filing one after the other through the crowd of hotel owners, freelance food journalists and hungry hordes from the outside world, they made their way to a raised platform. On normal weekdays this was where a string trio played Handel for the benefit of cream bun diners. Today there was not a cream bun in sight — perish the thought.

Honey said a silent prayer and crossed her fingers. She glanced over to a smirking Stella Broadbent and crossed her legs. Something bad was about to happen. She could feel it in the pit of her stomach.

Casper was spokesperson. Craning his long neck to reach the microphone, he bore a striking resemblance to a giraffe about to devour a large, black plum.

'Ladies and gentlemen.'

His voice was crystal clear, ringing to the rococo ceiling, ricocheting off the high arched windows. His piercing eyes swept the gathering to attention.

'The best chefs in Bath were given the task of producing a dish using chicken as its main component. They were allowed to choose the rest of the ingredients themselves . . .'

Honey looked at Smudger. His eyes were fixed on Casper, almost daring him not to pick him. Usually his complexion was pale pink; it was presently paler than refined white flour.

Setting down her wineglass, Honey stuffed her fingers in her ears and closed her eyes. What would it be? Celebration or commiseration?

Applause filtered through her fingers. She opened her eyes to see the top of a white toque bobbing up to the platform. Her heart sank.

Not Smudger. Smudger was about five-feet-ten. If he'd won she would have instantly recognised his blushing complexion and corn-coloured hair.

A beaming Oliver Stafford, five-foot-seven, possibly eight in his white kitchen clogs, stepped up onto the stage, accepted his prize and blew kisses at the audience.

'The best man won!' he shouted.

Applause erupted. Oliver Stafford played to the crowd, shaking men's hands, kissing those of women he didn't know, the cheeks of those he did. His eyes seemed to be everywhere. They settled on her. Again, that wink, the obvious appraisal and the salacious smile. The meaning was obvious. *I'm game if you are . . .*

Honey looked away to where Smudger was standing, clapping disconsolately, a blue, second-prize rosette pinned to his chest. If looks could kill, Oliver Stafford would have been stewed steak.

There was no time to lose.

Turning her back on events, she pushed her way through the crowd. 'Congratulations. You did very well.'

God, that sounds lame! She rethought her strategy. 'I think you're due a bonus.'

Smudger's scowl returned with a vengeance. 'I think that bugger's due a kick in the—'

'Quick,' she said, as though she hadn't heard. 'We've got to get to Abbey Green and get the best spot.'

'Clint said he'd do that.'

His voice lacked interest. His eyes were still fixed on Oliver.

Clint, real name Rodney Eastwood, their casual dishwasher, odd-jobber and general kitchen help, had indeed promised to grab a pitch and start setting things up. Smudger needed to occupy himself with something other than stamping on Oliver Stafford's head.

'But you need to be there to oversee things.' A lamer excuse.

Smudger didn't budge.

Honey followed his gaze. A beaming Oliver Stafford was posing for photos, holding his silver cup above his head while wedged between two scantily clad blondes.

'Come on. No time to lose.'

Honey began packing things up, knives first. They were the most dangerous. A vision of Smudger and the egg whisk flashed into her mind. She found room for that in with the knives.

'Over here, over here.'

Oliver, the blondes and a bevy of photographers and other interested parties barged over to the row of steel tables.

'Behind the table please, Chef,' ordered one of the photographers.

Before taking up position, Oliver kissed one blonde then the other and gave each a quick squeeze. 'Won't be long, darlings. Keep it all hot for me, won't you?'

Honey tried to grab Smudger's arm. Too late. Smudger had hold of Stafford by the ears.

'Let go of me!'

Some of the photographers carried on clicking.

Casper pushed through the crowd. 'Please control your chef, madam! How dare he grasp that man's extremities!'

'Smudger, let go of his ears!'

Smudger growled. 'He should thank his lucky stars it's only his ears!'

There was uproar all round and through it all the paparazzi kept snapping. Muttering various reasons why he shouldn't disconnect Stafford's ears from his head, Honey tugged at Smudger's arm. Angry eyes glared above strawberry-pink cheeks — though they weren't nearly as red as the other chef's ears. There were only inches between their faces.

'I know what you did, Stafford, and I'll get you for it. You hear me? I'll get you for it.'

Finally, he let go.

'He's bloody mad,' said Stafford, vigorously rubbing at his bright-red ears. 'You're mad, Smith. Right bloody mad!'

Up until Stafford had opened his cakehole, Smudger had been responding to her urgings to get out.

Now he lunged again, fists ready to deal damage to the other chef's face.

Honey flung herself forward in a rugby tackle, hanging onto his waist, her cheek resting against his buttocks. She lost her shoes, and her legs splayed out. Graceful it was not, though she must have shown some skill, judging by the applause from the crowd. Her love of banoffee pie had a lot to do with her carrying enough weight to pull it off. Legs dragging behind her, she clung on for all she was worth.

'Come on, Smudge,' she muttered against a mouthful of his starched cotton jacket.

He looked down over his shoulder at her and frowned. 'Blimey, it's like being hugged by a sack of potatoes.'

'Charmed, I'm sure.'

She daren't let go, while Smudger's eyes still followed Oliver Stafford, whose overinflated ego was being smoothed down by his boss. 'Bling' Broadbent's peachy complexion glowed with inner light as she tossed a contemptuous sneer in Honey's direction.

'My, my. Taking defeat lying down and with your legs open. Well, that's par for the course, from what I hear.'

Honey struggled to her feet. Now it was her turn to lunge . . .

'You bitch!'

. . . And Smudger's turn to hold *her* back.

Stafford made a flamboyant gesture of dismissal. 'Bad chefs make bad losers!'

Honey felt her skin tightening. She looked hastily around her. She'd put the knives away, but what about the steak mallet? A whack in the middle of the forehead and *hey presto* — no more pesto from that chef!

Smudger was frighteningly calm, the kind of silent calmness that happens before a storm. She had to get him outside before the storm broke and he flattened Stafford's nose. She grabbed his arm. 'Come on, Smudge. Let's get going.'

She tried pushing him. He was like a rock, totally immovable. He pointed an accusing finger at the other chef. His voice was steady. 'That prize was mine. You robbed me, Stafford. I bloody well know you did. But I'll get you; mark my words if I don't!'

CHAPTER TWO

Emma Pearce stifled a yawn. She'd been on reception duty at the Beau Brummell since three that afternoon. It was now close to eleven, but tonight she'd had to stay.

Oliver Stafford, the hotel's head chef, had emerged victorious over a number of other excellent chefs in today's competition and celebrations were still going on.

The sound of laughter, popping champagne corks and the reassuring clink of toast after toast filtered from the lounge bar. If past performance was anything to go by, they'd still be at it in the early hours.

Sighing and stifling another yawn, she eased her right foot out of her sensible shoe and rubbed it against her ankle. Her feet were killing her. The night porter was late but would be here soon. She couldn't wait. There was no point in asking Mrs Broadbent if someone could stand in for her. Mrs Broadbent expected her staff to stay until relieved — like tired, loyal troops holding an important bridgehead.

A blast of air came in as the main reception doors swished open.

Emma prepared to plaster on a smile before raising her head and welcoming the late returning guest. Instead her jaw dropped.

'Good evening, miss. I have come to see my wife. We got married back in Texas when she came over on vacation. Invited me to come over and run this hotel — as a partner — in bed and out.' Adopting a wide grin, he tilted back his head and looked around. 'Old place, huh?'

Emma tried to retrieve her jaw. She couldn't possibly say a single word until she did. Was she dreaming? She blinked hoping that if she was she'd wake up at home in bed and quickly fall asleep again.

He was at least six-foot tall, lantern-jawed and was wearing a Stetson, stone-washed jeans and cowboy boots — complete with a pair of jingling spurs.

Suddenly it came to her. 'Oh. You're a strippergram! Sorry, I wasn't expecting . . .'

'No, honey, you've got it wrong I'm the real thing.'

He shook a leg. 'Do you hear my spurs?"

Emma's eyes widened 'I . . .'

Her tongue stuck to the roof of her mouth.

'So where is she?' asked the man. 'It's been a while but I got here as quick as a rattler in a cornfield. So where's Stella?'

Emma swallowed. 'Can I take your name?'

'My name. Tell her Chuck is here. Chuck Rogers.'

A sudden explosion of laughter came from the bar. The tall, muscular lamp post of a man turned his head in that direction. 'Hold telling her I'm here. I'll tell her myself.'

Emma nodded, her throat too constricted by surprise to say anything. If this was a wind-up, it was a good one. She giggled. Mrs Broadbent was not the best boss she'd ever had. Fuelled with half a dozen pink gins, she could be downright nasty or totally oblivious to what she was doing. The possibility that she'd got so tanked up that she'd married a cowboy would certainly put a dent in her pride.

He strode across to the wide double doors leading into the bar. At the same time a Japanese couple came through the front door. They'd been chattering away about the play they'd just seen at the Theatre Royal. Their chattering and their progress to the reception desk came to an abrupt end. They stared then grinned. 'Hi, cowboy!'

Ignoring them, she half skipped, half ran to keep up with him.

'Howdy, all,' he cried out as he entered the bar. All sound ceased — except for the crash of the odd wine glass hitting the ground.

All eyes turned in his direction.

Stella Broadbent took another swift gulp before focusing her attention. At first she looked puzzled, and then she began to laugh. 'OK, who booked the stripper? Come on. Was it you, Oliver?'

Though a smile played around his lips, Oliver Stafford's eyes narrowed. He wasn't one for making snap appraisals. 'Not me,' he said and took the cork out of another bottle.

With a swagger and a tipping of his hat, the cowboy strode up to Stella.

'My,' she said, looking him up and down and playfully stroking his arm. 'You're a big boy, cowboy, and those muscles are certainly in the right place.'

Titters of amusement ran through the onlookers.

'Hey, Stella. Ain't you going to give your old man a big hug?'

He held his arms wide and addressed the onlookers. 'We met back in Texas. It was one helluva night. Woke up in bed together the next day and I offered to make an honest woman of her. We married at a very pretty watering hole. Ain't that right, Stella? We did tank it up a bit. Had to get married after all that. I told you I'd follow you over and here I am. Pretty hotel,' he said looking round. 'I'm looking forward to taking charge here.'

There was still some laughter, but not everyone. Stella was livid.

'I've had enough of this! You've been put up to this by the same person who daubed graffiti on the front wall and damaged our guests' cars. Who put you up to it? Go on! Tell me!'

The man named Chuck Rogers looked hurt. He shook his head dolefully. 'Come on, Stella. We did agree to divide all our worldly goods between us. I got a few head of cattle and you got a hotel.'

The tittering of amusement dissolved into disbelief. Was this entertainment or was this man for real? The latter view seemed to be gaining ground.

Stella Broadbent seemed to grow small — all head and high-heeled shoes, face puce and eyes saucers. She inflated briefly and then exploded.

'Get out! Get out! Get out!'

There was pandemonium. People shouting, laughing — some shouting for the police to be called, others laughing and ordering more drinks.

A burly security guard came rushing in.

'That man,' Stella shouted, by now surrounded by friends and guests. 'Get him out!'

Shouted at and jostled from all sides, the security guard lost his cap. In his quest to retrieve it from the floor before it was squashed, his hand was trodden on. By the time he was upright, the cowboy he'd been called to throw out was gone.

* * *

'This way.' Unsure of why she felt so responsible for the tall man, Emma rushed him outside.

The sound of a police siren panicked them both.

She shoved him into a rusty old Toyota parked near the entrance. 'This is my car. Stay there till it's over.'

Snuggled down out of sight on the back seat, the man who'd introduced himself as Chuck Rogers fell asleep, satisfied with a job well done.

He didn't know what time it was when he awoke, only that his limbs were stiff from being folded up like a seaside deckchair.

Stretching his long legs through the open door, he peered cautiously around him. Nothing. Few lights were burning in the hotel.

Everything was in order, he decided, as he rubbed his aching back, except . . .

His right hand was empty.

'Shit! Where's my hat?'

Movingly slowly towards the entrance of the hotel, he peered through the doors. Seeing no one at reception, he cautiously crept inside.

The smell of cooking had permeated the very fabric of the building. He wrinkled his nose. Hopefully this passageway led into the main building. Whatever, he had to find his hat. It had his name inside. His real name.

On his way down the hall, he heard voices coming from the kitchen. He pressed his ear against the door. Someone was arguing — a man and a woman.

He backed out. They might hear him. He turned and saw the security guard sitting at reception. *Damn! He wasn't there a second ago!* He moved quickly further down the passageway and found a back door. Outside he skirted the building, avoiding the front doors. On his way he saw his hat lying on the ground and picked it up. Time to go.

* * *

Stella was being a cow, but Oliver was used to it. He knew she wouldn't take the news well, but didn't care.

'After all I've done for you,' she screamed, her eyes blazing.

Before she knew it, her chin was being clutched by his fingers.

'Whatever's been done I've done for myself. You were just a stepping stone. That's all.'

'All that money . . .' she began.

There was still some fire in her along with the pink gins.

She winced when he pinched her more tightly.

His eyes blazed. '*I* saw the opportunity. *I* made you the money. I deserve a better reward.'

She looked uncomfortable, and her lips were squeezed out of shape. 'But what about me?'

Oliver Stafford had two sorts of smiles — one sort could make a woman go weak at the knees, the other could strike a chill in the bravest of hearts.

'You've had me, darling. Isn't that enough? Now it's off to pastures new. Fallow pastures, you could say.' He had a new girlfriend, something fresher and younger than Stella. She'd been his meal ticket to more money, influential people and a better life.

'I made you what you are. I made you wealthy with my connections,' she shouted.

He eyed her sidelong, like he had when first seducing her. 'Yes, you introduced me. But I have their ears now and under my terms. I'm calling the shots. You're just their lackey.'

She stared, eyes blazing. 'You'll be sorry. You mark my words.'

'And you keep your mouth shut,' he said, pointing an accusing finger. He saw the blood drain from her face and knew that just for a while she would keep her mouth shut. The trouble was that once the booze was in her, she couldn't control her tongue. It would get her into trouble. What he was up to could do the same. *But I'm cleverer than her,* he told himself. *I know how to handle them.*

'Anyway,' he said with a grin. 'You married a cowboy.'

The door slammed so hard a saucepan fell off the wall.

He drank a toast to her after she'd gone. Today had been such a good day. He also drank a toast to Mark Smith, head chef at the Green River Hotel.

'And to his butcher,' he added. 'Nice bit of chicken, that.'

Draining the glass, he threw it into the sink, where it smashed to pieces. That was when he noticed a pan left in to soak. A Kitchen Devil, a sharp knife used for all manner of tasks, was left in it.

Oliver scowled. All chefs are trained to put things away — especially knives. And in his kitchen, you did what you were trained to do. His expression darkened. 'You little shit. Wait till I get hold of you, Carmelli.'

He threw the knife onto the steel table, where it slid and pirouetted before coming to a halt.

There was also a bag of rubbish left by the door. Carmelli would be mincemeat by the time he'd finished with him. But in the meantime . . .

His hands worked with malicious zeal, spreading the rubbish out onto the clean table, rubbing coagulated gravy and fat onto its shiny surface.

He looked up when the door opened, saw who it was and smiled. 'If you've come to try and persuade me to knock it on the head, you're wasting your time.'

Turning his back, he surveyed the cooking ranges to see what other tasks he could set to make life difficult for his errant apprentice.

He opened the oven door. Ovens were buggers to clean. Bending down, he hooked out a shelf, meaning to lower it onto the bottom one. Two shelves for cleaning were much more work than one.

So intently was he concentrating on making more of a mess that he almost forgot about his visitor, only remembering as the knife sliced through his throat. After that, oblivion.

* * *

Smoke charged with delicious aromas had drifted across Queen Square all evening from all manner of food stalls set up by restaurants and hotels. Honey breathed in the smells deeply, then sighed. This evening had been heaven compared to the event that afternoon at the Pump Rooms. Smudger had recovered — if you could count a lack of communication and a glum expression as a sign of recovery. Recognising he was disappointed that he didn't win, Honey did her best to take his mind off things, finally giving him a twenty to take himself off to the nearest bar.

She and Clint continued to run the stall, churning out steak and langoustines, pasta and pasties until just before midnight. Just as the last item of paraphernalia was loaded into the back of the van, she recognised a figure wearing a leather jacket, a black shirt, faded jeans and five o'clock shadow. Steve Doherty was off duty and heading her way.

She'd decided she liked him so it was OK to wave.

His expression lifted. He looked pleased to see her.

'I've just come off shift,' he said.

'I've just come from a battle zone . . .'

His eyebrows lifted questioningly.

She shook her head. 'No matter. You look tired.'

'So do you.'

There was a pause. On first meeting they'd hardly been the best of friends. But things had changed. Awkward silences were a sign of a shift in attitude. It was just a case of who took the next step, a step that would narrow the gap between them.

'Can I tempt you into accompanying me to the nearest wine bar?'

Her tiredness lifted and she smiled. 'I'm easily tempted.'

'Good.'

'OK with you, Clint?'

Clint said he would take care of things. For a price.

They went to a little wine bar called Lautrec's just off Kingsmead Square, one of Honey's favourites. Toulouse Lautrec posters decorated the walls between gas lights almost as old as the building.

'I like these black dolphins,' said Steve, nodding at the paintings while the Burgundy glugged from the bottle.

Honey frowned. 'What black dolphins?'

'Those.'

He pointed at the black-stockinged legs of La Goulue and the other can-can dancers from the Moulin Rouge.

'Steve, those are dancers' legs. They're doing the can-can. Can't you see the rest of their dresses and their features?'

He looked embarrassed. 'It's just a load of scribbles — and bubbles.'

She laughed. 'Spots. Spots on a dancer's dress.'

He huffed a bit. 'Can't see it myself.'

'Are you colour-blind?'

'Of course not. Are you?'

'Women aren't usually colour . . .'

She would have gone on to tell him that women didn't generally suffer from colour blindness, but Doherty's phone began chirping like a parrot with laryngitis. Like Wyatt Earp, he was a blur of action as he got it from his pocket. If it were possible to shoot someone with a mobile, whoever was at the receiving end would have been dead by now. They were halfway through the bottle of wine, but she knew by the look in his eyes that they wouldn't be finishing the rest right now. She eyed him speculatively. His expression had changed. A dark thoughtfulness appeared in his eyes.

'What is it?'

His phone was quickly returned to its holster. His eyes held hers. 'We've got a murder at the Beau Brummell Hotel.'

Don't be silly, she told herself as a cold shiver ran down her back. 'It wouldn't be a chef by any chance?'

He frowned. 'How did you know that?'

'I didn't.' In her mind she was wondering where Smudger had got to. 'Just guessing,' she said with a nervous smile. 'It's been that kind of day.'

CHAPTER THREE

Beau Brummell was a Regency buck and social climber, a Mr Fixer to Regency gentry; whatever they wanted, he could get or fix.

The hotel bearing his name was a Victorian architectural hotchpotch of fake Florentine and birthday cake madness situated in Weston Lane on the eastern side of Bath. What it lacked in Georgian elegance it made up for in amenities, chief among them being its own car park. What Honey wouldn't give to have a hotel car park at the Green River. But there it was; car parks weren't pencilled in on the eighteenth-century city plans.

Honey counted the cars with undisguised envy. It helped to keep her mind off Smudger, the chicken breasts and the unbridled rivalry between the two chefs, and dare she think it, the question of murder.

'Damn the woman. She's full! Why couldn't the chef have got killed when it was empty?'

Doherty attempted to hide his amusement and kept walking. 'So you could gloat that she wasn't full?'

She glowered at him, noticing the smirk playing around his mouth.

'She would if it was the other way round. Bling Broadbent is a cow.'

'Now, now, Honey. You're on official business. Serious business. Time to put the claws away.'

'It won't matter to Bling Broadbent. She'll smile and ask how I'm doing and I'll say, "So-so", and she'll say, "Well, actually, dahling, I'm terribly full at the moment." It's "dahling" when she's sober. An earful of expletives when she isn't.'

She shoved her hands in her pockets, a symbolic act that wasn't lost on Steve. He smiled. 'This business is more cut-throat than mine.'

He didn't meet her eyes: best to plead ignorance rather than sour a blossoming relationship.

It was two in the morning, and although the blue lights on the police cars continued to flash, most hotel guests slumbered on.

A disgruntled security guard wearing a surprised expression and a wrinkled uniform heaved a wooden barrier to one side.

A glow of amber light fell through the plate glass doors of the hotel entrance. A policeman stood guarding it. All attention and their footsteps were diverted to a sign saying *Trade Entrance*, beneath which a figure bobbed about like a plump hobgoblin.

'Here! This way,' said Stella Broadbent in a loud whisper, waving her arms. Gold chains flashed around her neck; a diamond the size of a bricks sparkled on her fingers. Her face was pink. She smelled of French perfume and strong wine.

'Bling Broadbent? I'm Detective Sergeant . . .'

Stella Broadbent's eyes fixed him with the sort of stare that could nail bare feet to the floor. 'My name is *Stella* Broadbent.'

Steve apologised. 'This is a night for corrections,' he said with a wry smile. 'I should have said Detective *Inspector* Steve Doherty. My promotion was only recent.'

'Congratulations.' Her eyes narrowed and her pursed lips reminded him of the rear end of a cow.

'Follow me. The rest of your men are already here causing bloody havoc. It's most disconcerting and bloody inconvenient. *Hic.*'

Steve raised his hand in a drinking motion to his mouth and looked at Honey.

'You bet,' she murmured. Though she may not have had money problems, gossip was rife about Bling Broadbent's problems with drinking and men.

'This way,' she repeated, ushering them down the side of the building. 'I apologise for using this entrance, but I can't have you disturbing my guests. It's bad for business.' She gave a brief nod in Honey's direction. 'It's good to see that the Hotels Association is keeping its finger on the pulse.'

Honey gave a weak smile back. 'I think we all know how important it is.'

'More important than whose chicken breasts belong to whom,' said Stella with a haughty toss of her head. She turned back to Steve. 'My chef was threatened today by her bloody chef. He's a temperamental sod! You should arrest him right now. Stands to reason. That's who did it, all right.'

Honey didn't meet Steve's questioning look. To his credit, he handled the situation pretty well.

'All avenues will be explored and anyone that ever threatened him will be questioned.'

'Glad to bloody hear it,' said Stella and hiccoughed again. She threw a sour look at Honey before motoring on towards the kitchen.

'I thought you said her name was Bling,' Steve whispered as they followed the hotel owner past an army of green wheelie bins and a large bottle bank.

'Bling is what she wears,' Honey whispered back. 'Didn't you see it flashing?'

'Ah!'

The tape around the crime scene fluttered like bunting at a second-rate carnival. The police were on one side of the tape, and the specialists — Scene of Crime and Forensic — were on the other.

The kitchen had a red quarry-tiled floor; Honey looked for the bloodstains. There were none. So where was the body?

She craned her neck. The usual gang in jumpsuits were picking around for evidence. Centre of attention was a flat-top Falcon heavy-duty commercial cooker. There were two of the sturdy beasts standing side by side. The other had five burners. Saucepans could be moved from the cooler edge of the flat-top to the red-hot middle, a boon to a busy chef. The last of the kitchen heat hung in the air, lying heavy on the chest. So did the smell of the waste spread over one of the stainless-steel worktables.

The oven door on the flat-top was open. A body was being eased out of the oven and into a body bag.

A horrible thought occurred.

No! Please!

'Carefully now.'

The head of the corpse flopped back as he was lowered into place. A collar of blood seeped from a deep neck wound, staining his chef's whites.

'I won't faint,' muttered Honey once she was convinced that Oliver Stafford did not resemble a well-roasted suckling pig.

'What?' asked Steve.

'Oliver Stafford,' she said.

'And Smudger didn't like him?'

'That's putting it mildly. They were rivals.'

Zip went the body bag.

Another mutter. 'Thank God for that.'

'For what?'

'That I didn't know him very well. I'd hate to think of my friends or family having their throats cut.'

'My mother used to cut chickens' throats,' said Fleming, the on-duty pathologist, who was already drawing his pension but keeping his hand in. 'She used to knock them on the head with a piece of wood to stun them before cutting off their head. Otherwise they run around without their heads.'

'Is that right?' said Doherty with surprising curiosity and not a hint of revulsion. 'Would the deceased have done that then?'

'No. I don't think so.'

Honey blinked. Did they have to be so offhand about it all? It was as though she were standing in the midst of a freezing-cold cloud. Her legs had turned to clouds too, puffy and floating and no longer attached to the earth.

Steve noticed. 'You all right?'

'Is this a nightmare or is it real?'

Someone chose that moment to drop a load of knives that were being taken for testing.

Doherty rolled his eyes and swore.

The clatter of steel against tiles did something to her nervous system. The cold cloud rolled away.

She found her voice. 'So you're looking for a murder weapon?'

'Looks like,' said Steve.

Stella Broadbent's impossibly high heels came clattering down the corridor. She looked what she was: pompous, plump and pickled to the eyeballs.

'Excuse me, officer, but I do require you to be finished and off the premises before my guests come down for breakfast. Now, do hurry up. There's a good fellow.'

Honey's jaw dropped, and she reminded herself that sensitivity wasn't part of Stella's make-up. Still, at least the bad language had ceased.

Steve Doherty had been dealing too long with the public to be surprised by Stella's attitude. He cut her off at the knees. 'No, I won't hurry up. It'll take as long as it takes.'

He turned his back on her and addressed Honey. 'I think Forensic will agree that a pretty big knife was used, one with a wide blade, if that neck wound is anything to go by.'

Stella tugged at his sleeve. 'Don't turn your back on me, you bloody wanker. I want you to sod off. I've got a bloody business to run.'

Cool as iced cola Steve turned to face her. 'Madam, if you continue to use that language, I'll have to arrest you for being drunk and disorderly.'

Stella's eyelids flickered like the pop-up numbers on an old-fashioned cash register.

'But . . .'

Steve was adamant. 'Madam, you can have your kitchen back when I'm good and ready. And not before!'

She made an effort to drag herself up to her full five-feet-four-inches. 'I shall not acquiesce to your demands!'

Steve frowned.

'*Agree*,' said Honey. 'She's not willing to agree to your demands.'

'I know that,' he muttered.

'Sorry, I thought you were having another *bling* moment.'

An angry flush seeped through Stella's Estée Lauder foundation and rouged cheeks. 'Stop this muttering. Get out of here and arrest that obnoxious sod she employs in her kitchen!'

She made a stab towards Honey with a red-tipped fingernail.

Steve squared her up. 'All in good time, madam. You will not tell me what to do. I will tell you. First, I want you to round up all members of staff and guests who were on the premises tonight.'

'My guests?'

Her eyes nearly popped out of her head.

'Your guests.'

'But what's it got to do with them? Most of them were asleep in their beds when this happened.'

'Then they can sign a statement saying so. If they're still in bed, do it in the morning.'

Stella exhaled a breath so deep she resembled a deflated beach ball. 'Right. I will gather everyone still up together in the lounge . . .'

'And your staff.'

'Yes. My staff.'

'And yourself.'

'Myself? But I'm the owner.' Her head spun round as though it were fastened on a clockwork spring. 'Honey! You represent the association. Do something!'

Smarting from the accusations and implications already being flung around, Honey resisted the urge to scratch Stella's eyes out. Instead she'd enjoy the damned woman's discomfort.

'Stella,' she said, adopting a soothing, sugary tone, even though it threatened to choke her. 'Look at it this way. Make a statement in your own place or make one down at the police station. Imagine if anyone sees you down there! What are they going to think? Your social standing will be ruined forever.'

Stella's eyelids fluttered nervously.

Honey continued, her sugary voice becoming as gooey as melted toffee. 'Now, tell me truly, which would you prefer?'

'A few questions to kick off,' said Doherty. 'Did the deceased have any enemies?'

Stella held her hand out in front of her. A huge diamond, the one Honey had thought was the size of a brick, flashed on her finger. 'See that diamond? That's what Oliver was. A diamond among chefs. The best in Bath, perhaps even in the country. That's why other chefs hated him. Isn't that right, Mrs Driver?'

The red lips curled back from the ultra-white porcelain. It wasn't a smile, more of a snarl. Bling Broadbent had seen and heard everything that had gone on at the competition.

'I told you who did it. Speak to her chef,' she spat, one polished claw pointing at some place between Honey's eyes. 'He threatened to kill Oliver yesterday. Ask her! She knows it's true!'

'He didn't mean it like that,' Honey said to Steve. 'He was upset because Oliver had stolen his breasts.'

Steve's eyebrows jerked upwards.

Honey explained. 'Chicken breasts. He reckoned Oliver had swapped them. Ours were best quality and theirs was . . .'

Stella sprang from a deflated crouch into a feline attack. 'How dare you! What would we want stealing from a second-rate establishment *and* a second-rate chef!'

Now it was Honey who sprang. Steve got in between them.

'Now ladies!'

With a bit of help from other officers, the two were prevented from clawing each other's eyes out.

'Take her through there,' said Steve, nodding towards the hotel reception. 'I'll take this one outside.'

'No fornicating with floozies on my premises,' shouted Stella as she was propelled firmly but politely out of the room.

Steve wrapped his arms around Honey, lifted her off her feet and took her outside.

'Put me down.'

She landed with a scattering of gravel.

'Cow,' she muttered to herself. 'She ought to strangle herself with that bloody gold chain. Or put it through her nose like they do with cows.'

'That's bulls,' said Steve. 'They put rings through the noses of bulls, not cows.'

'Well *that* one's a cow,' said Honey, thrusting her arm in the direction of the hotel entrance. A light came on in a ground-floor window. She could see right into the bar through the hugely elegant oriole window. Stella was perched on a bar stool accompanied by a bottle of something and a large glass. She poured, drank and poured again.

'*And* a lush,' she added.

She felt his eyes on her and knew they were full of questions because he'd taken on board everything Stella had said. Too many witnesses had heard Smudger threaten Oliver Stafford. But surely he couldn't be the only one. Chefs were competitive by nature. They made enemies easily. She imagined Steve's questions. *How many people had wanted to see Oliver Stafford dead? Is it true that your chef threatened to kill him the day before?*

Drat! She hadn't spoken to Smudger yet. Could she hold Steve off long enough to speak to Smudger first?

'I haven't congratulated you on your promotion,' she said suddenly, smiling and throwing her arms around him.

'That was ages ago.'

'How would you like to celebrate?'

She kissed him long and deep. Although looking taken aback, he kissed her back, the tip of his tongue tickling the back of her throat.

She retreated coughing and gagging.

He eyed her accusingly. 'That's for trying to change the subject.'

'No need to choke me.' She told herself not to look up into his eyes. *If you do, you're lost.*

She did and she was. He had such deep-set eyes, like pools you wanted to dive into — or better still just dive into bed with the attached body and study the eyes at leisure.

But she couldn't give in that easily. 'Smudger didn't mean it. He wouldn't kill anyone.'

'I'll need a statement from him.'

She sighed. 'I knew you'd say that.'

CHAPTER FOUR

Smudger had an alibi, or so he said. Honey caught up with him after having a quick word with Clint, who seemed to know the darkest dives that people might frequent — especially people he knew.

Smudger was exiting a nightclub and looking slightly the worse for wear.

She grabbed his arm. 'A word in your shell, like. Have you been in there all night?' she asked him.

'No,' he replied, shaking his head, his breath covering her in an alcoholic mist. 'I went to Sam Weller's first.'

Sam Weller's was a pub named after the character of the same name from Dickens.

'Are there witnesses that can verify that?'

He stopped in his tracks, looked at her and frowned. 'Why?'

Taking a tight grip on his arm she headed him in the direction of Manvers Street police station. 'Oliver Stafford's been murdered.'

His face broke into a grin. 'Couldn't happen to a worse bloke! Give the guilty bloke a medal. Where did it happen?'

'He was found with his neck partially severed and half stuffed into his own gas oven.'

Smudger looked more pleased than it was healthy to be. 'So someone finally cooked his goose!' He laughed at his own joke.

'It's not funny, Smudger. You were heard threatening to kill him. The police want a statement — now!'

'I've got an alibi.'

'You'd better have.'

He looked totally unfazed. 'After I left you, I bumped into Reggie Banks, an old mate of mine. He can vouch for me. We were playing pool.'

'You'd better be telling the truth.'

'Stay cool! Stay cool!'

Honey seethed, grabbed him forcibly so they were face to face and almost shoved her finger up his nose.

'Don't tell me to stay cool! I am cool — more or less.'

He shrugged. 'What's the worry? I couldn't stand Oliver Stafford, but I wasn't the only one. I didn't kill him. Why would I?'

Honey eyed him sidelong. 'Professional jealousy? He beat you in the competition.'

Smudger made an indignant snorting noise. 'I didn't need to kill him for that. I've got nothing to prove. I *know* I'm better than him!' He grinned suddenly. 'Perhaps it was someone who didn't like his cooking.'

'That's poisonous.'

'So was he.'

She shook her head in desperation. Smudger was a good chef, but like most good chefs, incorrigibly cocky.

* * *

A female PC with glasses and acne took Smudger's statement and another bod took his fingerprints.

Steve Doherty came in just as they were leaving. He glanced briefly at the fingerprint sample.

'Nothing positive to say at present,' said the fingerprint guy, his eyes and experience keen enough to make a swift judgement. 'We'll have to see if they match prints at the murder site.'

'Of course, Inspector Doherty.'

Honey watched as the policewoman's cheeks turned pink.

'One of your groupies?' she asked Steve once the woman was out of ear shot.

He grinned and noisily scratched his stubbly chin. 'They can't resist.'

It was too early in the morning to bring him down with a sharp comment. 'We can go now?'

'You can.' He offered up an apology as to why he couldn't give them a lift back to the hotel. 'Too busy following up leads,' he said, throwing a warning glance at Smudger, who was looking far too complacent for someone who'd been prime suspect only minutes before.

She told him it was OK. They'd walk. 'We both need to clear our heads.'

Not too good an idea, as it turned out. It was four in the morning and pouring down. The rhythm of the rain accompanied the sloshing of their footsteps. Her shoes were killing her and her hair was plastered to her head.

By the time they'd reached the Green River Hotel, they were both wet through.

Smudger had his own flat in Walcot Street, a Bohemian enclave where antique shops and delis rubbed shoulders with small cafés and owner-occupied craft shops. It was too late for him to go home.

Circumstances, such as functions that didn't finish until after midnight, sometimes necessitated him using a room in the hotel. Sometimes he had a few drinks to unwind before going to bed. Sometimes so did Honey.

'We're having a night cap,' she said.

'It's not night. It's morning.'

It was hardly a protest.

'Who cares?'

She unlocked the door to the bar and pushed it open. The muted smell of rich liqueurs and varied malts came out to meet her.

'Drink.'

She handed him the Jack Daniels and took a sip of the vodka and tonic she'd poured for herself.

After sinking into the springy comfort of a leather chesterfield, she set her empty glass down on the table in a businesslike manner.

'So! Who did it? Who hated Oliver Stafford enough to kill him?'

For the briefest of moments she sensed hesitation.

Smudger's ultra-light lashes brushed his cheeks before he looked up at her.

'Do you want a list?'

'Possibly. Casper will be on the phone first thing in the morning wanting to know details and to hear what I'm doing about it. The Hotels Association is very touchy about murder. It affects bed occupancy. And bank accounts.'

'Where do I start? I know, I'll start with saying that he was a right arrogant ba—'

'That description covers every chef I've ever known.'

The blue eyes opened wide with surprise. 'Am I arrogant?'

'Are you a chef? A good chef?'

He made a *humph* sound before emptying his glass.

She rested her chin on her hand, her elbow on the chair arm. Her eyelids were heavy but she was curious. Bed could wait.

Smudger looked thoughtful, no doubt giving his image a mental makeover.

Honey began to focus more on bed.

'So? Come on. We don't have all night.'

Smudger flicked a finger at his bottom lip as he thought it through. 'He was a bully in the kitchen. Now, you can't say the same about me, can you!'

It was a statement not a question. A truthful statement, as it turned out. The kitchen staff thought Smudger was fun. Only the suppliers felt bullied by his fastidious inspection of catering supplies — especially the butcher.

'Did he have family?'

'Married.'

'Poor soul.'

'I told you, he was a right—'

'I meant his wife. What a shock.'

'Hmm.'

Hardly a word, but there was something about his tone that grabbed her attention.

'What does "hmm" mean?'

He shrugged. 'Just rumours.'

Honey took a guess. 'He was an out-and-out womaniser.'

Smudger looked surprised. 'Who told you?'

'Call it womanly intuition.' Honey recalled Stafford's behaviour at the contest. She knew a womaniser when she saw one. She'd been married to one. Carl Driver had hired an all-female crew for his fifty-foot yacht. But sailing mid-ocean can get boring, and the sails weren't the only things that got pulled down on a regular basis.

'Really?'

'A woman can tell. Anyway, gossip travels fast in Bath. It's a small city.'

She would have quizzed him about it further, but her eyelids were getting heavy and her head wanted to assume the horizontal position.

She yawned, and weariness began to get the better of her. She lay back, barely aware that her head was sinking lower onto her hand and that her elbow was slowly sliding along the back of the settee.

She didn't hear Smudger shuffle off to bed. She didn't even hear the early shift coming in to prepare breakfast or the guests descending the stairs, lured by the smell of grilled bacon and Cumberland sausages. She heard nothing until the trilling of a ring tone permeated her right ear.

At the same time as blinking herself awake, she tried to work out where she'd left her phone. It took a few more seconds of blinking before she realised that she'd been using her handbag as a pillow and her phone was inside it.

'Hello?'

There was no answer at first — a matter instantly rectified once she'd turned it the right way up.

'Where are you?'

She recognised her daughter's voice.

'I'm in the bar.'

'I thought you'd stayed out last night.'

'No. Here I am.'

'Right.'

The line went dead.

The door to the bar wasn't usually opened until mid-morning. Lindsey, to her credit, didn't enquire as to why her mother was lying semi-comatose on a couch in the bar at the same time as bacon and eggs were cooking.

Her worried face appeared around the door.

'Mum. I need to talk to you.'

Honey blinked herself to wakefulness. A couple of matchsticks would have helped, but she didn't smoke. She imagined they were propped open, and they obeyed.

It might have been her imagination, but Lindsey looked a little drawn, a little too white even for breakfast time.

Honey pretended to study her reflection in a gilt-edged mirror. She looked as though she'd been dragged through a hedge backwards, her hair lank and lifeless and her mascara smeared across her cheekbones.

'I look as though I've died overnight. Do you think I look forty-something, or fifty-something? I suppose thirty-something's a bit much to hope for.'

Her eyes slid sidelong to the edge of the mirror, the frame and the girl pacing the carpet.

Lindsey was fiddling with her hair, eyes darting all over the place.

Something was wrong. A mother knows. Over the years Honey had learned not to rush things. She wouldn't pry. She wouldn't hound her daughter into telling her everything. The aim was not to end up sounding like her own mother. A softly, softly approach was best. Give her time, she'll tell you all about it.

Lindsey began to speak, though haltingly. 'Everyone's . . . talking about Oliver . . . you know . . . Oliver Stafford. He was murdered last night. Smudger told us.'

Lindsey looked down at the floor. Honey guessed she was chewing at her bottom lip, just like she'd done when she was ten and had hung a school bully up on a coat peg.

A sense of foreboding trickled down her spine. 'What is it?'

Without lifting her head, those lovely eyes looked up at her from beneath a jagged, tulip petal fringe. 'I think the police will want to question me.'

The trickling sensation became a mountain torrent. She didn't ask why. Heart thudding in double-quick time, she waited for Lindsey to continue.

'Well,' she said, settling herself back on the chesterfield, nerves on edge but expression controlled as she waited for her daughter to continue.

'I knew Oliver Stafford — quite well, as a matter of fact.'

Honey nodded as she took it in, knowing instinctively that she was not going to like what was coming next. 'Knew in the biblical sense?' she asked, desperately keeping her voice even.

Lindsey sat down in the chair opposite, legs tightly together, hands resting on knees.

An unidentified emotion surged in Honey's chest. Anger? Shame? She didn't know.

'You bloody fool!'

At last Lindsey raised her eyes. 'I didn't know he was married. I chucked him when I found out.'

'When?'

'Two months ago.'

'When did it start?'

'Six months ago.'

Honey groaned and hid her face in her hands.

A member of staff tapped at the door. 'Mrs Driver, there's a policeman here.'

'I'll be right out.'

'He wants to talk with Miss Lindsey.'

CHAPTER FIVE

They gathered in the small conference room at the end of the first landing.

'Any lead on the fingerprints?' Honey asked Steve.

He shook his head. 'That kitchen's like a bus station. Everybody's in and out and their fingerprints are everywhere, though none on the knife except for those belonging to the deceased. The kitchen porter who worked under Stafford mentioned Lindsey having had a relationship with the dead chef. Is that true?'

Looking quite dejected, Lindsey nodded. 'For a time.'

Honey, unable to control herself, asked Lindsey why she'd been attracted to a philanderer like Oliver Stafford. The effort of trying to control her emotions made her voice sound taut even to her own ears.

'He liked history,' Lindsey answered.

This was not quite the answer Honey had envisaged. 'And that was it?'

Lindsey sighed and gave her that look, the one teenagers seem to have borrowed from their grandmothers, the one that reminded Honey that they shared the same size bra cup.

'Mother, adult relationships are about people having things in common — a bit like you and Steve.'

Honey exchanged a brief glance with Steve. 'OK, yes, we've got crime in common . . .'

'No, you're roughly the same age and you both have a collection of Abba LPs hidden away in a cupboard.'

'I admit it, though I'm not sure about Doherty . . .'

'That's beside the point,' said Doherty, his face taut, jaw firm. 'You have questions to answer.'

Honey noted the pinkness in his cheeks and touched her own. Hot. Same colour, no doubt. 'Should we get a lawyer?'

Steve opened his mouth to answer. Too late, his response was halted by the opening of the door. 'What's going on here? Who wants a lawyer? What for?'

A cloud of French perfume preceded the entrance of Gloria Cross, Honey's mother. She was wearing a linen dress of Italian design cinched with a brown leather belt at her oh-so-slinky waist. Hell of a looker for a septuagenarian.

'Look,' said Steve, a little snappy now because he hadn't yet got round to asking a single question, 'all I want to do is get you to answer some questions about Oliver Stafford — how you met, what he told you, and who his friends were.'

'This sounds interesting. Shift up,' said Gloria, pushing her rear into the spot between her daughter and granddaughter. 'Has my granddaughter turned into a femme fatale?'

'You don't need to be here,' said Steve.

'Of course I should be here,' she retorted. 'I've watched *NYPD Blues*. And *The Sweeney*. I know your sort, Doherty, and I won't have my family being intimidated!'

Gloria loved old cop shows.

Doherty adopted his very-good-cop mode. 'Look, ma'am, all I want to do is ask Lindsey a few questions about the murder victim.'

'Murder? Who got murdered? And don't call me ma'am,' she added, fixing him with a warning frown.

Steve rolled his eyes.

Honey went ahead and explained. 'A chef's been murdered. The one who beat Smudger in the competition yesterday.'

'Is that so! I expect he was very good indeed to have beat Smudger.'

Honey interjected without thinking. 'Don't let Smudger hear you say that. You know how temperamental he can be . . .'

She leaned close to Steve and whispered in his ear, 'Can you forget I said that if I'm very nice to you later?'

Steve sighed, closed his eyes and rubbed his temples. 'Your attempt at bribery is noted, though I'm too dog tired to write it down. A cup of coffee would be good — black with plenty of sugar.'

Honey would have sympathised if Lindsey hadn't been involved. She wanted this over and done with. 'Sod the coffee. You're supposed to be taking a statement.'

He yawned. 'Have pity, Honey. I've been on duty all night.'

'I insist you take my daughter's statement.'

The pad and pen he'd brought with him was in danger of sliding out of his lap. He clutched at it before it escaped and thrust it into Honey's hands. 'You do it. She's *your* daughter,' he said, then folded his arms and closed his eyes.

'This is hardly professional.' Honey rolled her eyes, then gave in. 'Let's start at the beginning,' she said, brandishing the notebook. 'What made you get involved with this jerk in the first place?'

Lindsey glanced at her mother. 'As I said, he told me he was something of an amateur historian, and you know how I am with history.'

Honey thought of all the times Lindsey had gone to lectures on the Tudors and concerts of medieval chamber music when her peer group were getting legless and laid in a night club. 'I'm curious to know his chat-up line. What was it? Come and see the size of my codpiece?'

'Costume matters,' said Gloria. 'I get turned on by costume drama; did you ever see that Jane Austen adaptation when Colin Firth comes out of the water all dripping wet with his trousers sticking to his loins. My, you could see everything. And then Sean Bean playing Sharpe on TV.

What was he like, especially from the rear; the best bum I've ever seen . . .'

Honey found her patience failing. 'Mother!'

'Am I digressing?'

'Worse, you're fantasising.'

After checking Steve Doherty's half grin, she turned back to Lindsey. 'Right. You didn't know he was married.'

'No. I didn't want to get involved with him, but he was such a charmer. And how many men do you know who are interested in history?'

Honey thought. 'John Rees. The guy who owns the bookshop in Rifleman's Way.'

'He's ancient.'

'He's two years older than me,' growled Honey through gritted teeth.

'I know quite a lot of men who are interested in history,' said Gloria. The most ungrandmotherly-looking grandmother had a faraway look in her eyes.

Honey groaned. This was getting them nowhere. 'Mother, the men you know are *part* of history.'

Her mother drew air up her nose with all the ferocity of a psychotic vacuum cleaner. 'Hannah, I shall leave if you continue to insult me.'

Recognising the altogether vitriolic tone in the way she pronounced 'Hannah', her given name, Honey apologised. She attempted to get her thoughts in some kind of professional order — now she was Honey Driver, super sleuth, not Honey Driver, hotel owner.

'Lindsey, where were you last night, say between the hours of eleven and midnight?' She held her breath as she awaited the answer.

The moment Lindsey smiled Honey knew she was in for a stark revelation. Why could teenagers sometimes make you feel as though you were younger than them, or worse, about to become a permanent resident in an old folk's home?

'Mother, I was here. You were out gallivanting with Smudger while I was holding the fort. Mary Jane can vouch for me. She was reading the tarot cards.'

'Well that's good enough for me,' said Gloria, getting to her feet. 'Mary Jane may be a little eccentric, but she always tells the truth.'

To Honey's ears it sounded a bit of a contradiction, but she gave it no mind. Lindsey's revelation had left her feeling let down. She couldn't hide her anger. She couldn't face the disappointment of not knowing, not being told. This sort of thing happened to other people's daughters. Not hers. Not her beloved Lindsey.

Honey felt something land on her shoulder. Steve had fallen fast asleep.

The women looked at him. Lindsey carried on. 'By the way, Casper phoned.'

'Oh! The word's got round.'

'He asked you to call in when you're passing.'

Honey bit her lip. Casper would want to know the details of the murder.

She cupped Steve's face in her hands and laid his head back as she got to her feet. 'I'd better get round there.'

'What about him?' Lindsey jerked her chin at the sound-asleep policeman.

Honey thought about it. 'He's quiet enough.' She placed the notebook and pen back in his lap. 'Wake him up when he starts snoring.'

'Are you going to see Casper?'

'Yes. And then I'm off to ask Bling Broadbent a few questions. That cow! Do you know her car park was chocker last night? That cow actually employs a security guard to oversee her bloody car park.'

Lindsey smiled ruefully. 'Now, now, Mother. Remember to play nicely.'

'I'll play rough if I have to, and talking of rough . . .' She kissed Steve gently on the forehead. His jaw dropped open and a resounding snore erupted from his open mouth.

'Shall I . . . ?' asked Lindsey.

Her mother shook her head. 'Not yet. Give me a head start. Then do it.'

CHAPTER SIX

On her way to the underground garage where she parked her car, Honey conjured up how best to put 'Bling' Broadbent in her place. Having her arrested on suspicion of murdering her own chef would be good. The delicious vision of wiping that supercilious smile from Stella's bright-red lips would not go away. Unfortunately she had no evidence to support that particular theory. Maybe she'd had a thing for her head chef. Jealousy was always a good reason to murder, but she checked herself. Conviction must be based on evidence not personal prejudice. Murder was serious. Even the likes of Stella Broadbent didn't deserve to be locked up for something she didn't do.

Stella was one of those people who had to be like the Christmas Fairy, always on top of the tree looking down her nose at everyone else. She could never bring herself to like the woman, but neither could she condemn her out of hand.

Her reverie was interrupted by yet another call from Casper. She put it on speakerphone.

'I need you *heee . . . re.*' He spoke low, deep and slow, the last word as drawn out as a bowed double bass string.

'I'll be right there as soon as I've spoken to Bling — I'm sorry, *Stella* Broadbent.'

'Here! Now!'

There was something pleading in his voice. There was class, there was confidence, but today there was also something else. Puzzlement? Confusion?

Her eyes were drawn to a notice board, and her intention of calling on Stella Broadbent flew out of the open car window. Bonhams were holding an auction of collectables. Clothes were included.

'I won't be long.'

'Honey? Honey?'

A car pulled off the single yellow lines in Queen Square and she pulled into the space, turned off the engine and locked up. With a spring in her step, she dodged the traffic to the other side of the road and into Bonhams.

'More voluptuous underwear, hen?' asked Alistair, the Scottish clerk behind the counter. His smirk of approval was lost within the confines of a bright ginger beard.

The last time she'd been in Bonhams, Jolly's as it was then, she'd purchased a particularly large pair of undergarments, said to have been worn by Queen Victoria. Alistair remembered the purchase. He made it his business to know what everyone collected.

She paid for a catalogue.

'Anything interesting?' she asked as she thumbed through the shiny pages. If there was anything, the employees of the company would have spotted it. Experience equals grandstand knowledge.

'I did see a very nice pair of garters fashioned from French lace and festooned with ribbons in a particularly fetching strawberry shade.' He spoke slowly and eloquently, the richness of his accent turning the verbal equivalent of flat pancakes into fruit-filled Genoa.

'You sound as though they quite took your fancy.'

Standing at six-feet plus in his lace-up shoes, Alistair smiled through his thick red beard. 'Not for me, hen. I would have preferred blue myself — to match my eyes, you understand.'

'Anything else?'

He clapped his hands over his chest. 'A salmon-pink Berlei from the fifties.' He used his finger to describe it. 'Sewn round and round, and round and round into a conical shape, just like Madonna used to wear at the height of her career, only bigger. Much bigger.'

Her phone rang again as she headed into the auction room. Bidding had already started. She didn't have time for a proper look round so would have to trust Alistair's judgement. The garters came first. Bidding started at twenty pounds, a ludicrous amount for apparel never likely to be seen.

Bidding climbed steadily. There was a middling crowd. If she craned her neck she'd see who she was bidding against. But she wouldn't. Bidding called for deep concentration. All that mattered was getting what you came for.

She waited until the bidding reached thirty-five before going in at forty.

'Forty. Do I see forty-five? Forty-five anywhere? Now come on. These were said to have been worn by a dancer at the Windmill Theatre in London. During the war it boasted that it never closed. Got to be worth more, surely?'

The auctioneer's eyes scoured the room for a potential punter. No one stepped in. She smiled. The garters were hers.

'Going once, going twice . . . Fifty, madam? Fifty pounds. A fresh bidder at fifty pounds.'

Honey bid fifty-five. The other party bid sixty. Honey bid sixty-five. Her rival bid seventy.

Seventy? For a pair of faded garters?

Despite the condition of the intriguing items, she might have pushed the bidding further if her phone hadn't rung again. Casper!

'I need you here right now!'

'Casper, there's just one more lot . . .'

'Honey, I have a man here who I think you should speak to. Remember, my dear, you're the one liaising with the police on behalf of the Hotels Association. Do I have to remind you of the benefits . . . ?'

His comment hit a raw nerve. Perks came with the job. She got priority bookings via the committee, recompense for involving herself in tourist-related crime. 'I'll be right there.'

She sighed. So much for the garters, but there was still hope for the salmon-pink brassiere with conical stitching.

Alistair had come out from behind his counter and was standing at the back of the room. She knew he would be bidding on behalf of people who for whatever reason couldn't be there. It was a fair bet none of them were involved in a murder investigation.

She handed him her bidding card. 'Last bid for lot 132. Go up to fifty for the Berlei.'

'Och! You couldn't resist the *brazier*, could you, hen?' He grinned, but his eyes remained fixed on the auctioneer.

She smiled at his pronunciation of *brassiere*. 'No, I couldn't. I suppose you thought it would suit me?'

'Och! No, hen. Though you could use it as a bowling ball carrier . . .'

Her eyes widened. 'That big?'

He nodded. 'What the Germans would call a *büstenhalter*.'

Enough was enough. 'Don't bother.' She grabbed the ticket from the bunch he was clutching and tore it into shreds.

'See you, hen,' said Alistair, his eyes still fixed on the auctioneer and his head nodding in time with the bids.

Casper's hotel, La Reine Rouge, was a stone's throw from Pulteney Weir and a pleasant walk from the auction rooms.

A party of Dutch kids, in the UK on an exchange scheme, trotted past chattering happily as though they were the only people in the world. Whether they noticed the grandeur of their surroundings was questionable. They were away on a jolly, out of school, and that was all that mattered.

She darted between people aiming digital cameras and barely missed being run down by a hire car driving on the wrong side of the road. The driver wound his window down.

'Excuse me, can you tell me where the Pump Rooms are?'

She pointed round into Quiet Street. 'That way, but you'll have . . .' Too late. The window was wound up.

The last she saw was the car mounting the pavement and around the bollards barring access to Quiet Street. Horns were blowing. People were shouting. Quiet Street was far from quiet.

Never mind. The air was balmy, summer was here and everyone was out enjoying themselves.

Neville, Casper's head receptionist, was on duty behind the highly polished mahogany desk. Honey glanced at her watch as a brass-faced grandfather clock struck eleven in time with the wall clocks lining the stairs to the upper floors. Casper collected clocks.

Neville was resplendent in a red silk waistcoat embroidered with birds of paradise. Regency style was *de rigueur* at La Reine Rouge, suiting the ambience of the elegant building. The tourists loved it.

The phone rang and he pointed to the stairs leading down to Casper's office before answering the call.

Intrigued, Honey made her way down, knocking before entering the subterranean suite that served as offices.

The first thing she saw on entering was Casper's pale complexion.

'My goodness. You look as though you've seen . . .'

Casper's visitor rose from his chair.

Honey's jaw dropped. Her head tilted back to accommodate the man's height. Over six foot. Good looking too. Simply dressed, jeans and light blue pullover, the sleeves of which were tight over his muscles.

She heard Casper clearing his throat. He probably couldn't believe it himself.

'This gentleman tells me he has important information regarding the murder of Oliver Stafford.'

'My name's Peter Jones.' He held out his hand.

Honey shook it and nodded slowly while she tried to find her voice. He was good looking, a bit like a film star whose name she couldn't fathom, but not quite up to scratch. Good looking all the same.

'Have you been to the police?'

He shook his head. 'No. I would have but got talking to Neville at the club last night. He was telling me about what happened at the hotel.' He shook his head. 'I could be involved; I mean I was there as Chuck Rogers — a cowboy — an act I was paid to do. You know, like a party stripper-type of thing, but without the stripping. I just had to act. That's what I really want to do . . .'

Honey was getting impatient. 'Can we cut to the chase, Pete. Now why didn't you go to the police?'

'The police make me nervous, but I think I should explain why I was there, you know, so I can be excluded from enquiries. Neville suggested I come here and speak to his boss.' He flashed a smile at Caspar. 'For which I'm extremely grateful.'

'Right!'

'Do you think we can sit down?' she said, her neck already aching from having to adopt such an acute angle. The guy was tall. Handsome too.

'Certainly.'

'And this evidence can you tell me exactly what it is?'

'Well, I was there as a cowboy.' He emitted a light laugh. 'I'm not really. Furthest west I've been is to St David's in Wales. I'm not a real cowboy.'

'I get that.'

'Right. Well, I was supposed to pretend to this woman that we'd got married when she was drunk and I was entitled to half the hotel.' He grinned. 'She didn't really swallow it — well I don't think she did. Anyway, I heard my so-called wife arguing with Mr Stafford. She was calling him many rude names and threatening to destroy him if he didn't continue to "play ball".'

Honey looked at Casper for help. He looked just as shocked and puzzled as she felt. 'And your wife was supposed to be Stella . . . ?'

'Yes. Stella. But she's not really my wife. The story I was told to repeat was that she we met on holiday in Texas and she got drunk, I proposed and she agreed. We got wed. That was the story.'

'And that's it?'

'I was paid to do it.'

'That figures.'

'But I did overhear an argument.'

'He's given me the details,' said Casper, a perplexed look sullying his usually calm expression. He related a few details.

'I can't go to the police about it.'

Honey asked the obvious question. 'Who paid you?'

He shook his head. 'I cannot divulge my clients' particulars. It's private. Confidentiality and all that.'

Honey took a deep breath and reminded herself that this was a serious business. Murder was involved, plus the reward of substantial bed occupancy at the Green River Hotel for taking on the job in the first place. 'And you definitely heard her threaten Mr Stafford?'

He nodded. 'I managed to sneak in. I heard her screaming at him to do as she said. There was no security guard, at least at first.' He frowned. 'He appeared later, but I avoided him.'

Honey made a mental note to have a word with the security guard — that was after she'd had a word with Bling Broadbent.

'You have to tell the police,' said Honey.

A sense of panic moved him. 'You tell them,' he said, backing towards the door. 'I don't want to get involved. That's why I came to see you and not them.'

'Do we have your address?'

'I'll be around.' He was gone, the door swinging behind him.

'Oi!' Honey raced after him while Casper reached for the phone.

Once outside, she looked up and down the crowded street. There was no sign of him. Traffic was flowing well. He could have jumped into a taxi or even on a bus. Steve Doherty would have to deal with it. They had to find him again. They also had to find out whoever had paid him to do it.

CHAPTER SEVEN

The atmosphere between mother and daughter was subdued. They were each efficiently carrying out their duties around the hotel, only speaking when the need arose and never, ever alighting on the subject of Oliver Stafford. The relationship rattled between them. It had happened, but both were having difficulty dealing with it.

Getting out cleared Honey's head, but because this case was so personal, the details never ceased to whirl in her mind.

She and Doherty were having a lunchtime drink in the public bar of the Garrick's Head next door to the Theatre Royal. For once it was Honey who had called him to arrange the meeting.

'His wife could have hired a hitman,' Honey said.

'It's possible. Or Mr Mark Smith could have done it.'

'Nooo!' She said it emphatically and low. 'Not Smudger. Anyway, his alibi checks out.'

'For the most part. Did you know he visited Stafford's wife on a regular basis?'

Honey looked away. She hadn't known about her daughter's relationship with that rat Stafford, and she hadn't known about Smudger's relationship either. It rankled that neither her daughter nor her chef trusted her with their secrets.

'I'll take that as a no,' said Steve. 'How are your hotel bookings?'

'Great.' She continued to admire the Regency décor, the old posters and pictures of stars who'd trod the boards of the old theatre. The famous Sarah Siddons and David Garrick himself had played to packed houses in Regency times, and Sarah Bernhardt and Lily Langtry at a later date. The big names still came, taking a break from the stage with a gin or two.

Honey knew she was dwelling on this case, but she couldn't help it. Even if Casper hadn't been putting bookings her way as reimbursement for liaising with the police, she would still be doing the job. But should she be? Was she neglecting her family — notably Lindsey? She wanted to find Stafford's murderer for no other reason than to serve her own misgivings. The high-flying chef was a sexual predator; that alone could have resulted in his murder. No stone must be left unturned. After that? Well . . . she'd wait and see how she felt.

'You need more fun in your life,' Steve said suddenly.

Still with her eyes on her drink, she nodded. A thought occurred to her and suddenly she began to smile.

'Any luck tracing the cowboy?'

He shook his head. 'Your friend Stella and her premises have been the target of a hate campaign for some months. To my mind this is just an extension of that.'

'You're probably right.'

'Never mind. We'll find him.'

'First stop, a few questions at the Beau Brummell?' she asked brightly.

'Did I invite you?'

'No, I invited myself.'

CHAPTER EIGHT

The Beau Brummell always struck Honey as a three-star building striving for five-star excellence. OK, she was biased. She loathed Stella Broadbent. Couldn't stand her. Not at any price.

And the bitch had a car park.

The car park was covered with gold-coloured gravel. Today it dazzled under bright sunlight. Honey put on her sunglasses.

'The sun's not that bright,' said Steve.

'I'm doing it to protect my eyes from Stella's jewellery,' she growled.

'Ouch,' said Steve, and pretended to cower inside his jacket.

A few hire cars were parked out front. So was Stella's sporty Mercedes alongside a white Rolls Royce.

The same security guard was still in situ, looking less surprised and more at ease.

'You back again?' He was making an effort to sound welcoming, but it came across only grudgingly.

'Yes. To see you,' said Steve, flashing his warrant card. 'You haven't made a statement yet.'

The man shrugged his bulky shoulders. They were rounded and heavy like the rest of him, not so much a good physical specimen as a very large one.

'I didn't see anything.'

'You were here all night?'

'Yes.'

The man's eyes flickered. Honey noticed and pounced. 'But you must have taken a leak. Or supper? Or fallen asleep?'

He turned on her. 'I didn't fall asleep.'

He sounded defensive. She knew he was lying. His complexion had turned apple red.

'I want a statement from you,' said Steve, pointing at him with a stabbing action.

The big man seemed to shrink in size, and they carried on past him.

'I can't wait to see her face when we mention this Peter Jones,' said Honey once they were inside. 'It's the stuff of tabloid journalism — middle-aged woman acquires exotic husband . . . I know it's not true, but . . .'

'Honey, behave yourself or I won't let you stay.'

'Did you say stay, or play?' She nudged his arm.

'Behave.'

Stella was in reception. Honey had the impression she'd been waiting for them, watching as they'd questioned the security guard.

'A few more questions,' said Steve once the formalities were out of the way.

Stella studied her wristwatch, an aloof look on her face. 'Well, I can only spare you twenty minutes. I need to apply myself to contacting Shifty Chef, the catering staff recruitment agency, in the hope they've got a decent head chef on their books. I know it may sound a bit mercenary so soon after Oliver's death, but I'm off on holiday in two months and need to have everything running smoothly by then. And you know how long it takes to advertise, interview and arrange a start date.'

'Where are you going?' asked Honey.

'Borneo, to see the orang-utans.'

Honey sucked in her lips to stop herself from bursting out laughing.

'I'm very keen on conservation. One can adopt or sponsor an orang-utan, you know.'

'How romantic.'

Stella's wonderfully made-up face never gave into expressions — especially nervous ones. It cracked into a smile on occasion, mostly when she was taking the money of overcharged guests. She tried to smile now. It still came across as nervous.

'Perhaps we'd better go into my private *lounge*.' She said, the invitation directed at Steve. She pronounced 'lounge' as though she were swallowing a lozenge. 'Perhaps you'd like to wait here,' she said to Honey.

Honey's smile was for real. She was enjoying this. 'Oh no, I'll come in too. I need to hear the evidence and I particularly wanted to ask you about—'

'Best you stay here,' said Steve Doherty with a warning look.

Honey was left gaping. How could he do this to her? But they did. They left her there.

'You can't just stand there, you're in the way of paying guests,' said the receptionist. Her tone was as plummy as her uniform. Honey spotted the name Perdita Fordingby emblazoned on her breast.

Honey plastered on a smile. 'Your congenial hospitality is quite overwhelming.'

The receptionist sniffed and flapped some papers. Honey took herself outside.

The nose of a butcher's van was poking out from around the side — just below the sign saying 'Trade Entrance'.

The driver appeared and got in the van. Gravel flew up from beneath the squealing tyres as he accelerated from nought to forty in half a second.

'Oi!' she shouted as a sharp stone hit her on the cheek. 'Ow!' She gingerly touched the sore spot and felt blood. The flow trickled down her cheek.

'Damn.'

She was wearing a taupe top with a contrasting white collar. Two minutes and it was likely to turn polka dot. Loath to reacquaint herself with the smug-faced receptionist, she headed for the entrance to the storerooms and kitchen. From her last visit she remembered there being a staff toilet in the vestibule outside the kitchen.

Muffled conversation came from the other side of the kitchen door. She pushed open the one to the toilet, turned on the water and dabbed at her face. The water turned pink. She looked for a paper towel to staunch the blood. There was none. Toilet paper? None of that either. The only item remotely useable to wipe her face was a pillow and a sleeping bag rolled up in the corner.

A slow smile spread over her face. A sleeping place. She'd been right. The security guard had been lying.

She still needed something to staunch the blood, so headed for the kitchen, knocking on the door before going in.

Richard Carmelli, now in command of the kitchen — at least for a time — was in conversation with a man she instantly recognised and instinctively loathed: Roland Mead, well-known catering butcher and currently a close friend of her mother's. The two men stopped talking and looked at her.

She gave them both the once over and nodded an acknowledgement. Carmelli, a youngish man with dark eyes and dark hair, was wearing a red bandana around his head instead of the traditional toque, and his name was embroidered across his chest in flowing script. The other man was wearing a denim shirt and matching jeans, both of which were too small for his robust flesh. Likewise the toupee that sat like a pancake on top of his head.

Piles of vac-packed meat sat on the table in front of them. At the other end of the table were round white tubs. She glanced at them and saw the handwritten labels.

Coronation chicken. Carmelli had been batch cooking. Four days' supply of the tubs would go into the cooked meats fridge for immediate use. The rest would be frozen down and brought out when needed.

Her attention returned to the two men. The older man looked determined; the younger looked intimidated, as though the other guy had said something he didn't want to hear.

'Sorry,' she said. 'But there are no paper towels in the loo — or any paper at all for that matter. I've cut my face.' She lifted her fingers momentarily to indicate the bleeding.

The chef handed her a piece of kitchen towel. 'What happened?' He sounded genuinely concerned.

Honey explained. 'The driver of the butcher's van is out to get a place on the Ferrari racing team.'

The big man in the toupee faced her. 'Do you mean my van?' His whole demeanour was bluff and blunt.

'Do my eyes deceive me, or did it say *Roland Mead, Meat Trader* on the side of that van?'

'Aye.'

'Then I *do* mean your van. That driver's a maniac.'

Roland Mead eyed her with sceptical disdain, one eye narrowed. The other eyeballed some point between her chin and eyebrows, as though seeking a secret doorway into her brain. He seemed to weigh things up before speaking. Sympathy wasn't on the menu.

'If you're thinking of filing an insurance claim and looking for compensation, you'll get nowt from me.'

He spoke in a broad Yorkshire accent — or it could have been Lancashire. Honey had never been too hot on North Country accents. He turned to the chef. 'Give me a call if you want to reconsider my offer and I'll sort things out.'

He threw her a warning glare before exiting the kitchen through the opposite door.

'What a charming man.'

'Right,' said the chef. His sarcasm was obvious.

'I take it that's his Rolls Royce out front?'

Carmelli grimaced. 'Well, it certainly isn't mine. Not on the wages I get here. *Do this Richard, do that Richard. How about a rise, Mrs Broadbent? Certainly not, Richard.*'

'Yep. That sounds like Stella. Generosity has never been her middle name.'

She wondered if Oliver Stafford had asked for a rise after winning the competition. Could Stella have slit his throat in one angry moment?

The young chef interrupted her thoughts.

'Is your face all right now?'

She dabbed with the kitchen towel at the sore spot and looked at the results. 'It seems OK.'

'Good. We've had enough blood spilt on this floor.'

It was impossible to tell by his tone whether he was glad or sorry that Stafford was dead. She chose to take the negative line.

'I take it you didn't like Oliver Stafford.'

He nodded. 'That's about right. And I've got the scars to prove it.'

'Are you serious?'

'The man was a jerk. Ask his wife.'

Asking his wife anything was something she would try to avoid, and not just because the poor woman must be upset. Her own daughter had been 'another woman'. Even though Lindsey had been innocent of his marital status, it made her angry; angry at Lindsey, but also angry with Oliver. And then there was Smudger. She still hadn't got up the courage to ask him about his relationship with Oliver's wife. There seemed to be enough on her plate at present.

'He had this thing about being superior to any other chef in the city,' Richard went on, pacing backwards and forwards to the open fridge with bundles of the vac-packed meat. 'That meant taking anything they valued — and I'm not just referring to recipes.'

Honey frowned. 'I'm not with you.'

Richard picked up another pile. 'Wives. Girlfriends.'

'So you're saying it was all just a game to him?'

Richard shook his head. 'Olly had a big appetite — not for food, mark you. He took care of his health and went to the gym and all that stuff — when he could fit it in. He wanted *things*. The trappings of success. Money, flash cars and flash birds. Material man, that was our Olly. He wanted to prove to the world — or rather other chefs — that he was better than them in every possible way. Oh. And he was a bully.'

Honey jumped when he slammed the fridge door. There was no need to ask Richard whether he'd been the victim of Oliver Stafford's tantrums. Actions spoke louder than words.

'Where were you on the night he died?'

Richard stopped transferring the meat to the fridge and laid his palms flat on the stainless-steel tabletop.

'That bastard came back here crowing about beating the pants off the other chefs. He'd been drinking champagne with Mrs Broadbent and was full of himself. He reckoned he was going places, and the likes of me wouldn't be allowed in his kitchen. He started pushing me around. I'd had enough. I went home.'

'Is there a witness who can verify that you went home?'

He nodded. 'Two witnesses. The security guard and my girlfriend, Sasha. We've got a bedsit in the Old Dispensary.'

'Why do you think he was boasting like that?' she asked him.

Carmelli grimaced. 'He reckoned he'd played his cards right and was becoming a partner in the hotel. I couldn't see it myself. Why should he be?'

Why should he, indeed? Honey looked at the table. Some packs of meat remained.

'You've forgotten some.'

'That's pork. They're stored separately to steak.'

'The coronation chicken smells nice.'

'It's not as good as you think. Oliver made it. I'm ditching it and making my own. Have some. Compliments of the house.'

She thanked him. Because 'the house' was Stella Broadbent, she wouldn't normally have accepted it. But Richard had such a captivating smile.

She tucked the tub into her bag. The bag was a wonder; she could hide a puppy in there. It came with her everywhere. 'You were saying?'

'Oliver. Yes.'

She sensed he wanted to get Oliver Stafford and all that he'd stood for off his chest.

'These chefs whose girls he was knocking off, were any of them in the cooking competition?'

'Brian Brodie's wife. It didn't stop Brian from trying to ride on Oliver's coat-tails, though. Oliver was Brian's role model. Poor sod!'

She took a beat before asking the young chef the burning question. 'How do you feel about getting Oliver's job?'

Turning from sideways on to face her, Richard Carmelli cocked his head — a sure signal for sudden or deepening suspicion.

'How come you're so curious?'

She thought about blustering, but decided to speak the truth. 'I liaise with the police on behalf of Bath Hotels Association.'

Abject realisation came to his face. 'Oh! You work for Smudger Smith — sorry, I mean Smudger Smith works for you.'

Far from needling her, the comment had hit on a well-known truth: a hotel and restaurant's reputation depended largely on its chef.

She smiled and decided she couldn't help liking this young man. 'No need to apologise. It does seem the other way round on occasion.'

'Right.'

She sensed her source of information was closing down. It occurred to her to offer him a job at the Green River if anything came up, but decided now was not the appropriate time. In any case, she'd have to ask Smudger.

'Thanks for your help.'

'No problem.'

'Thanks for the kitchen towel.'

She asked if Oliver had been confident about winning the competition.

Richard nodded. 'At least, he was before hearing that Casper had replaced Sylvester Pardoe. Pardoe's good, but Casper is fastidious. Nothing gets past him.'

He was absolutely right. Nothing *did* get past Casper. After his death he could donate his taste buds to science, they were that sensitive.

'So why did Pardoe opt out?'

'Couldn't say. Sorry. Have to go. Work to do.'

She couldn't help feeling she'd been dismissed. She also couldn't help noticing that Richard's attitude towards her had changed the moment she'd mentioned Sylvester Pardoe. She made a mental note to check it out. Hopefully she'd remember.

* * *

After she'd gone, Richard Carmelli glared at the last packs of meat sitting on the table. His fingers tightened around the knife handle. He hadn't meant to say that much. He certainly hadn't meant to mention Sylvester. Now he regretted it.

'Damn! Damn! Damn!'

With each word the knife thudded into the meat again and again. Blood oozed out through the jagged openings, ran across the table and dripped onto the floor. It spattered his fresh whites and flicked up into his face. Once the packs were no more than a sodden mess, he threw down the knife, rested his elbows on the table and dug his knuckles into his eyes.

CHAPTER NINE

It was mid-afternoon when Honey Driver entered the elegant foyer of La Reine Rouge, intending to ask Casper for the addresses of Brian Brodie and also Sylvester Pardoe, the two names Richard Carmelli had mentioned.

Her mother had arrived at the Green River just after lunch full of information about her latest beau and his white Rolls Royce. It wasn't the first time her mother had found herself a boyfriend. Her demands were minimal when it came to character or age; as long as they were rich, she didn't give a hoot.

Honey didn't want to hear all the gory details. In her haste to escape she'd grabbed the first pair of shoes she laid her hands on and raced out. They were the wrong pair, too high and too pointy. Her feet were killing her.

Her phone rang, causing her to hesitate between the outer and inner doors of La Reine Rouge.

'You've got the brazier,' said Alistair, the clerk from the auction rooms.

She pictured a cast-iron tripod full of burning coals.

'Not me, Alistair. I didn't bid for any brazier. I've got central heating.'

'The upper-decker wobble-checkers. The *büstenhalter*.'

The cone-shaped monstrosity of a fifties brassiere, the cup sizes big enough to take a pair of prize-winning turnips or tenpin bowling bowls. She didn't want it and told him so.

'Alistair, you've made a mistake. You saw me tear that slip up.'

'Sorry, hen. You must have torn the wrong one up, and I was a bit too busy to notice. You've got yourself a brazier big enough to fit the Fifty-Foot Woman!'

This was not good news. Yes, she collected vintage underwear, and conical-type bras were definitely in that category. But no one could look sexy in *that* particular pair, with the possible exception of a Jersey cow.

No point in arguing. 'I'll be round for them.'

First the information. The fact that Oliver Stafford had been a ladies' man didn't surprise her. She remembered the look of him: average height, solid, trim build, classic features, come-to-bed eyes. Mightily self-assured and oozing sexuality. Mr Super Stud — in his own eyes, at least.

Thinking of him set her teeth on edge. How many women had he seduced? She remembered Lindsey and shuddered at the thought of it. She didn't stop to ask herself whether she should tell Steve of her conversation with Richard Carmelli. Sod him! He'd blanked her out at the Beau Brummell just because she wanted to make Bling Broadbent squirm. Now it was her turn. She wanted to find Oliver's killer if only to shake his hand. This was personal, her revenge on behalf of Lindsey.

She'd asked Steve what Stella Broadbent had said about the cowboy.

'She reckoned someone hired him from a strippergram agency and that it was all a huge joke.'

'And where is our hunky cowboy?'

'Don't know,' he'd said. 'Someone was out to make her look stupid. Apparently she'd been experiencing a lot of that kind of thing — you know, wrong deliveries, guests not turning up, parties of school kids arriving for cream teas.'

Honey couldn't help smirking. Stella's upmarket hotel and school kids were worlds apart.

Casper was perusing a copy of the *Western Daily Press* when she was ushered into his presence by Neville.

'Have you seen this?' he demanded without looking up, his tone strident and none too pleased.

She didn't wait for a chair to be offered but sat herself down. She sighed. 'Well, it's only to be expected that it would make the front page.'

The paper rustled indignantly as Casper reappeared. 'But that's just it, my dear girl. We have most certainly *not* made the front page.'

Honey frowned and screwed her head to one side so she could get a look at the front page. The headlines were there. *Prize-Winning Chef Found Murdered.*

'Yes it is.' She dabbed her finger at the headlines.

Casper sniffed disdainfully and fixed her with an accusing glare. 'I *meant* the competition results. No mention of the Bath International Taste Extravaganza until page three, and then only a few oddly chosen words. "Grande Epicure chef wins local award." *Local* award! How dare they! And on *page three*!'

'That's what I wanted to talk to you about: the competition. I need the address of one of the chefs who took part in the final cook-off.' She got her notebook out from her bag. 'His name's Brian Brodie. I'm also interested in Sylvester Pardoe, who I understand you took over from.'

'Correct.' Using just the tips of his fingers, Casper folded the newspaper and placed it to one side. Layering his hands beneath his chin, his piercing eyes fixed her with a challenging stare.

'I don't think I need to tell you that we could do without this very adverse publicity. The committee and I had envisioned an approach from a television channel — you know the sort of thing — cook something up in twenty minutes from basic ingredients. They tell me such programmes do very well. As I am not in the habit of watching television, I have to accept this information second-hand, but I presume the food tastes good enough. Not that it matters that much. It's the publicity that counts.'

'Add butter, salt, garlic and oil and anything tastes good,' Honey murmured. It was true. Every television chef she'd ever seen enriched their recipes with those ingredients.

Casper shrugged. 'Whatever. We could still be in with a chance.' Casper leaned forward, his eyes more piercing than before. 'I want you to deal with this, Honey. I want it wound up and finished with before we get a call from the BBC or any of those other wretched people.'

As usual Casper was at pains to ensure that the city of Bath's prosperity was not blighted by bad publicity. He handed over a list of names. 'Finalists and semi-finalists.'

She saw Oliver Stafford's name and address. She also saw Smudger's.

'And Pardoe?'

He almost purred the information. 'He was a judge. I replaced him.'

'But why did he opt out?'

Casper waved an elegant hand. 'In my view he wasn't up for the job. Got last-minute jitters, I suppose.'

'Do you have his address?' she asked.

He sighed.

She sensed he'd scheduled their meeting to last no more than five minutes. Casper was as fastidious about time as he was about appearance. Everything had to be perfect.

He pressed a button and Neville appeared.

'Get me the folder regarding the BITE competition,' he ordered.

Neville scurried off but was back in no time. Casper passed her a piece of paper.

'Here.'

Closing his eyes, he lay his head back and spun his swivel chair. The interview was at an end.

Honey thanked Neville on her way out.

Sylvester Pardoe ran a restaurant in the Cotswolds. Instinct told her to speak to him first. The coincidence of him opting out of the judging intrigued her. She'd bear it in mind, but for now, back to the Green River.

Her feet were killing her, her toes squashed to distraction within the wickedly witchlike toes of the spiky-heeled shoes. It was choice between barefoot or taxi, and there were no taxis around.

A third alternative came jogging into view. Some clever soul had started up a sedan chair service from the Royal Crescent and all places en route down into the city. Luckily for her a guest of La Reine Rouge had taken advantage and was being dropped outside.

Slipping her sore feet out of the instruments of torture, she waved them over.

The two men carrying the sedan chair were dressed in period costume, tri-corner hats, thigh-length waistcoats, knee-length britches and white stockings. They seemed only slightly breathless. Luckily for them the trip had been downhill all the way. Just as luckily, their passenger was on the plus side of eighty and the minus side of 110 pounds.

Honey eyed the chair with curious intent. Should she? In the hope of losing weight, she tended to walk as much as possible. Bath was a compact city, surrounded by green hills and nestling at the side of a river. But it was getting close to rush hour. Traffic was building up and she'd give anything to rest her aching feet. Besides that, she needed time to think, and a gentle jog home might be just the thing.

'Hey,' she said. 'Can you take me to the Green River Hotel?'

They eyed her up and down as though she were the nicest thing they'd seen all day. For a brief moment she felt flattered until the truth hit her. They were working out whether they could lift her. She felt like a side of pork in a 'Guess the Weight' competition.

'It's flat all the way,' she added by way of incentive. 'Well, most of the way.'

They exchanged looks and took a few deep breaths.

'Right you are, madam,' said one of them, a ruddy-faced chap with thick, dark eyebrows and shoulders the width of a decent-sized doorway. 'That'll be fifteen pounds.'

She balked at the charge, calculating that a taxi would be less. A taxi would also be quicker, but not nearly so much fun. And her feet were hot — almost steaming. And there was that thinking time. Watch the crowds enjoying themselves and plan what to do next.

'OK. Fifteen pounds. And don't spare the horses.'

Even the face of the rosy-cheeked man visibly paled. 'You don't mean that, do you?'

She shook her head and smiled. 'No. Just kidding. Take it as slow as you like.'

She paid her money, they took their places fore and aft between the shafts, and she clambered in.

The sedan chair swayed and rocked in time with the trotting bearers. The inside was lined with blue brocade. If it wasn't for the traffic wardens and fat women in tight shorts, she could almost believe she'd travelled back two hundred years.

At sight of the passing sedan, heads turned and hands scrabbled for digital cameras.

'Hey, Arnold would you look at that!'

The same comment — without the Arnold — was voiced in German, Japanese and a whole host of other languages.

The swaying of the chair began to make her seasick. *Fix your eyes on a steady point; that's what Carl used to say.* But nothing seemed fixed. It hadn't worked when she'd gone sailing with her husband, and it didn't work now.

So, concentrate on something important.

Gulping down the bile, Honey sank back against the upholstery and thought about the dead chef. What had been her immediate impression of him? Good looking. Yes, she had to admit it. She could understand why women fell for him. She recalled the wicked wink and the way his eyes had swept over her. She'd blushed. Oh yes, Oliver Stafford had been a charmer. A mere glance and a few sweet words could make a woman feel on top of the world. Not a woman of her age, of course. Older women didn't fall for flattery quite so easily, at least that was what she told herself.

A shout from the street caught her attention.

'Hey, is there someone important in that there chair?'

Important? Yes! This could be fun. She'd play at being important.

Sitting bolt upright, she adopted the regal pose; nose high and hand waving like a slowed-down metronome.

Of course I'm important, she told herself and felt her spirits soar. It was the best she'd felt in weeks.

They passed from the busier hub of the city and into Great Pulteney Street. Minutes from home. Seconds in a taxi.

Guests coming out of the Green River Hotel stopped in their tracks, gawping at the liveried bearers and their swaying chair. Some ran back inside and returned with ever more gawping tourists.

The crowd loomed closer, cameras at the ready, batteries whirring in unison.

The bearers set down the chair.

'Is that the Queen?' someone asked.

Coming to a sudden halt brought Honey down to earth. She didn't feel like a queen — not any kind of queen.

'I feel sick,' she said as she squeezed herself out of the narrow door.

'It's the motion,' said one of the bearers. 'A lot of elderly people have trouble with it.'

She threw him a killer glare. 'Thanks a bunch.'

Lindsey pushed her way to the front of the crowd gathered around the chair. 'Mother!'

'I'm all right, dear. I just need a bit of fresh air.' She patted her face and waved her hand. Her cheeks felt hot. It seemed the whole world was a carousel, its spinning slowing as her eyeballs stopped pretending they were hitting tilt on a pinball machine.

Lindsey's expression was unchanged — something between exasperation and irritation.

'You might be OK,' she murmured, 'but Smudger isn't.'

Bump! Her eyeballs and everything else snapped back to reality. 'What now?'

'I think he's going to murder the butcher.'

'Really?'

Unbelievable.

The Davis brothers had been her meat suppliers since the very beginning. They were old-style butchers and gentlemen, and although Smudger sometimes had a go at their delivery drivers, he'd never had a serious set-to with the butchers themselves. True, the steaks were sometimes returned if he wasn't impressed with the ratio of marbling to meat, but on the whole things were congenial.

And why shouldn't they be? Mr Glyn Davis was seventy-eight but still raised his own steers, and after the slaughterhouse had done the necessary, he butchered them himself. Mr Trevor Davis, his brother, took care of the general administration. 'He's got more of a head for it, being younger than me,' Glyn had once explained. Trevor was only seventy-six.

'Poor Mr Davis,' said Honey as they headed for the kitchen.

Lindsey put her right. 'Not Mr Davis. Mr Mead.'

'What happened?'

'He tried to persuade Smudger into buying our meat from him.'

'And?'

'Smudger simmered and showed him the door.'

The kitchen door swung on its hinges. Smudger appeared looking as though his head was about to explode.

Honey prepared herself. Lindsey followed.

Smudger was red in the face and glared when she came in. 'Tell whoever the duff nut is on reception that the next time they send a supplier into my kitchen without telling me first, I'll pickle their nuts in vinegar!'

Lindsey mumbled an apology.

Honey sensed her daughter's awkwardness.

'No nuts,' said Honey. 'Lindsey didn't know he didn't have an appointment.'

Eyes like billiard balls, Smudger glowered. 'Just don't!'

Muttering to himself, he stormed back to the kitchen. She raised her eyes to heaven. Why do I put up with it?

The answer came in parts. Number one, he was a good chef. Number two, firing him and employing another meant getting used to someone. Compatibility was important. And Smudger and she were compatible — most of the time.

She considered all this as she and Lindsey returned like smacked pooches to reception.

Sighing, Lindsey picked up a pen, fiddled with it and poked it through her hair to an itchy spot on her scalp. She avoided meeting her mother's eyes, bit her bottom lip and looked apologetic. 'The phone rang before I could tell Smudger that Mr Mead wanted to see him. As I answered it, he sneaked through into the kitchen. He said Grandma had suggested he pop in.'

Honey rolled her eyes, wishing her mother would keep out of her business and not have recently fallen in love with Roland Mead.

First things first. Smooth the ego of the head chef.

Placating difficult customers was as nothing to placating difficult chefs. Like wild animals, they were extremely territorial. No one was allowed into their space without permission.

'OK, OK. I'll sneak out there and go on bended knee.'

Usually, Lindsey would have responded, saying something like, '*He's only a chef, not the Queen*,' or '*He only bites when there's a full moon*.' Today she said nothing. Honey knew how she was feeling; neither of them could melt the ice that had formed between them since Oliver Stafford's death and Lindsey's confession.

* * *

It was gone two in the morning and Brian Brodie sat alone at a table in his own restaurant staring at a dark spot on the wall where the damp was coming through.

He'd sat staring a lot since Oliver Stafford's murder, wondering what he should do. Was there any real point in talking to the police?

The sound of something moving in the kitchen made him shiver. He knew instinctively who it was. Flight and fight fought unequally inside him. He couldn't do either. He just had to stand and face the music, simply because there was nowhere and no one to run to.

Shaking like a jelly, he got up slowly, droplets of sweat hot on his forehead but freezing instantly. His hands were moist. He rubbed them down his thighs as he stared in the direction of the kitchen. He had to go out there. He had to see. He had to explain that he wouldn't relate anything Oliver had told him.

The kitchen was warm and almost dark. By the blue hue of the fly zapper hanging in a dark corner, he looked around him. The stainless-steel equipment shone icily cold in the bluish glow. Shadows fell blackly onto a greyish floor. The kitchen was empty, and yet he wasn't sure . . .

'I've not spoken to the police,' he said, his voice tremulous and a looseness in his bowels. 'I won't say anything.'

No response. He sighed with relief, his heart hammering against his rib cage. No one. No one at all.

He went across to the oven. Tins of dough were proofing prior to being baked into bread. He peered in; two tins had been pushed too far to the back. They'd burn once the oven came on. He reached in, his head resting on his arm, half in and half out of the oven. A heavy object came down on the nape of his neck, severing the spinal cord.

He lay like that among the proofing loaves until five o'clock, when the timer clicked and the oven came on.

* * *

At breakfast time, Honey was humming her way around reception. On spotting Lindsey she felt a surge of motherly love, that old protectiveness that makes a tiger out of a pussy cat.

'Lindsey, I'm sorry . . .'

The phone rang. Lindsey pounced on it, and her mother knew why. The phone ringing was like a chance to draw breath, to prepare herself for some home truths and all the old tears and apologies between parent and child.

Lindsey's expression altered as she took the call. Raising her eyes she looked directly at her mother.

Honey's nerves went on full-scale alert as she read Lindsey's expression. Something bad had happened.

'It's Steve Doherty. Another chef's been found murdered.'

'Jesus!' Honey closed her eyes and tried not to imagine another cut throat, another life lost.

Lindsey seemed to read what she was thinking. 'It's not the same as the other one.'

Honey opened her eyes. Lindsey looked right back at her but didn't say a word. Honey read her expression. Not the same method, she read there. But something worse. Much worse.

CHAPTER TEN

At first they wouldn't let her in. 'Extenuating circumstances,' said the uniformed constable standing outside. He wouldn't let on what extenuating circumstances, but a nervous tic developed beneath his right eye when she pressed him. Never mind. She'd find out in due course.

To while away the time she went around the corner to Bonhams in order to collect the 'brazier', as Alistair insisted on calling it. She loitered on the way, welcoming the smell of greenery in Queen Square, where office workers and young women with babies were sitting on the grass in the sun. The trees were rustling in the breeze and the traffic was lazy but not too congested.

An empty bench lured her into sitting down for a while. She rummaged in her bag and brought out Sylvester Pardoe's address in the Cotswold town of Broadway, a place of haute cuisine and high prices. OK, this was a police investigation, but there was nothing to stop her phoning him and enquiring as to the reason why he'd dropped out of the judging panel. She could say she was a journalist and not give her real name.

Strike while the iron's hot.

'Hello?'

The voice on the other end of her phone put her through to Sylvester Pardoe. She rattled off the lie, but wished she'd thought it through a bit more when he asked her for her name.

'Mary Jane Jefferies,' she said.

'I suppose you know that the winner of the competition was murdered,' she added. 'Would you like to comment as to why you withdrew? I mean, did you have a premonition that something bad would happen?'

She winced at her own lies. They sounded so lame.

There was a pause.

'Are you for real?'

Honey panicked. 'Of course I am. Why shouldn't I be?'

A pause again. She could almost feel his distrust coming over the airwaves.

'Personal reasons.'

'May I ask what they were?' Honey asked.

'No. You may not.'

The line went dead.

'Friendly,' she muttered, pushing her phone down inside her bag. What next?

It was a hop and a skip from there to Bonhams and the ugly bra that awaited her, but a few more minutes to unwind wouldn't go amiss.

A man she thought was vaguely familiar joined her, sitting at the far end of the bench. Unfolding a brown paper bag from his pocket, he began to eat a crusty roll. Recognising a free lunch when they saw one, a host of pigeons converged around his feet. One of them was more resolute than the others, attacking its comrades each time they dared dive at the same crumb it fancied.

The man laughed at their antics. She looked at him. He looked back.

'I knows you,' he said in a broad West Country accent.

Honey frowned. Did she know him? Did she want to admit knowing him? He had bright-red cheeks and thatched eyebrows.

'You knows who I am,' he said expansively, spreading his hands palms outwards.

She stared blankly. Did she?

'Of course, of course, of course,' he said, on seeing her expression. 'You don't recognise me without me clothes.'

There was something about that statement that wasn't quite right. He was wearing corduroy trousers and a denim shirt. He wasn't *without* clothes. He was *wearing* clothes. And she didn't recall seeing a red-faced man naked — not lately, anyway.

'I'm sorry?'

He reached down and retrieved something from the paper carrier bag he'd placed on the ground. He placed it on his head.

Honey recognised the tri-corner hat of the sedan chair bearer. 'Now you knows me,' he said with a cheery grin.

'Ah, yes. Of course I do,' she said brightly.

'I used to run a pub. Got fed up of that though. Good class of customers, but that don't mean they ain't no bother. We had bother, all right, though not too often. You got a hotel?' he asked seemingly as an afterthought.

She told him she did.

'Got chefs to deal with, then. They can be right aggro, they can. I remember one real bad set-to. Two chefs going hammer and tongs at each other. Award-winning chefs too, they was. They'd 'ave killed each other if I 'adn't stepped in and sorted them out.'

'I can see that.' She certainly could. His shoulders were as broad as his accent.

Her appraisal was too evident. Looking pleased as punch, he rolled his shoulders. 'I need broad shoulders for what I do now. And they suits the costume, don't you think?'

It was on her mind to say that the three-cornered hat and the Marks and Spencer polyester-mix trousers didn't go that well together. He seemed to read her thoughts.

'I'm on half day today.'

She had visions of one bearer struggling with the sedan chair all by himself.

'There's three of us. We take it in shifts. You know one of our bearers.'

He handed her a business card, the sort created by any half-decent software package.

'I do?' She looked for enlightenment on the grubby card. All it said was Sedate Sedans and gave a telephone number.

'Clint — you know, Rodney Eastwood.'

Her jaw dropped. Clint did the washing up on a casual basis, was a bouncer at the Zodiac in the wee hours, and helped out at Oxfam when needed. She shook her head in amazement. 'How many jobs does that boy have?'

The man grinned. 'At least he works for his bread. Can't say fairer than that, eh? There ain't no shame in having more than one job. I got more than one meself. Sometimes I do a bit of furniture bumping for the antiques auctions — you know, lifting stuff from lorries and getting it into their auction rooms.'

A vision of voluptuous underwear sprang to mind. Lot sixty-nine or whatever it was. Honey made her excuses to leave.

'I'll see you around some time.' Bits of his conversation — a certain bit in particular — caused her to pause.

'You don't happen to know the name of the chefs who were fighting, do you?'

'Once met, never forgotten,' he said with a jerk of his head and a shake of a finger. 'Oliver Stafford and Sylvester Pardoe. Hated each other, they did. Pardoe was a regular customer. Stafford was chasing one of my barmaids.'

'Par for the course, from what I hear,' she said, walking backwards before turning to head more quickly in the direction of Bonhams.

'Any time you want two burly men to pick you up, just give us a ring,' he shouted after her.

Misinterpreting what was actually being said, curiosity appeared on the faces of the lunchtime crowd.

Blushing like a virgin bride, she ran past the mothers with babies and the office workers with brie baguettes and Diet Pepsi. She arrived at Bonhams still red in the face, but more so from breathlessness than embarrassment.

Alistair was sitting at his desk some way behind the counter.

'I came for my purchase.'

He got up slowly from his chair, stretching each limb in turn and not moving towards her and the counter until he was sure he'd reached full extension.

'I thought you might have put them into the next auction, seeing as you don't want them,' he said, eyeing her in his slow, perfunctory manner.

'The thought did occur to me, but then I considered making them part of a fancy-dress outfit — you know, Madonna on tour.'

Alistair pursed his lips and gave her what her mother called an 'old-fashioned' look. With slow deliberation, he pulled the unwanted article from beneath the counter.

Honey stared. They were salmon pink and conical, with ever-decreasing circlets of stitching finally ending in sharp points, as unlike the shape of breasts as it was possible to be. And they were large. Not handsomely, lustfully large, but horrendous, Hammer House of Horror large.

She shook her head as she held them up before her face, her arms at full stretch. 'I don't know anyone that size.'

Alistair had that deadpan expression even when he was happy or sad or just nothing. But his eyes twinkled, though his voice was flat as a pancake.

'Do you go tenpin bowling?'

She shook her head.

Alistair shook his too.

Honey held them up at eye level and eyed them thoughtfully. 'A pair of hanging baskets?'

Alistair nodded. 'They'd take a good few geraniums.'

CHAPTER ELEVEN

Ambience, thought Honey as she entered the latest catering establishment to boast a dead chef in its kitchen. Steve had been loath to give her the details, except the name Brian Brodie. His restaurant was the Samuel Pepys, named so after the great seventeenth-century diarist.

'That's two chefs who took part in the Grande Epicure dead in suspicious circumstances,' she said excitedly, her mind working overtime. 'Two dead and one to go.'

He looked puzzled. 'What's this *Grandie* thing got to do with it?'

'Grande Epicure. It's a contest run in France for top-flight chefs. The competition's fierce. A chef would kill to win it.'

There followed a pause.

'Would they now? Was your chef one of the participants, by any chance?'

She made a face. Why couldn't she engage her brain before opening her mouth? The genes of course. Her mother was just the same.

'He had an alibi.'

'For both murders?'

She stuck her neck out. 'I'm almost certain.'

'Almost?'

Suddenly she didn't like the tone of his voice. 'I trust Smudger.' She knew she sounded defensive, but she believed in supporting her staff. This usually amounted to inter-staff disputes or customer grievances. Murder wasn't usually on the list.

Now she had something extra to tell him. Sylvester Pardoe and Oliver Stafford had had a fight.

Before leaving the Green River, she'd told Lindsey to inform Casper of the latest murder. She was expecting him to ring and prepared herself accordingly. No sign of it would filter into his voice, but he wouldn't be pleased. She'd bet a pound to a penny on that.

Her phone played a snatch of the *1812 Overture*, a thunderous and apt introduction for a man like him.

'Casper.'

'Are the press there?'

She glanced out at the small crowd gathering on the pavement, recognising a few freelance reporters and photographers.

'I'm afraid so.'

Casper grunted an acknowledgement. Casper St John Gervais never allowed sympathy to get in the way of practical considerations. Still, what he said next was a bit surprising.

'On the plus side the Samuel Pepys will have its fifteen minutes of fame.'

Well that was to the point. Honey couldn't help a hint of sarcasm creeping into her voice. 'Quite so, Casper. I can just see a full-page advertisement on the "Dining Out" page in the *Bath Chronicle*.'

'Quite. Let me know the details *tout de suite*.'

He rang off.

She pulled a face. She really couldn't believe that Casper *would* consider an ad in 'Dining Out'. My, but the man was mercenary. For her part she was feeling regretful on two counts. Number one, she and Lindsey had just been about to make a breakthrough in their lately strained relationship.

Number two, she wished she'd visited Brian Brodie before this happened.

The Samuel Pepys was notable for its terracotta floors and exposed stone walls. An interior designer with a Chelsea background and the right connections had been engaged to upgrade the décor when Brodie had bought the place. Oak Windsor chairs had been replaced by designer wickerwork, stained-dark tables by light oak and dripping candles by twelve-volt LED lighting.

'Must have cost a fortune,' Honey muttered as she took everything in.

Someone went to fetch Steve, who was still exchanging details with the initial forensic team. She spent the waiting time peering at a wall-mounted menu.

'British-based cooking . . . emphasis on home-grown produce . . . free-range Suffolk chickens, Dublin Bay prawns and Wye Valley salmon and asparagus . . . happy lives . . . optimum taste.'

'I doubt the chickens, prawns and salmon would quite see it that way,' she muttered, then realised what she was doing. 'I must stop talking to myself, I must stop talking to myself, I must—'

'Honey. Are you talking to yourself?' Steve had been fetched quicker than she'd expected. Day-old stubble contrasted with deep-blue eyes and overgrown dark hair curling over his collar. A little longer and he'd need to tie it back 'Tom Jones' style — Tom Jones the eighteenth-century rake, not Tom Jones the singer.

Her smile was as ready-made as baked beans and not quite natural. 'Whatever makes you think that?'

His eyes ran over her like maple syrup over ice cream. 'You're looking good.'

She was wearing jeans and a sailor-type top with an interesting neckline — just a hint of cleavage rather than the Rhone Valley.

'It's the latest thing for murder scenes and straight from the Paris catwalk.'

'Nice.'

Nice was the height of flattery coming from Doherty and made her glow. It also made her fancy him more, though she wouldn't tell him that. He got too cocky if he thought he had the upper hand. Letting him know how much she fancied him would *definitely* be giving him the upper hand. She turned flippant. 'So what's on the menu?'

'A dead chef. Cooked to perfection.'

She pulled a face. 'Are you serious?' All her enthusiasm for telling him about Pardoe turned to smoke.

'Yep. As crisp as a turkey, though without the trimmings.'

It wasn't funny and he hadn't meant it to be. His expression was deadly serious. Being flippant helped him cope.

Honey gulped down her revulsion and followed him. They went through a door that led into a corridor with a red quarry-tiled floor. Halfway along another door opened into the kitchen. The aroma of roast pork drifted out each time it swung open. She sniffed and immediately felt sick. There was something odd about it, a hint of toasted aftershave. She didn't need anyone to tell her the nature of the meat.

Steve held his arm across, roughly at the same height as the police incident tape. 'You can't go in. None of us can until this lot have done their thing.'

On the other side the Scene of Crime people and Forensic team were doing their thing. The medical examiner was first to emerge. It was his job to formally state that the victim was dead, though how anyone could not be dead after roasting overnight on gas mark 7 would be a miracle.

He spoke directly to Steve.

'Most definitely dead. Blow to the back of the head. Can't say when it happened but can say when his head began to cook. He was already dead when the oven came on.'

Honey felt her stomach heaving. How could anyone say that without throwing up?

She'd never get used to this kind of thing. Finding a perpetrator was one thing. Actually seeing the dead was something else. It was the puzzle that intrigued her. The victims only made her sick and a little sad.

Steve looked perplexed.

The medical examiner went into detail. 'The oven's got a timer on it. The commis chef says that it's always set to turn on automatically for five o'clock in the morning. They make their own bread, you see.'

The thought of bread and the smell of roasting meat on an empty stomach was too much. Honey was vaguely aware of the floor coming up to meet her nose.

She was also vaguely aware of being hurried along the corridor.

'He got hit on the back of the head and fell forward onto a shelf,' Steve explained once she'd come round and vowed never to eat pork ever again. She was sitting in a fashionably minimalist club chair, Steve's arm hovering protectively around her.

As her eyes began to focus, they alighted on a slim blonde with an orange suntan and a skirt that showed more than it covered. She was sobbing into a man-size handkerchief — or it could have been a napkin. She caught herself hoping that they had a good laundry service.

Steve saw where she was looking. 'That's Sandy Brown, Brian Brodie's girlfriend.'

She recalled her conversation with Richard Carmelli, the commis chef at the Beau Brummell, but couldn't remember the details too clearly.

'Not his wife?' Her voice sounded hollow as though she were speaking from the bottom of a rabbit hole.

His smile kind of floated in and out of her vision as he shook his head. Her eyelids felt heavy.

She sighed. 'I feel like going to bed.'

A smile smothered his face. He whispered in her ear. 'Just name the time and the place.'

She threw him a *you should be so lucky* kind of smile designed to put on the brakes. Her hormones were going full gallop and won the day. 'I don't suppose I'd kick you out,' she said as an afterthought. He liked that. She could tell by the way his fingers brushed against the side of her breast.

And the smile. Christ, how could he smile with all this going on? That poor chef. Even at his most irritating she had never considered roasting Smudger in his own oven.

'Come on.' Steve sounded concerned.

She made a firm effort not to fall against him as he helped her to her feet. 'I'll be OK.' He looked a bit put out when she waved him away, but her attention was firmly fixed on the sobbing girl.

The male members of the team investigating the murder scene were also paying attention to the delectable Sandy. The girl's skirt stretched like a black bandage across her willowy thighs. A white-cotton gusset winked with each strangled sob and the crossing and re-crossing of her mile-long legs. She was wearing an off-the-shoulder white top, too tight to be decent. No bra. Her nipples were like dark eyes peering through a fog. She was about twenty.

Sandy Brown was sitting at one end of a wickerwork sofa. The wickerwork was bronze, the cushions beige and sprinkled with gold thread. Very tasteful. And very expensive, Honey guessed.

She fingered the chair arm and the cushion before sitting down and guessed it was designer.

'It's Fiona Davenport,' said the girl, referring to the trendy sofa, almost as though it were a star of stage, screen and television.

Honey made a face. 'Wow. The guy must have been loaded.'

'Brian liked nice things.'

It occurred to Honey to ask in more detail how Brian Brodie could have afforded the services of an interior designer whose efforts were often featured in *Country Living* and *House Beautiful* magazine.

'The restaurant must have been doing extremely well.'

The sobs had turned to a well-rehearsed simper. 'The best in Bath. He did *ever* so well.'

But not well enough, thought Honey in response to the defensiveness in the girl's voice. Her eyes flitted over the restaurant, mentally counting the number of *couverts* and coming out at around forty. Forty at around forty pounds per head? One hundred pounds per head? And how often was the restaurant full? Generally it was safe to base the turnover rate at around twenty-five per cent capacity. But the hospitality industry was notoriously optimistic.

The girl blew her nose loudly. Honey winced. Just as she'd guessed, close up the large handkerchief turned out to be a table napkin. Not hygienic, but forgivable in the circumstances.

'Was Brian ever married?'

'He was.'

'So how long had you two been together?'

'Two weeks.'

'I see.'

'His wife left him two years ago,' sniffed the girl, pre-empting Honey's next question.

'And you moved in with him?'

The girl pulled a face. 'Not straightaway. Not until his other girlfriend moved out.'

Honey sized her up. She instinctively knew that this was not the girlfriend Oliver Stafford had been having an affair with. This was eye candy. Not even that. More like a cuddly toy, something silent and cute to cuddle up to.

'Do you know who'd want to kill him?'

The girl shook her head. 'He was a lovely man.'

Steve threw her a quick nod of understanding. There was nothing this girl could say to assist them in their enquiries. Honey nodded back. Steve turned to the gathered professionals.

'Anyone available to take this girl home?'

A host of hot-blooded Scene of Crime officers, plus two paramedics who'd been called out and had stopped for coffee, rushed forward like a human tsunami. The paramedics won.

'You need a lie down, love.'

They steered her towards the waiting ambulance.

Honey and everyone there looked on. 'I suppose that's what they call community spirit,' Honey remarked to Steve.

He grinned and passed her a glass of cold water poured from a blue bottle. He also ordered her to stay put while he oversaw the removal of the corpse and the reintroduction of his wayward officers to their duties.

Honey lay her head back, closed her eyes and gathered her thoughts. Two chefs dead. Both had taken part in the same competition. Only one of them had won, so there was no case of jealousy to answer here. So why these two chefs? Perhaps there was going to be another competition, and one chef was whittling down the opposition beforehand. *Please don't let it be Smudger.*

Her thinking was disrupted.

The uniformed police guarding the door were arguing with two big pieces of brown furniture that had sprouted heads, arms and possibly even legs. She couldn't quite see from her laid-back angle, so jerked herself upright to see more clearly.

The police were telling the walking wardrobes that they couldn't come in. The wardrobes were talking back and saying they had every right to come in and collect their property.

Closing her eyes, she resumed the reclining position. It was none of her business. She had no rights getting involved. Then one of them mentioned the magic words.

'It's our salamander, and the payments are in arrears.'

He did ever so well.

Honey shot up and charged over to the new arrivals. Sandy Brown knew nothing.

'I'd like a word with you guys.'

The big guys turned their ugly mugs in her direction. So did the boys in blue.

'Steve Doherty will OK it,' she said to the latter.

The two wardrobes, their arms bursting from the sleeves of their coal-black T-shirts, ambled into the restaurant. They looked her up and down.

'I'm working with the police,' she said. 'There's been a murder.'

If their faces could have paled they would have. Instead their chins kind of retracted into their jaws. 'That's nothing to do with us,' one of them said.

'So you won't mind answering a few questions.'

She studied them as they thought it through. They'd looked almost identical when viewed at a distance. Up front there were subtle differences. One had a cauliflower ear and the other had a broken nose.

Cauliflower ear exchanged a look with broken nose before proclaiming their decision. 'S'pose not.'

'How much did Brodie owe you?'

Broken nose adopted an indignant look. 'Not enough to kill for. We don't do things like that. We just repossess.'

'Yeah, repossess,' echoed his partner.

'We want the salamander.'

'Yeah. The salamander.'

They both spoke as though their tongues were too big for their mouths. And they were very big, almost round. Tweedle Dee and his brother.

'Do you know what a salamander is?' she asked them.

They looked at each other before one of them answered. 'It's something in the kitchen.'

'A grill,' she said. 'Wait here. I'll check that the police are finished.'

Luckily for the repo guys, the salamander — chef terminology for a large wall-mounted grill — was in a separate part of the kitchen that could be entered through another door, so they wouldn't be contaminating the crime scene. After disconnecting the gas, the two guys unbolted it and heaved it onto their shoulders.

'Why do I think I should be humming the funeral march,' she muttered as she watched them progress sedately out of the door.

One of Steve Doherty's team heard her. 'Sorry, did you say something?'

'Tell Steve I have to go, but I'll be seeing him.'

He promised he'd do that.

Despite him being busy, Honey hoped that he'd call and ask her out tonight. Depending on staffing levels, the dishwasher and whether she could find something to wear, she'd be up for that. She was in need of a night out after a day like this.

She stepped out of the restaurant and walked along Quiet Street, a stone's throw from Queen Square.

The city air was as fresh as a mountain stream after the smell of death. She thought about sitting a while in Queen Square again. That was until she saw her mother coming the other way, arm in arm with a man whose identity wasn't quite clear, though vaguely familiar.

'No thanks,' she muttered, heading off in the opposite direction, half thinking that she might turn vegetarian.

CHAPTER TWELVE

Having avoided her mother and her new lover boy, she made for a seat in Abbey Churchyard, reckoning she needed the break after what she'd been through. The smell of singed flesh lingered in her nostrils.

Purchasing a coffee from Starbucks en route, she sat down preparing to enjoy the passing scene. It was like taking a seat at the United Nations but without the speeches. Everyone was enjoying themselves.

A crowd of French students huddled together while a colleague took a photo. Their smiles were cheesy. Were they saying 'cheese' or '*fromage*'? Whatever, they were interesting to watch — chic, even, in their youth.

Steve rang. 'Are you OK?' He sounded worried. She pictured him trying to disguise the fact. It made her feel better though slightly naughty. For a second she toyed with the idea of encouraging even more sympathy. No. Not fair. She made an effort.

'Fine. No breakfast this morning. You know . . . an empty stomach and all that.'

'Get some fresh air.'

'I am. I'm sitting in Abbey Churchyard.'

'Alone?'

'In Abbey Churchyard? Are you kidding?'

'I meant close companions.'

Was he jealous? The idea was quite thrilling.

'None.'

'By the way, you dropped something when you keeled over.'

Did she? She couldn't remember and hadn't noticed. Her keys? Her purse?

'I hadn't noticed.' She did a brief rummage of her copious tan shoulder bag. Everything seemed in order.

'Hmm.' For a brief moment she was sure she heard a trace of amusement. What the devil could be so funny after finding Brian Brodie like that?

'Never mind,' he went on. 'I'll bring it along to the Zodiac tonight — if you're up for it.' He sounded tired.

The Zodiac was one of their favourite haunts, subterranean and dingily impersonal. It was open until the wee hours and was a place where hard-pressed hoteliers, restaurateurs and pub landlords gathered to unwind once their own businesses were closed.

'I'm afraid it's got to be around the witching hour.'

'Yeah. I guessed that.'

He hung up.

There was nothing she could do about the time. During their brief relationship, he'd insinuated she was too controlling, wanting to oversee everything at the hotel until most guests had gone to bed. She hadn't argued with that. Delegating responsibility wasn't her thing. If that was controlling, then that was her.

Tonight he'd brief her on what he knew so far. She wondered at Brian Brodie's previous girlfriend. Funny him being shacked up with a bit of fluff so soon after she'd left. Seemed like he and Oliver Stafford were tarred with the same brush. Both liked to play around. What about Sylvester Pardoe? She made a mental note to check up on him when the hotel and other pressures allowed.

Now, what was it Steve had picked up that she'd dropped? She delved into her bag again. Nothing important was missing. Never mind. He might be mistaken.

* * *

The facade of the Green River Hotel gleamed like gold in the late afternoon. It was her favourite time of day. She looked along Pulteney Street, admiring the hard black shadows falling from one side of the street and the honeycomb colour of buildings on the other. Mary Jane, their resident doctor of parapsychology, was right. If you squinted it was easy to imagine women in bonnets and empire line dresses, and Regency bucks in tight-fitting trousers and riding boots. The smell would be different, though — waste from a horse's rear end rather than the exhaust pipe of a BMW.

Lindsey looked up from behind the reception desk. She managed a weak smile.

'I didn't expect you back so early.'

Her expression made Honey think she'd taken her off guard. She looked slightly panic stricken, her hands seeming to be buried behind the high top of the reception desk.

'Now what? What's gone wrong?'

Lindsey looked hurt. 'Nothing's gone wrong.'

She sounded defensive.

Honey counted to ten and drove the suspicious thoughts away. Lindsey had made one big mistake. Honey was still trying to deal with her disappointment, but it wasn't easy.

She didn't mean to march so swiftly to the counter. She also didn't mean to be so obvious about trying to see what Lindsey was hiding.

'These are for you,' her daughter said suddenly.

Dark-red roses nestled against white freesias and dark-green leaves.

Normally Honey would have had to scrutinise a tiny booklet to see who had sent her the flowers. In this instance she didn't need to. The card was flat and white and said simply, 'TO MY MOTHER. WITH LOVE.'

Honey bit her lip. Red roses with velvety petals always brought a lump to her throat. Carl had bought her such roses back in the good old days before they'd married. He'd bought her the same for each and every anniversary and when Lindsey was born. Then they'd stopped and bunches of indiscriminate flowers had arrived via Interflora, yellows and pinks and purples. She'd known he hadn't chosen them, knew that what had been something special had become no more than a duty.

Silently, Honey wrapped her arms around her daughter. 'I'm sorry.'

'So am I,' said Lindsey, hugging her back.

They both sniffed as they parted.

'Any messages?' Honey at last asked.

'Nothing important.' Lindsey suddenly turned all furtive, looking around her and dropping her voice to just above a whisper. 'Mary Jane wants to see you.'

'What's wrong?'

'Shh! Grandma will hear you.' She took the flowers. 'Here, let me take them. I'll put them in water.'

Honey frowned. 'What does Mary Jane want?'

'She wants to give you some advice.'

She was shoved into the storeroom just behind reception. Mary Jane was sitting cross-legged on the floor. How a woman of her age ever got in such a position was a mystery. It was a wonder she didn't break something. She was in one of her trances, head back, elbows bent, palms upwards.

'What's going on?'

'As you are no doubt aware, Grandma's got a boyfriend,' said Lindsey.

'Yes, and he's got a Rolls Royce. You know how she is about that particular make of car. I'm not opposed. It'll keep her off my back.'

She made to leave. Lindsey pulled her back. 'Grandma's not a very good judge of character.'

Honey eyed her daughter and paused that bit too long. Her mother stepping out with Mead the butcher was surprising. But this was no corner shop outfit he owned. He had 'brass', as northern folk would say — warehouse interests, property and foreign supply depots.

'Anyway,' Honey added without thinking, 'we all make mistakes with men at some point in our lives. Some of us worse mistakes than others. It's probably hereditary.'

'OK. So perhaps I inherited my recent lapse from her,' said Lindsey in the glum manner she'd adopted of late.

'I'm sorry, I didn't mean . . .'

An indignant Mary Jane threw her hands up in the air, her batwing sleeves causing one hell of a draught.

'Nice flowers,' she said, opening one eye. 'However, I'd appreciate if you guys could shut your traps. Give me silence and I'll tell you what the future holds.'

Honey shrugged at Lindsey. In response her daughter dragged her over to the door and whispered.

'Mary Jane's already done the tarot and given a verdict. She reckons Grandma's new boyfriend is up to no good. And he's younger than her.'

'Younger as in?'

'At least sixty.'

Honey heaved a sigh of relief and waved her hand in front of her face. 'Thank goodness for that. For a moment I thought you were going to say that he was forty-six.'

'I'm worried about Grandma,' said Lindsey.

'She's old enough to look after herself.' The old saying, 'There's no fool like an old fool' ran through her mind like ticker tape.

'I don't know what she sees in him,' whispered Lindsey.

'He drives a white Rolls Royce.'

Lindsey nodded sagely. Everyone knew that Gloria Cross went weak-kneed at the thought of a man with a Rolls Royce. Not the chauffeur, of course, but the owner; it proved he had the bank account to afford the fuel and parking fines.

Honey gave what she thought was a philosophical appraisal. 'Perhaps the guy's up front and just wants a bit of company. He's not likely to be after her body at her age — unless he's an amateur undertaker.'

Lindsey was more blunt. 'No. We know he's not. He's a butcher.'

'Butcher by trade, butcher by nature,' Mary Jane said suddenly.

Cripes! Honey rolled her eyes. Suddenly she wanted to be up on the ceiling, away from all this madness.

'I think he's got an ulterior motive,' said Lindsey.

Honey folded her arms, resigned to listening no matter what. 'OK. Shoot.'

'I think he's after our meat order.'

CHAPTER THIRTEEN

Although there were far more important things to think about, the fact that her mother was in a relationship with Roland Mead stayed with Honey all evening. Those words Lindsey had uttered, '*He's after our meat order*,' were worrying.

Was it possible? Could the man be that conniving?

She couldn't help but confront him when her mother entered the hotel excitedly proclaiming that they'd booked a table in the restaurant.

His handshake felt warm and moist and lingered too long. His smile stripped the clothes from her body. Her worst fears were realised.

'I'm going to chance the steak,' he said in a way that left Honey in no doubt that he intended finding fault. 'It won't be up to my standards, no doubt, but I'll be lenient in my judgement.'

His smile was wide, his toupee was neatly straightened and his eyes dove down the front of her dress. Perhaps that was why he didn't appear to recognise her from their meeting in the kitchen of the Beau Brummell. She didn't enlighten him. Her mother seemed too enthralled with Mr Toupee to notice.

Honey had a strong urge to hit him between the eyes.

'My daughter's a widow too,' said Gloria Cross with surprising frankness. 'And the silly girl's had such wonderful opportunities. You would never believe how many eligible men I've introduce her to. Rich, of course. All professionals. But will she listen? No! She's like all these youngsters nowadays. They all know better than their elders.'

'Happen you're right, petal. There's no substitute for the University of Life.'

Honey cringed when he kissed her mother's hand. Bowing slightly from the waist sent his toupee tipping forward.

Her mother went off to powder her nose. 'Won't be long my big Aberdeen Angus.'

Honey couldn't contain her surprise.

Roland turned his attention back to her. 'Your mother likes bulls. I keep bulls — Aberdeen Angus. They're chunky, slow-growing and well-muscled.' His grin suited his trade — thick and meaty. 'A bit like me.'

'Is that so?' It was quite true that Mead was as big as a bull, but the look in his eyes was pure Big Bad Wolf.

Roland Mead had the kind of smile that's not really meant for anyone but himself. There was a definite flicker of interest as once again his gaze dipped into her cleavage.

'Must say I agree with your darling mother,' he said, his wet tongue lashing along his slippery lips. 'You need a man. A big man, I should think. One built like a bull.'

'I'm engaged,' Honey blurted, making a mental note to have a word with her mother. What did she see in this man? Ah yes! A white Rolls Royce.

She wondered what her mother would say if she knew he was coming on to her. The guy didn't know who he was dealing with.

She thought of him later still when she wriggled herself into a little black dress that always made her feel slimmer. Whether it actually did that was another matter. But never mind. Every little bit helped.

Two bubbles of fat spoiled its smooth lines just a bit higher than her hip bones. Love handles, people called them. Love? Were they kidding?

She retrieved a certain item of underwear from their hideaway at the bottom of a drawer.

It's only temporary, Honey told herself. *I'll lose four pounds by the end of next week. Definitely.*

As she pulled on the slinky spandex, she averted her gaze from the full-length mirror and flipped her mind back to basics. Was it really just a coincidence to believe that Roland Mead had wangled his way into Smudger's domain and now he was playing court to her mother?

She wasn't meeting Steve until late, so hung around welcoming guests and diners into the restaurant, one eye always on her mother's bewigged man friend.

She warned Smudger beforehand.

'He's going to order steak. You know the score.'

Smudger grimaced. 'Judge a good restaurant by its steak.'

'He's just trying to get our business.'

Smudger's jaw dropped big time and he spluttered as though about to explode. 'That bloke supplies meat to this place over my dead body!' With a loud bang, he brought a steak mallet down onto a piece of pale-pink veal.

Honey retreated.

The smell of night and the lights of the city beckoned. Restaurants close to the Theatre Royal were still busy. So were the pubs, their doors wide open, their patrons spilling out onto the pavements.

As usual the eyes of the doorman at the Zodiac peered out through a slit at eye level before letting her in.

'Are you in fancy dress?'

She recognised Clint's voice.

'No. Should I be?'

'It's optional.'

'Then I choose not to participate. Let me in.'

The door opened and Honey was mildly shocked to see Clint dressed head to toe in bandages. She looked him up and down. 'Have you had an accident?'

'Course not! I'm an Egyptian mummy.'

'So I see. Have you been raiding the first-aid box?'

He grinned. 'I'd need a lot more than one box of bandages to cover me. The boss hired this for me from a proper fancy-dress place. He reckoned it suited my image.'

Honey nodded a questionable agreement. Clint had a shaved head and scary tattoos. He also wore earrings and a ring through his nose.

She made her way to the bar and perched on a stool. Steve hadn't arrived yet, so she ordered a vodka and slimline for herself. She looked down at her legs. Was this dress too short? Yep. She spied a hole in her stockings a few inches above the knee. Never mind. She took another sip of her drink then tugged at the hem of her skirt to cover the hole. It didn't do much good. Thank God for dim lighting.

The place was filling up. Despite their efforts at fancy dress, she recognised a few hoteliers. Jim Sadler, financial director of a big hotel group, was dressed as a rabbit. A colleague — or it could have been his wife — was dressed as Alice in Wonderland, complete with Alice band on her head and wearing a blue dress. The dress was low cut, the skirt short. Honey frowned. She couldn't remember Alice ever having such a deep cleavage or wearing white stockings held up by frilly garters. Oh well.

She heard laughter that wouldn't have been out of place coming from a hyena. She saw Bling Broadbent draped over a big Samoan who she recognised as a player with the Bath rugby team. He didn't look comfortable with Stella's attention, but Stella didn't seem to notice. She was sozzled and sprawled over the thick thighs that formed his lap.

'I like manly men,' she slurred, running her hand over his chest.

'So I noticed,' Honey murmured into her drink.

The Samoan stood up. He was built like a battleship. Stella slid off him like a bundle of wet seaweed.

'Hey, big boy! You off already?' Her voice was slurred.

The Samoan stomped off, chairs and tables scraping the floor as he sidled through them — as best as anyone of his size could sidle.

Stella's gutted look followed his progress, and her eyes met with Honey's.

'Shit!' She was coming over.

Honey took a sip of her drink and averted her eyes. Hopefully Stella's vision was on the wobble and she wouldn't see her as long as she kept her head down.

'You,' she shouted and pointed a bejewelled finger. 'You! Honey bloody Driver!'

Too late. There was nothing for it. Honey raised her eyes.

Stella staggered across with far less agility than the rugby player. A chair or two toppled over and one or two of the patrons she bumped into ended up wearing their beer instead of drinking it. They shouted at her to watch out. She totally ignored them.

'I want a word with you.' She spat the words. At the same time she attempted to scramble onto the next stool. Her scrambling attracted some attention. Her skirt, a silky brocade number — definitely designer — rode halfway up her thighs. She was wearing fat knickers, the firm sort designed to keep everything under control, the legs ending a few inches above the knees. The height of the stool proved too much. She ended up resting her arms on it, buttocks prominently jutting behind her.

Her smudged make-up was the good stuff. Her gold earrings were the size of toadstools and matched her necklace. Her eyes were narrowed, like a sharpshooter taking aim. Her tongue was totally out of control.

'You've been slandering both my good name and that of my establishment,' she said, making a wobbly stab at being sober.

This was new. Slandering the woman? Well . . . not really . . .

'Slandering you? A woman of your expertise? No. Certainly not. You're quite capable of doing that for yourself.' This was hardly the time for sarcasm. Stella's brain wasn't quite in gear.

She looked puzzled — vaguely aware that Honey had said something clever, though not quite understanding what it was.

She finally seemed to cotton on. Her look darkened. 'You've been spreading rumours that I married a man I met in Texas. That bloody stupid cowboy.'

Honey picked up her drink, swirling the liquid so that the ice clinked against the glass. 'No, but that's what I heard.'

Stella's brows beetled over her nose. 'So who told you?'

Honey took her time answering. Slowly she set her drink down. Slowly she twirled the lemon round with her finger. 'It could have been true. We all do stupid things when we're drunk.'

Stella's indignation was like a spluttering firecracker fizzing all over the place. 'He . . . is . . . not . . . my . . . husband! It's a put-up job. Somebody is out to get me.'

She said it emphatically. She said it loudly. Heads turned. Whispers passed from one curious ear to another.

Honey was relishing this. 'Are you sure? You always did like a big man. Big man, hot Texas night and — and plenty of booze, of course.'

The colour running down Stella's throat matched her rouged cheeks.

'I may have had a drop too much to drink, but I did not sodding marry him! *I did not sodding marry him*! Someone put him up to it. The same outfit doing all the other sodding stuff. You, probably!'

'Not me!' Honey shook her head emphatically.

A whole sentence of nothing but expletives issued from Stella's mouth.

A hushed gasp ran among those who'd heard.

'OK,' said Honey, indicating the crowd with a toss of her head. 'Now everybody knows.'

Stella was livid. Unable to contain her anger, she clutched the handle of her Lacroix handbag and swung it through the air, aiming it at Honey's head. Honey ducked. The back swing of the handbag took Stella with it. She overbalanced, landing flat on her rear, legs in the air.

Honey gasped. So did a lot of other people. Stella's secret was out. Beneath the designer facade, she was wearing 'fat' knickers.

Accompanied by subdued sniggers, a couple of off-duty hotel managers helped her to her feet. The manager of the Zodiac also appeared, his expression as flat as a frying pan.

'I won't have trouble,' he said. His mouth clacked shut like a spring-loaded letterbox. He nodded in the direction of Clint and one of the other doormen. The latter was dressed like Russell Crowe in *Gladiator*, but looked more like a bigger, blonder Brad Pitt.

Cruelly self-satisfied, Honey ordered another drink and watched as Stella was carried out through the door that opened onto North Parade Gardens. The public entrance to the gardens was locked at this time of night, but there was a seat just outside the Zodiac's private exit.

Honey imagined her out there all alone — Stella the hostess with the mostest! She chuckled and raised her drink in a silent toast. Poor Stella. Sitting out there in her designer outfit until she'd sobered up.

The club got stickier as the crowd increased. A bunch of fairies complete with pink tutus, magic wands and five o'clock shadows trouped through to rousing applause. One of them was wearing a pair of rigger boots. Judging by the dust and dirt clinging to the soles, his day job involved manual labour.

Faces she recognised flitted past. Some acknowledged her. Some were too drunk or too wrapped up in the people they were with.

She glanced at her watch. Steve was late. He'd phoned earlier to say he might be held up. He'd phoned last night as well and also around three o'clock this morning. The job was taking its toll. He'd been on duty too long. He was losing track of time.

When she looked up she saw him pressing his way to the bar.

'I forgot where I left my phone,' he explained. 'Had to find it.'

She ordered him a drink and slid it beneath his hand. He looked floppy and worn out. If she'd had a heart or been twenty years younger she might have offered to firm him up a little. As it was, it was getting late and she was doing the breakfast shift in the morning.

'OK. Tell me all about it.'

He yawned. 'No luck with Jones the six-foot-plus rhinestone cowboy.'

'Don't exaggerate. He was only six-two, I think.'

'Big enough.'

He sounded grumpy. She reckoned it was due to the fact that he wasn't much above five-eight himself. But nicely put together.

'Never mind,' she said, patting his hand. 'Big isn't everything.'

'I don't suppose it is, dressed like that bloke was. But somebody must know where he is.'

She'd expected a more sexual riposte, but Steve blew hot and cold. She liked the hot best. His gaze wandered to the fairies, the Roman soldiers and the Jane Austen lookalikes. The latter in particular held his gaze. She could see why. Would Jane's bosom have ballooned out of a 36D cup?

Her mind ticked over as her eyes followed the swirl of crazy outfits. Fancy dress. She felt her face reddening. Was that all Peter Jones had been?

'Shit!'

Steve looked at her. 'I'm sorry?'

Sighing she pushed her drink away and hid her eyes. 'OK, we know the cowboy wasn't for real, but he must have got that costume from somewhere. He might have hired it.'

Steve glanced at the mix of people and outfits. 'You could be right. How many fancy-dress outfitters are there in Bath?'

'One I think, and a few more in Bristol.'

'That shouldn't take you long, then.'

'Me?'

'Yeah, you check it out. Women and clothes go together.'

'That's nonsense and you know it . . . but I accept the mission.'

A grin lit up Steve's weary face, swiftly replaced by a yawn.

'You're tired.' She rubbed his shoulder. Usually he would have taken advantage of that, suggested they find a private place where she could rub him some more. Instead he lowered his eyes. Something was wrong.

'What is it?'

'I need another talk with your chef. I'll be there just before lunch. By the way, you dropped this.'

The tired red eyes glittered wickedly as he brought the conical brassiere out of the carrier bag he was carrying.

She grabbed it and shoved it into her bag.

'It's not mine — I mean, I don't wear that size.'

Steve grinned. 'I'm not blind. I noticed.'

She caught herself blushing. It was kind of nice knowing he noticed as much about her as she had about him.

Still, she mustn't lose sight of the professional side of their relationship. Something was up. Her stomach churned. Had Smudger lied about where he was? She hoped not.

* * *

Out in the North Parade Gardens, Stella Broadbent's eyes flickered, fluttered and flitted between shutting and opening. The world was presently a bleary place, and there was no one to talk to. Why wasn't she in bed, she wondered? She couldn't remember getting ready to go out but knew she was out. She was just a bit unsure of where.

It was night-time, that much was for certain. The sky was black like the inside of a coal lid. The lights up on the road didn't seem as bright as usual, and the facades of the Regency buildings wobbled as though they were made of rubber.

'I need a drink,' she muttered.

No one brought her one. Didn't they hear? Had everyone gone home?

Her eyes flickered one more time and then shut. Unfortunately the buildings were still there wobbling around behind her eyelids. She was unaware of the stealthy footsteps, the figure emerging from the shadows. Her eyes popped open as a hand was clamped across her mouth. Her voice was stifled by another hand around her throat. She tried to scream. Her lips wobbled — just like the buildings.

His breath was moist against her ear. 'No talking to the police, Stella.'

She tried to say that she hadn't been talking to the police.

'Or anyone involved with the police,' he said, as though he'd read her thoughts. 'Leave the sauce alone and keep your mouth shut.'

The tips of iron-hard fingers dug into her throat. She felt the breath being choked out of her body, the world blackening around her.

She fought for air and, at the same time, emptied her bladder.

Just as suddenly as they'd arrived, the hands were gone. She could breathe. She coughed and spluttered, taking great gasps as she tried to refill her lungs.

Huge tears erupted from the corners of her eyes, taking her make-up with them. Ashamed and soiled, she struggled to her feet, terror following like a snarling dog at her heels. She ran through the passageway that bypassed the bar and went straight to the exit.

The doorman asked her if she wanted a taxi.

She said she didn't. 'I've got my car.'

She didn't see him frown. Neither did she hear him remark that she really shouldn't be driving. She had to drive. She had to get away.

CHAPTER FOURTEEN

Sleeping had weighed heavily on Honey's mind — and on her eyelids. She struggled from bed at around eight, wriggling her toes into her slippers before making her way into the shower.

Water cascading onto her face helped clear her head. That was when she looked down at her feet and realised her head hadn't been clear enough. She was still wearing her slippers.

Slippers in bin, body in clothes, she made her way to reception. Smudger wasn't due in until ten.

She phoned her mother. 'Are you up?'

'Of course I am.'

Her mother sounded indignant.

'How did things go last night?'

'Not too good, actually. Roland got called away on a matter of business. Someone called him from the warehouse. He had to go.'

Honey offered her sympathy though secretly thought it the best thing that could have happened. It was nothing to do with jealousy, she told herself. She was just looking after her mother's welfare.

'He's making it up to me. He's taking me for a drive in the Cotswolds.'

Honey's attention clicked in. The Cotswolds. That's where Sylvester Pardoe lived.

'Today's Wednesday. I thought Wednesday was your day for Secondhand Rose.'

Secondhand Rose was a dress shop her mother ran with a few other well-heeled, fashionable women. Dresses and other items bought for a fortune were brought in by women who had to have the latest fashion. The items they brought in were sold at a knock-down price. The sum received was divided between the shop and the customer. Her mother never missed a Wednesday in the shop, where gossip sparkled as brightly as sequins on a cocktail dress.

'I changed shifts,' she explained.

'Mother, don't you think you're getting a bit too involved . . .'

'Mind your own business.'

The phone went dead.

This was worrying. The dead chefs were worrying. She forced herself to concentrate and figured she was doing pretty well. Although not quite up to speed, things were chugging along well enough — or so it seemed. Wake-up time was imminent. She had just made up a bill for a three-night stay for two Canadians presently checking out.

One of them, a retired accountant, perused his bill and raised his eyebrows. 'Hell, am I paying for gold taps in that room?'

Not quite getting the implication, Honey eyed him through narrowed, burning eyes. 'Sir, we don't have gold taps.'

'So why such an expensive bill?' he asked, pointing to the four-figure total.

Honey apologised profusely as she scribbled over the extra nought that had appeared from out of the blue.

Seeing her mother being a dunderhead, Lindsey muscled in. 'Let me do that. Why don't you go and have a lie down?'

'I can't.'

'Try.'

They exchanged a mother–daughter look of understanding, the old warmth wrapping around them both.

Honey was touched. Her eyes moistened when she smiled. 'OK.'

She headed for the door marked 'private' that opened onto the path leading to her quarters in the coach house. Just as she reached for the door, she heard that old familiar hiss, similar to the sound of a gas leak.

'Psst!'

She looked round. A dismembered head was hissing at her. The rest of the body was behind the tapestry screen dividing her private door from the main reception area.

A pair of blue eyes sparkled through layers of fine wrinkles.

'I need to speak to you,' said Mary Jane in a hoarse whisper.

A long, thin finger beckoned her to follow.

That was it. The quick nap wouldn't happen. She smiled at Mary Jane and followed her crooked finger into the lounge.

Mary Jane was tall and gaunt, favoured wearing pink and had decided she was living forever. A wrinkled hippy, she drove a pink 1963 Cadillac which had been shipped over just after she'd settled in England on a permanent basis. Driving on the left-hand side of the road in a left-hand-drive car had proved a bit of a problem at first, but eventually both Mary Jane — and the city of Bath — had got used to it.

The conservatory was empty of other guests, but still Mary Jane's voice remained just above a whisper. 'Polly came to my room last night hammering on my door like a demented banshee.'

Honey frowned. Did she have a member of staff named Polly? Casual perhaps? She started to apologise. 'Oh, I'm so sorry, Mary Jane. I'll look into it.'

Mary Jane's wrinkles disappeared in a look of amazement.

'Hell no, Honey darling! Isn't that what I came here for? Having my friends from the other side cross over to visit me?

Polly's never quite got the hang of walking through walls. She still thinks she's alive and can't do any of that stuff.'

The penny dropped. Pennies dropped a lot with Mary Jane, seeing as she mostly lived in another world.

The 'crossing over' she referred to had nothing to do with flying across the Atlantic. She was talking about the dearly departed who seemed inclined to drop in to see her on a regular basis.

'I'm sorry, I thought you were referring to one of the chambermaids,' said Honey as Mary Jane pressed her into a chair.

'I *was* referring to a maid,' exclaimed Mary Jane, her bright eyes aglow, her expression animated. 'Apparently, she was a foundling left on the doorstep and Sir Cedric's wife took her in. And before you ask me which wife, it was his second. You know how it was with Sir Cedric.'

Honey adopted the most serious expression she possessed and nodded. Of course she knew how it was. According to Mary Jane, Sir Cedric, a man of means who'd died round about 1750, had married three times and seemed to have chased anything wearing a skirt. Mary Jane claimed to be his direct descendant.

'I see,' she said, as though she'd just been told that next door's cat had got run over.

For the umpteenth time since Mary Jane had first descended on the Green River Hotel, Honey asked herself why she was listening to this drivel. But she kept listening, eyes wide open. Sir Cedric was not the only resident ghost, it seemed. Ghosts were forever asking her opinion as to where they'd gone wrong in their lives. 'Sometimes I'm kind of an agony aunt,' Mary Jane had explained. 'And sometimes I'm just someone they want to impress.'

'Of course.'

It wasn't outrageous, just plain unbelievable. But Mary Jane was nice, and she didn't want to upset her.

'Anyway,' Mary Jane went on, 'Polly is adamant that she has second sight and can read the cards and what have you. Whether that makes her a bona fide clairvoyant or not, I don't know.'

Neither did Honey.

'Anyway, she tends to materialise in the rose garden just beside the sundial.'

Now, this was something new. Had her mother secretly introduced a cluster of hybrid tea roses without telling her? If she had she must have done it in the last few minutes.

'We don't have a sundial — or a rose garden, for that matter.'

'You don't *now*,' said Mary Jane, her wrinkled hand patting Honey's as though she hadn't long started school. 'But back when she worked here there was a rose garden and a sundial.' She looked up at the ceiling, a normal aspect of her thought-collecting process. 'Now, what was I saying? Ah, yes! She's made a prediction that someone who used to be married but isn't any longer is about to come to a sticky end. She says they're to be wary of travelling in a carriage, especially if there are no horses pulling it.'

Honey blinked. 'A horseless carriage. A car.'

Mary Jane closed one eye and took a few seconds to think about it. 'A car. Yeah. I see your point.'

'Do we know the name of this person?' Honey asked her.

'She'll appear just as we say . . .'

Mary Jane's sentence was cut off in mid-stream. The door swung open and Honey's mother made a grand entrance.

Gloria floated in accompanied by a cloud of perfume and the clicking of her kitten heel shoes. She was dressed in a light lavender outfit liberally sprinkled with hand-sewn silver rosebuds around the hem.

Honey threw Mary Jane an ominous look.

Mary Jane threw one right back.

Gloria did a twirl between them and the French doors.

'Guess what? Roland is taking me to a Freemasons' lunch at Grover Park.' She paused for effect, hands together, her eyes bright with enthusiasm. 'IN HIS ROLLS ROYCE!'

Honey and Mary Jane exchanged more startled glances. Her mother was a prime contender for Mary Jane's prophesy.

'You can't!' exclaimed Mary Jane.

'Do you have to?' Honey's scepticism was reflected in her tone. She didn't want to believe Mary Jane's warning, but still, you couldn't be too careful.

Her mother's bottom lip trembled. Her eyes glittered. 'Have you any idea how long it's been since I rode in a real Rolls Royce with a handsome, attentive man?'

That look! Something between a petulant child and a bulldog about to bite your backside.

In her mind, Honey was telling herself that Mary Jane's ghosts were just figments of her imagination. And so were their prophesies. Weren't they?

This would be a balancing act. Much as she had no wish to upset her long-term guest, she recognised her own cowardice. 'OK, OK. Enjoy yourself. What do I care about the way he might drive? What do I care if he careers along at ninety and you hit the back of a bus and . . . ?'

'Hey there! Just hold on.' Her mother looked horrified.

'It was Polly,' explained Mary Jane, her glittering eyes unblinking, her expression tense. 'She's Sir Cedric's maid — or rather his wife's maid — and she said . . .'

Gloria pulled herself up to her full five-feet-four-inches. 'Mary Jane Jefferies, you are out of your skull! Get a life! Get real! Get a *man*!'

She marched off, got as far as the door and turned round. 'And you,' she said, pointing her finger at her daughter, 'are just plain jealous. You'd have liked Roland's attention yourself. God knows you've had enough opportunities with some really suitable men I've put your way. But you've blown it with them all. You're just like your father. He never listened to me either. But never mind. I've got my man. AND YOU HAVE NOT!'

The door slammed.

'I'm sorry,' said Mary Jane once the echo had died away. She was biting her bottom lip, the corners of her eyes downturned. Coupled with her wrinkles, it made her look like a sad bloodhound.

Honey didn't remark on the fact that her mother's efforts at matchmaking were insufferable and that the men she'd found for her daughter were as interesting as a garden full of limp lettuce. She shook her head. 'No need. You know my mother. She pleases herself.'

Mary Jane was holding her head to one side as though she were listening for something. Her eyes had that glazed, 'I'm not in this world' kind of look.

She frowned. 'Polly tells me to take a rain check on this. She reckons the accident may already have happened and that the person may have already crossed over.'

She nodded sagely, like some big-time newspaper editor who picks and chooses what stuff he's going to print.

'Right you are, Polly. You think she may already be there — and close too.'

She looked surprised, then tilted her head again, gazing at the ceiling.

'Polly asks if perhaps there's someone else you know who happens to be divorced . . .'

'My father's dead.'

'I know.'

'So why doesn't he come visiting?'

Mary Jane shrugged. 'Ain't got no need to? Besides, your mother's here. He might not want to rekindle that fire.

'When did Polly tell you about the accident?'

Her frown was deep and she bit her lip quite hard. 'It was late last night. She always comes just when I'm drinking my primrose tea beneath the moonlight out in the garden before settling down for the night.'

'Well, let's hope she's wrong.' Honey made her excuses and left her there. 'I'll get someone to bring you a herbal tea.'

Mary Jane nodded. She looked crestfallen. Honey made sure about the tea.

'With or without a teaspoon of medicine?' asked Lindsey.

'With,' Honey replied.

Lindsey added a dash of gin to the raspberry-flavoured tea. Mary Jane would never admit to it, but herbal tea without a dash of gin stayed in the cup.

The sound of saucepans came clattering from the kitchen. Smudger had arrived. Honey pushed open the swing door.

Smudger was already in his whites and was wearing a red bandana as a sweat band. It quietly complimented his pink complexion and corn-coloured hair.

His voice filled the kitchen. 'Okra, mange tout, squash and Jersey Royals.'

A trainee chef scuttled out to the vegetable store to fetch what was required. One of his commis chefs was already slicing up the *mise en place* — a salad selection for lunchtime use.

Her head chef looked surprised to see her. 'Is it Monday? Are we changing the menu?'

Entering his kitchen without a scheduled arrangement was never something to be taken lightly.

'I need to speak to you.'

A certain something about his face caused her to look again. Normally close shaved, a few days stubble shadowed his chin.

'Fine,' he said while slicing an eighteen-inch cucumber at breakneck speed.

'In private.'

His eyes met hers. He didn't say anything but followed her out into the hallway.

She cleared her throat and folded her arms. 'Steve Doherty wants to ask you some more questions. He's coming in just after lunch.'

He turned promptly away. 'Not a good time.'

'Mark!'

It wasn't often that she called him by his real name. When she did he knew he was in big trouble.

'Did you lie about that night?'

His expression hardened. He shook his head. 'No.'

Honey scrutinised his expression. Mouth defiant, nostrils narrowed, chin firm — no direct giveaway, but there was something about the look in his eyes . . .

'Is there anything else you want to tell me?'

He shook his head again. 'No.'

Again the abrupt turn. It made her angry, so much so that she had an urge to say something truly shocking to make him stay — something erudite but plucked out of thin air.

The best she could come up with was, 'What do you know about the Grande Epicure?'

Had she plucked the words from nowhere? No. Surely someone had mentioned it. Richard Carmelli? Whatever. They were enough to stop him in his tracks.

His hand had been holding the door open. Now he let it go. His face darkened.

'Who told you?'

Her heart raced. Smudger didn't frighten her — usually. 'I . . . um . . . think it was . . .' She shook her head. 'Never mind. Tell me what you know.'

He looked down at the floor and nodded as though he were remembering something and trying to get things clear in his head. 'OK. I will. After lunch? When our pet copper arrives?'

She reluctantly agreed. The door to the kitchen swung shut and he was gone. She heard shouted orders. Once more Smudger was lord of his own domain.

Honey wandered through reception, into the lounge and out into the conservatory. She was again the model hotelier, nodding and smiling at guests. In her head she was thinking of the two dead chefs. She'd seen Smudger's dislike of Oliver Stafford. She hadn't asked him about Sylvester Pardoe, though. She turned on her heel meaning to do just that. Lindsey blocked her path.

'I thought you were going for a lie down.'

It was daft feeling that she had to excuse herself to her daughter, but that was exactly how she felt.

'I'm all fine now.'

She beamed brightly.

Lindsey's smile was weak, thoughtful. 'You look fine. And we're both fine — aren't we?'

Honey looked out at the garden. Invigorated by her infusion of herbal tea and Gordon's gin, Mary Jane was practising her tai chi, her long arms moving like a willow in a breeze.

Honey smiled. Her thoughts were most definitely with Lindsey. Just a short time ago — not long after she'd taken on this crime liaison nonsense — she'd pressured Lindsey to forego chamber music concerts and go nightclubbing. 'Be a bit footloose and fancy free,' she'd said. And now that her daughter had kicked over the traces, who was she to condemn? It was just that Oliver Stafford had been married. If she cared to admit it, the generation gap was showing. People rarely stayed in the same relationship all their lives nowadays. She hadn't. Neither had her mother. They'd been the early birds breaking the trend.

She shrugged as she smiled. 'Just one of those things.'

Lindsey's dark eyes brightened. Her smile spread. 'So I'm your beautiful girl again?'

Honey hugged her and kissed her on the cheek. 'You'll always be that.'

* * *

Doherty rang her to say he'd be late. 'Should be closer to three.'

'I'm looking forward to it.'

'I always do.'

She could imagine the cheeky grin. My, but he was tempting. But not yet, she told herself. Not just yet. There was plenty of time.

Her mother wouldn't agree, of course. Gloria Cross never tired of telling her that she'd be left on the shelf.

'You'll end up a dried-out old spinster.'

Pointing out that she had been married and produced a daughter and that spinsters were usually virgins had cut no ice. Deep down her mother was a dyed-in-the-wool romantic. The pile of Mills and Boon books with titles like *The Italian's Virgin Bride* and *Taming the Lady Angela* on her bedside table was testament to that.

Over a quiet cup of coffee and a pile of unpaid bills, she asked herself why, in spite of all the flirting, 'it' hadn't happened between her and Steve yet. Time had a lot to do with it. When he wasn't involved in a big investigation, she was busily arranging next year's advertising or interviewing yet another batch of wannabe chefs or waiters or a prospective bride and groom wanting perfect arrangements for their perfect day.

And when a crime involved tourism and the hospitality trade in general, they were both strapped for time.

'Life's a bitch,' she muttered to herself.

The door opened. A draught of air sent paperwork fluttering in a white wave over the desk.

'Honey! Have you heard?'

Few people dared barge into her office unannounced and without knocking. But Casper St John Gervais considered the foibles of mere mortals beneath him.

White suit, panama hat, black shirt and carrying his signature silver topped cane, he waved the offer of tea or coffee aside with a grandiose flourish of a white-gloved hand.

'Have you heard?'

She flipped her own hand dismissively and made a face. *No comprende!*

Casper sank onto the sofa, hat and silver capped cane gripped with both hands, knees tightly together.

'Bling Broadbent. Speeding along the road on her way home, lost control and hit a wall.'

'Is she hurt?'

'Very, my dear girl. She's dead.'

A cold chill swept over her as she put down her coffee cup.

Casper prattled on. 'Her car was smashed flat and so was she. Cutting equipment was brought in and the car was dismantled into manageable bits. I suppose Stella was too. How dreadful!'

She instinctively invited Casper to stay for lunch, feeling a need to do something ordinary, everyday, a basic pleasure of life. Being alive and having no car park was preferable to being dead and having the best hotel car park in Bath. And an imposing hotel. And a chef (though recently deceased) who'd won the BITE competition.

Casper declined her offer. He explained that he was selling a few items at auction left to him by his father when he received the news. 'My father collected train sets,' he said in an off-hand manner. 'Not my cup of tea at all'

'I see,' said Honey. She did see. It explained a lot about Casper. It explained something about Mary Jane too, or at least about the ghostly Polly's prediction. She was still plodding her way through a pile of invoices when Steve arrived. She asked him about Stella Broadbent.

'Traffic told me they had to scrape her car off the road.'

Honey shivered. She presumed they'd had to do the same for poor Stella.

She sighed and sat further back in her chair. 'I saw her last night at the Zodiac. She was very drunk. *Very* drunk,' she repeated, fixing him with an intensity meant to emphasise the point.

She went on to give him a blow-by-blow description of what had happened. Ordinarily she would have laughed and mentioned what Stella wore beneath her expensive designer label clothes. But this was neither the time nor place. Her expression doubtless betrayed her feelings.

'There's nothing for you to feel guilty about.'

'I didn't know she'd driven home. I could have stopped her.'

'Could you?'

She forced herself to nod an affirmation. Rubbish. Nothing could have stopped Stella from doing exactly as she liked. A bit like herself, really. The realisation made her blood run cold.

'Poor Stella. Squashed flat like that.'

'Not entirely.'

When something was interesting, Steve's tone of voice altered. She looked at him with narrowed eyes. He was pensive, as though sifting through his thoughts.

'Her lower body was quite badly injured, but from the waist upwards . . .'

There! That thoughtful tone again. And she could see something in his eyes.

'What is it?'

'Well, it's not confirmed on paper yet, but the pathologist isn't happy about some marks around her neck. They look like finger marks.'

Honey pushed aside the thought that she'd once considered strangling Stella. This was for real.

'And?'

He shrugged. 'We'll see. Now!' he said, slapping his thighs as he got to his feet. 'Where's this bloody chef of yours?'

By three the kitchen was cleared of lunchtime debris and readied for the evening shift. Sometimes a chef who wasn't working that evening would stay on to do the prep. Today the kitchen was empty.

Steve stood in the centre of the kitchen and spread his arms. 'So where is he?'

'He must have forgotten.' She plotted murder in her mind. She'd promised Steve Smudger would be there. He'd let her down.

'You did tell him?'

She gave him one of her hardest looks. 'I stressed the fact.'

Her eyes were suddenly drawn to a dirty knife left hanging over the edge of the sink in the washing up area. The blade was smeared with something red. Not for the first time that day, her blood turned cold.

'What are you doing?' Steve asked as she swilled the knife off in running water.

'Washing up.'

He tried to grab the knife. 'Is that blood?'

'No!' She ran her finger along the blade and licked it. 'It's jam,' she said with an air of light relief. 'Just jam.'

To her great relief, it *was* jam, but that didn't explain why it had apparently been flung aside unwashed. Smudger was a stickler for cleanliness and everything being in its place, and if no one was staying on he was usually the last to leave. Something had happened to make him rush off. She'd tick him off about it later. So would Steve, judging by the look on his face.

CHAPTER FIFTEEN

Steve Doherty finally tracked Smudger down after the evening shift. His explanation for rushing out was plausible enough, if a bit flimsy — he'd had a headache. Except that Honey couldn't recall him ever having a headache, even after a few pints of extra strong pulled from a large oak barrel. Steve asked him what time he'd left the pub the night Oliver Stafford was killed. They were going to do a recheck because someone had mislaid the original statements. Smudger told him he couldn't remember but the barmaid would. Steve said he would check. He pushed his face close to Smudger's, jaw firm, eyes unblinking. 'I'm warning you, my son. You'd better be telling me the truth or your feet won't touch the bloody ground. Got it?'

Wary of the warning look, Smudger drew in his chin. 'OK.'

'Right. Let's start off with your whereabouts on the night Brian Brodie was killed?'

'With a friend.'

'A girlfriend?'

'You spent the night with her?'

He nodded again. 'You bet I did.'

Honey leaned against the sink, arms folded, listening with interest.

Steve looked at her. He didn't look happy and not entirely convinced.

'I'm going to believe him because he works for you. But I'm going to check everything with a fine-tooth comb. I'll be in touch.'

Steve left without throwing her a wink or a smile full of promise.

'I hope this girlfriend checks out,' Honey said once Steve had gone.

Smudger grimaced. 'She will. We're old friends.'

There was something about his eyes, just the merest flicker that made her think he hadn't divulged the whole truth. However, she didn't press him. What he did in his personal life was his own business.

'And the Grande Epicure?' she'd asked once Steve had left. 'You were going to tell me about it.'

He avoided her eyes. 'It's a competition in Paris.'

'For chefs?'

'Of course.'

Smudger had worked for a five-star hotel before coming to work for her. She'd sometimes asked herself why he'd left such an upmarket joint to come and work for her. The prestige of a five star always outranked a four. It looked good on the CV, just in case they got to open their own restaurant or end up with their own television programme.

He admitted that Oliver Stafford, Brian Brodie and Sylvester Pardoe were there too.

'Who won?'

He shrugged. 'I don't remember.'

He was lying. Of course he remembered.

'You're not telling me everything, are you.'

He shrugged and turned away, seeming to prefer the sizzling of a hot pan to facing further questions.

In the two years since he'd worked for her she'd never known him lie. But he was lying now. She was sure of it.

* * *

The following morning she kept her promise to Steve regarding the fancy-dress outfitters. The shop in Batheaston was her first stop; she hoped it would prove fruitful. Rumour had it that the woman who ran Fancy Pants and Fantasies had once been a stunt woman in Hollywood.

Batheaston, a village situated three miles to the east of Bath, seemed an odd place to have a fancy-dress shop. A steep hill swept down towards Bathford and the old route to Bradford on Avon and the A4 on to Chippenham. Narrow pavements divided old stone buildings from the road. What shops there were had blank frontages. Although the road wasn't so busy since the opening of the new bypass, it was still difficult to park.

To her left, steep lanes sloped up into a cul-de-sac and the village of Northend. She shot up the second one and found a parking space, not too much of a problem at this time of day when most folks were at work.

It was a fair walk back from there to the main road. The road was fairly empty of cars and the pavements of people.

An impatient-looking man at the bus stop was the only person in sight. He nodded a brief good morning. 'Bloody buses. None at all or three all at once.'

'That's the way it is,' she replied. She glanced up at the gold-and-green sign saying Fancy Pants and Fantasies.

'That used to be a pub,' said the man. He shook his head glumly. 'Nothing's the same as it used to be.'

He sounded like Marvin the paranoid android in *Hitchhiker's Guide to the Galaxy*. Feeling bad about Stella, the last thing she wanted was some misery bending her ear and making her feel worse. She pretended she didn't hear and pushed her shoulder against the shop door. There was a rush of air as it opened and a sucking noise from the rubber surround.

Andrea Andover, the proprietor, was sitting behind a green plastic counter. Rumour had it that Andrea had doubled for the likes of Carrie Fisher and Demi Moore in some of their trickiest stunts. The only thing she'd doubled since then was her size.

Andrea Andover wobbled. She had three chins, and her breasts were big enough to use as a bookshelf and likely to come into sight around a corner before she did.

She appeared to be rummaging up the rear of a bright yellow chicken costume. She looked up on hearing the door open.

'Can I help you?'

Honey eyed the chicken. 'Are you stuffing that?'

Judging by her deadpan expression, Andrea had never been asked to double for a comedian.

'I'm sewing its tail back on,' she replied in a voice that matched her expression. 'People do strange things when they're in costume. I blame television, myself.'

Honey cocked a surprised eyebrow. Coming from someone who had worked in Hollywood, it was a bit rich, but she wasn't here to debate the fact.

As she sewed and stuffed, Andrea's flinty eyes stayed fixed on Honey's face. Disconcerting was an understatement; she found herself searching her memory, just in case she'd hired and broken a chicken costume without being fully aware that she had.

Reason overcame her.

'I'm looking for a man who might have hired a cowboy costume from you. He gave his name as Peter Jones.'

'Yeah . . .'

'He's about over six-foot tall and good looking. Does it ring a bell?'

The chicken outfit ceased heaving as Andrea stopped what she was doing, closed one eye and fixed Honey with the other one.

'I told the daft sod not to do it. We got chatting, see? I thought it was crass, pretending to be someone's husband and that they married when they were drunk. Different if it was a party or something. Everyone knows it's just a giggle. But what he took on was not meant that way. I told him, "Peter, that man that's paying you is up to no good." It was a wicked hoax. The woman had a problem, and the guy who paid him all that money did it out of malice, not fun.'

'How much was he paid?'

'Five hundred pounds plus expenses, he told me. I only charged him seventy-five for the costume. T'aint much of a costume anyway — just a hat, a pair of cowboy boots and a rawhide waistcoat.' She cocked her head to one side, one eye closed again, the other looking thoughtful and all alone.

'It was a laugh and it wasn't a laugh; that was the way it was meant to be. Something was funny, but something was sad.' She shrugged and picked up the costume again. 'That's the way I saw it.'

'Peter Jones. Do you know where he lives?'

Andrea nodded. 'Sure I do. I've got his card.'

Shoving the chicken outfit aside, she tugged out a small cardex box with podgy hands and handed over a plain card with black writing on it. Peter *Francis Jones, actor, impersonator. Strippergrams a speciality.*

CHAPTER SIXTEEN

Before leaving Batheaston, she tapped in the numbers on her phone. There was no answer from the telephone number on the card, so she left a message. Was Peter Jones away on holiday or out acting, impersonating, or embarrassing some unfortunate soul whose friends thought it might be fun to make them squirm?

She phoned Steve and told him about it.

'We'll want to speak to him. Just how well did he know Stella Broadbent? I want to know.'

'I can understand that.' She told him she'd see him later. Nothing to do but go home.

After parking her car in a designated parking space, she headed for the exit. A sudden whirring sound made her look up. The light on a security camera blinked red. Had there been a security camera at the Beau Brummell? Pictures of the building clicked through her mind like the pages of a stiff paged Filofax. No camera? Wasn't that a little odd? Most good-sized car parks had them. She presumed Steve had checked it out.

She strolled back to the Green River through the lunchtime crowds. A short cloudburst had sweetened the air and, like the buds of spring flowers, people were emerging from shop doorways and arcades loaded with stuff they wouldn't have bought if it hadn't rained.

The sun warmed the pavements and the water turned to steam.

A horse-drawn carriage was coming towards her. They were regulars on the sightseeing circuit; ten pounds got you a slow ride round Bath, allowing a bit more time to take in the sights or be lulled to sleep by the gentle motion and the running commentary of the tourist guide. Picturesque and practical in a city built for sedan chairs.

The grey horse tossed its head, coming to a stop.

'Hannah! Hannah!'

Her jaw dropped. Her mother wasn't the type to do the tourist thing, unless you counted going first-class on a cruise liner. She was in the company of Roland Mead. They both looked happy. So much for the trip to the Cotswolds. Roland Mead had let her mother down again. Didn't she just know that would happen?

A sudden pang of something she couldn't quite identify hit her. Was it jealousy? She wasn't sure. She still couldn't forget that Roland had made a pass at her. She hadn't told her mother. Let her enjoy herself while she could.

Her mother beamed at her as Roland helped her down from the carriage. She was sharply dressed in a navy-blue suit edged with white piping.

'Hannah, we've had such a wonderful morning. Roland and I are off to lunch now.'

She turned and looked up at him.

Honey noted the adoration in her mother's eyes.

Roland was wearing an expensive suede jacket. A gold sovereign dangled from a thick chain around his neck. The man had money but no taste.

On top of bad taste he had bad form, daring to grab Honey's shoulders and kiss her on both cheeks.

She barely controlled the urge to wipe them off, but what he did next was unforgivable.

'How about your little girl joining us?' He addressed Gloria almost as though Honey wasn't there.

'Ask me,' said Honey, visibly grinding her teeth.

'Ask her,' said her mother. She didn't look too pleased about the deal.

The smile barely flickered. 'OK. How about it?'

Honey flinched. The last thing she wanted was to spend a precious lunchtime with her mother and her 'boyfriend', though *boy* was hardly the right word. The most boyish thing about him was the toupee. Was it real hair? If so, whose was it before he got it?

A sweet smile was called for. 'I wouldn't want to impose. I've got a business to run.' She glanced tellingly at her watch.

'Business! Yes! That's just what I'd like to talk you about,' said Roland.

Honey eyed the arm protectively draped around her mother's shoulders. The roguish look was still in his eyes.

'Me and your mother being so close, stands to reason I can give you a really good meat deal,' said Roland.

It pained her jaw, but she held on to the sweet smile. 'I wouldn't want to ruin your lunch. I think mother would prefer to have you to herself.'

Roland's white teeth flashed like a toothpaste advert. Were they real?

'A proper business date, perhaps?' he suggested with a fixed, wide smile. Flash, flash, flash!

Her mother jumped in feet first.

'Two's company, three's a crowd,' she said, tightening her grip around Roland's waist and smiling up at him like a lovesick teenager. 'We don't need kids out with us adults.'

'Well . . .' He glanced swiftly at mother then daughter. 'Another time, then.'

'Definitely another time.' *When hell freezes over.*

They sauntered off, her mother giving a cute little wave over her shoulder. 'By the way, Chef's not being very sensible. You need to have a word with him.'

Her stomach felt as though she'd been swallowing scrap iron. Please God, she hasn't upset Smudger, has she? Her footsteps quickened.

Her mother was walking out with a master butcher and she couldn't afford her meddling to affect the business. But there was something else.

Was it possible that she was missing her mother's spurious attempts at matchmaking? Dentists, accountants and stockbrokers — all offering money and security but precious little excitement, and sadly lacking in the eye candy department. She pushed the discomforting thoughts from her mind. First priority was Chef. Why was Smudger upset? Worse still, what part had her mother played in his unhappiness?

She caught Smudger reading the newspaper when she got back and prayed it wasn't the employment section.

'Everything OK?' she asked breezily and crossed her fingers behind her back. Don't mention anything until he does.

He turned his head slowly and fixed her with an accusing eye.

Nightmare scenarios flashed through her mind. Advertising for a new chef, interviewing, new menus, old customers' muted responses to new blood . . . the list was endless. Her blood ran cold.

'What have I done?'

His jaw shifted from side to side as he chewed over his thoughts, prolonging the agony. 'I'm not in favour of changing butchers.'

She was taken aback. 'Who told you we were changing? No! Wait. Don't answer that. My mother.'

She sat down next to him. 'Smudger. Whose hotel is this?'

'Yours.'

'Not my mother's. Mine. What did she say to you?'

He hesitated. Honey's stomach churned. This could be bad.

'She said that if Mead became part of the family then we'd be switching to him.'

Marriage? Her mother was talking about marriage? Had she taken leave of her senses?

'Over my dead body! Now listen to me. I value your judgement. Choice of supplier lies ultimately with you. OK?'

The rigid shoulders relaxed as the tension left him. 'OK.'

Honey gave a big sigh of relief.

'Right,' she said, getting to her feet. 'It's Lindsey's night off and mine too, so how about you cook us a delicious meal? We'll have it in the coach house. OK?'

She didn't add that it would be a kind of making-up celebration between her and Lindsey.

'I'll rustle you up something special. Coquilles Saint-Jacques?'

'Just the ticket!'

Feeling as though her feet were floating six inches off the ground, she sauntered off. Her mother's meddling had been fixed again. Everything was lovely — for a while. Surprise, surprise, Lindsey had plans.

'Sorry, Mum.'

She was going to a nightclub with a group of friends, including a guy she was quite keen on.

'Fine.'

But it wasn't fine. What was happening here? For some time she'd been encouraging her daughter to let her hair down; now she was doing exactly that, so why the peevishness? Lindsey had male company. So did her mother. *And there's the rub* . . . Daughter and mother had dates and she didn't.

Petulant, peeved and feeling left out, she slumped off to the coach house, making for the bathroom.

Have a long, luxurious soak. Do your nails. Do your hair. Pamper yourself.

Yes, a nice soak would do the trick. After stripping off she eyed her naked self in a full-length mirror. Did she look good naked? The lighting was good, the mirror sharp. The truth was nebulous.

'The jury's out on that one,' she muttered to herself, when suddenly something happened to make things better.

The hot water was still tumbling into the tub, the steam misting the mirror and blurring her image. A great improvement!

Now, could she scoff two portions of Coquilles Saint-Jacques with all the trimmings and a bottle of Chardonnay all by herself? Of course she could. Comfort eating would do the trick.

She eased herself down into the warm water, her head resting on the roll-top. The bath was Victorian, had lion's claw feet and was big enough for two. Her spirits rose. Now there's a thought . . .

Being alone this evening wasn't very appealing. Neither was telling Smudger that the special meal was off. His ego was still fragile. She didn't want to upset him.

Her eyes slid sidelong to her mobile phone. She picked it up and punched in Steve Doherty's number. Two murders. He was busy, but surely he could fit in a lovely meal and an available woman? Surely it must be as obvious to him as it was to her that they could easily become an item — with a little work on both sides.

'I'm all alone tonight and chef's cooking a special meal for two.'

'I'll be round at ten.'

Whooping for joy, she ducked beneath the surface. Mission accomplished.

CHAPTER SEVENTEEN

He was leaning on the doorpost when she opened the door, one hand flopped over his forehead, a blue tie hanging loose around his neck. Surprise, surprise, he hadn't shaved for at least two days, judging by his stubble. He drew a hand across his chin. The stubble made a rasping sound — audio testosterone. Honey's legs turned to jelly.

He looked tired, but his mouth lifted in a lop-sided smile. 'You didn't say whether it was a black-tie event, but I managed a blue one.'

She'd warmed to that smile shortly after she'd met him. Given half the chance she'd get a lot warmer, quite hot in fact. So far the right time hadn't materialised. But it would. Shortly.

The table was laid and the food was ready. All it needed was a little cooling off.

As she set out the first dish, Honey told him in more detail about her visit to the fancy-dress shop in Batheaston. Steve listened as he dealt with the wine. 'But no reply when you phoned him,' he managed between yawns.

'No.'

They clinked glasses. 'I was also going to ask you whether there were any security cameras at the Beau Brummell.'

He nodded. 'There are but they're well hidden. The trailing geraniums play a starring role.'

She took a taste of wine. 'Not the variegated ivy?'

He grinned. 'That too. We've got the video files down at the station. The security bloke isn't sure they were working that night, but we're going to check them anyway. He muttered something about maintenance.'

They sat down to their meal.

'There were other incidents suggesting that the hotel, the owner and the dead chef were the victims of a hate campaign,' said Steve, gently cradling a glass of wine in his hands. 'Stella Broadbent's car was treated to a spray job from someone who wasn't too hot on spelling.'

Honey saw the amusement on his face and sensed she was about to be enlightened.

'"F-U-K-ing cow" in purple and green. Similar thing happened to the chef's car; some of the customers' cars had punctures, coach parties had been misdirected — though that could have been accidental — but the rat in the pantry and the cockroaches in the rice sack were a bit suspect.'

Honey made a face. 'Killing the chef was a bit drastic. One hatred too many. And what about Sylvester Pardoe? How does he figure in this?'

Steve frowned and gulped back his wine in frustration. 'Now, there's the rub, as that bloke Shakespeare once said. Are we looking at two separate crimes? Both murders were carried out by the same person. Forensic are pretty set on that. But is the hate campaign connected to the murders?'

Honey sat down and sipped at the wine he handed her. 'Right. Let's take it that they are unconnected — in which case, my money would be on an ex-employee or someone she'd crossed in business.'

'Did she cross many people in business?'

She almost choked on the wine before answering. 'This is Stella Broadbent we're talking about. Flasher of everything she's got, rub-your-nose-in-it extraordinaire! She *made* people cross, that was for sure.'

He grinned. 'Like you, for instance.'

Honey made little mewing noises of discomfort and heaved her shoulders.

'OK. I was envious of her car park. Of her hotel too, come to that. She's got more rooms than me, and they're pretty swank by all accounts. She told everyone how much better they were than anything her competitors could offer. She told them to their face. The cow loved winding people up. Dracula drank blood. Stella thrived on envy.'

She noticed Steve's attention wandering between her eyes and her lips. She imagined he liked the colour of her eyes. She sensed him forcing himself back to the subject in hand.

'It's worth pursuing. We questioned the staff, but not her business rivals.'

Honey eyed him speculatively. She felt a task coming on when he smiled at her like that.

Steve held her eyes with his own. 'I'm sure you'd be better at that. You know which hoteliers she wound up the most. There may be something, or there may be nothing, but do it for me, eh? Just in case there is some connection.'

She narrowed her eyes. 'You're loading me up with a lot of work, Doherty. Do you know how many hotels there are in Bath? And don't think I don't know what you're playing at.'

'You're a hotelier. They're hoteliers. They might open up more to you than me. Birds of a feather gossip together.'

He smiled in that boyish, rakish way of his — Colin Firth as Mr Darcy but without the thigh-hugging breeches. On the other hand, he didn't need the tight trousers. His jeans already hinted at what was on offer. She could go with that. She also accepted that other hoteliers were more likely to confide in her than in Steve. She knew the game. After a few words with Casper, who knew everything about everyone in the hospitality trade, she would know which hoteliers to question.

As she considered who might come top of the list, she assessed the calorie count of the scallops before heaping salad onto her plate.

A thought suddenly came to her. '*Something funny, something sad.* That's what Andrea Andover said about the guy who booked the strippergram. Annoying that he didn't give her his name. She reckons Peter Jones knows. I've asked Andrea to let Peter know that I want a word with him.'

Steve perked up. 'The stuntwoman. I hear she used to double for a load of Hollywood stars. Did she look anything like Demi Moore?'

Honey grimaced at Steve's shallow moment. She threw him a disapproving look, shook her head and swallowed a new potato. 'No. More like Bruce Willis after a year of living on doughnuts.'

He pulled a face. 'Grim! Mind you,' he said, his gaze flowing over her body, 'present company makes up for the disappointment.'

She felt herself getting hot. Time to freshen up.

'Cheese?'

She left him with a wedge of St Augur and a box of crackers. She knew what he liked. No need for trimmings. He'd probably like her the same way, she mused on her way to the bathroom.

Gripping the bathroom sink with both hands, she leaned forward. The eyes she saw in the cabinet mirror were looking a little wild tonight — and it wasn't just due to the wine.

'Right,' she said, taking a deep breath and tousling her hair. 'It's now or never.'

Granted that their professional relationship was something of a barrier to their personal one, but once that was put aside it was no holds barred. Getting better physically acquainted was the spectre at the feast; the feast they never quite got round to.

Her bosoms surged against her neckline as she took a deep breath. Tonight could be the night. They were both tired, but also relaxed. Time to take the plunge.

Besides making sure the bedroom was tidy and the sheets fresh, she squirted extra perfume behind her ears, down her cleavage and up her skirt. *Who knows where things could lead?*

Recalling her naked self in the wickedly honest full-length mirror, she turned down the lighting — *less is more*. In this case, she hoped that less lighting equalled less bumpy bits and dimpled thighs. Before leaving the bedroom she tugged off the knee-length controlling undergarment and slipped on a black lace thong. The bulges that had been smoothed bubbled against her dress. Never mind, Steve had sunk two glasses of wine and eaten well.

She studied her reflection. Cleavage? Not enough but easily rectified. She undid the top button. Cheeks? Flushed. The wine was responsible for that. Shoes? Drat! Why hadn't she noticed earlier that she was wearing her flat black ballerina shoes? She swapped them for a pair of four-inch heels that she couldn't stand upright on for longer than fifteen minutes. Fifteen minutes should be enough.

Right! One last look in the mirror, and hey presto! She was sex on legs. Fabulous! Totally irresistible.

Sashay in. That was the thing. She stopped just before the door. Would sashaying be sexy enough to tempt him? Perhaps not. She tossed her head. Be a bit more alluring. Use everything you've got.

She ran her hands down over her ribs and her waist, carefully avoiding the 'love handle' areas. Well, the legs were good. Good enough for a dancer, a very sexy, alluring dancer.

Smiling, she hitched up her skirt. If this didn't impress him, nothing would.

'Da, da, da, de, da, da, da . . .'

Accompanied by her off-tune rendition of 'The Stripper' she slowly extended one near naked leg, then curved it around the door.

She'd expected some response like 'Holy Cow' or 'Wow'.

Nothing. She told herself he was dumbstruck.

Gradually, she eased her body round, ending up posed provocatively against the door post.

And there was Steve. He was lying full stretch on the settee, eyes closed, mouth open.

'Steve?'

Even an outright rejection would have been better than his sudden resounding snore.

There was only one thing left to do. The dishes were waiting. She gathered them up and took them to the kitchen.

CHAPTER EIGHTEEN

The day could have started better. First, the dishwasher was having one of its away days, thus the kitchen resembled a Turkish steam room.

'The rotation arm's not turning,' shouted the kitchen porter, his head emerging from the machine in a sweaty, hot haze.

Honey resigned herself to ringing the repair man. His answerphone gurgled into life, telling her that he was away on a cruise around the Mediterranean and wouldn't be back until the sixteenth.

She swore at the phone as she slammed it down. People could be so selfish. On holiday! Did he have no idea of her dishwasher's fickle temperament?

A lever arch file of useful contacts left by the previous owner was her next port of call. As thick and heavy as a volume of Encyclopaedia Britannica, she heaved it up onto the desk.

'I need to enter all this stuff on our database,' she murmured with a sideways glance at Lindsey. Her daughter's face was presently lit by the computer screen.

'That's impossible,' said Lindsey.

'Why?'

'You don't know how to.'

Lindsey had a point.

'By the way,' her daughter added, 'what's the decoration hanging from the ceiling fan?'

Honey glanced over her shoulder at the closed door to her private office. She remembered the huge brassiere she'd flung into the air on her return from the kitchen last night. She'd left her bag on her desk in the office behind reception. As she'd grabbed it the contents had spilled onto the floor. The 'brazier' had been among them. Irritated by Steve's snoring and now this, she'd thrown them skywards. More aerodynamically designed than she'd thought, it had flown higher than she'd envisaged and landed on the ceiling fan.

She searched for and found an unbelievable excuse. 'Those things have multiple uses, you know. Lampshades. Trendy, don't you think?'

After sorting out a repair man for the dishwasher, she rang Peter Jones again. There was no response, again. Shame. He was the only person who knew the identity of the bloke who'd hired him.

Honey recalled what Doherty had told her night before. Sylvester Pardoe fitted into this somewhere, but she hadn't figured that out yet. Neither had Steve, he admitted over toast and coffee that morning — that was, after apologising for falling asleep. She'd made him suffer a bit, showing her displeasure, though not letting on about the floor show he'd missed. It could be a while before she was that keen again.

Totally out of the blue, Roland Mead turned up and sent the morning into a nosedive. Talking business with a supplier that her chef so obviously disliked was close to financial suicide. She didn't want this.

'Am I expecting you?'

'Of course you are. And you'll be glad I came. I'm going to make you an offer you can't refuse.'

He was big, bluff and overconfident.

'My regular butcher rings to make an appointment if he wants to see me.'

Roland shook his head and made a hissing, disapproving sound. 'Strike while the iron's hot, that's my motto. And anyway, Hannah, I'm not a *regular* butcher. I'm a wholesaler with a wide range stored in a cold store at Avonmouth. I can supply you cheaper than your *regular* butcher.'

His familiarity with her name put her back up. 'My name's Mrs Driver. Only my mother calls me Hannah.'

His smile was like that on the face of a rag doll, the stitches showing around the edge — too ragged to be real.

He eyed her appraisingly, drawing himself up to his full height in an effort to impress her. 'A woman who sticks to business. I like that. That's why I know you'll be glad I came. No one can touch me for price. It stands to reason. You can't afford not to try me. I know you're tempted,' he said, clicking his teeth and tipping her the wink. 'Go on. Admit it. You can't resist.'

Was that a double entendre?

'I'm afraid I can resist,' she said, her tone meant to leave him in no doubt that she'd sooner be sunbathing in a ditch full of snakes.

She drew a deep breath and deftly buttoned up the top of her blouse, which had come undone. 'I leave the choosing of suppliers to my chef, and he's very happy with the Davis brothers.'

Roland guffawed as though she'd just cracked a huge joke. 'They're past it.'

'Their meat isn't.'

Roland's eyes hardened and fixed on her face. Leaning forward, he dared to place his beefy palm on the open lever arch file. His fingertips edged towards hers.

'Let me remind you, sweetheart, that you employ that chef of yours, not t'other way round. Get on top of 'im, darling, before he gets on top of you — in a manner of speaking. Take my advice.'

'Take mine, Mr Mead. Remove your hand from mine.'

He grinned. His hand remained.

Her fingers were already over the paper punch. She clobbered his knuckles. The rag doll smile hung on by a few loose stitches.

She purposely turned her back on him. 'Now, if you'll excuse me, I need to attend to my website.'

Lindsey had got up from her chair to use the photocopier. She looked back in horror as her mother took her place.

Roland lingered.

Honey pressed a few keys. A string of gobbledygook raced across the screen.

Roland leaned as close as he dared, none too sure of what she was likely to do with the computer screen if he got too close. 'Think on it and give me a call when you're not too busy. You know it makes sense.'

'Will you tell Grandma that he was making a pass at you?' asked Lindsey after he'd left.

'Was it that obvious?'

'Dead right, it was. Are you going to tell Grandma? Come on. You have to do something, surely?'

Honey thought about it. What would be gained by telling her mother that Roland Mead was a creep? The answers were easy-peasy. There was a fair chance that her mother wouldn't believe her, and besides, her pride would be damaged, her ego pinched like a pair of too-small shoes. And if she did believe her, there was an equally fair chance that she'd chuck him and revert back to finding a new man for her widowed daughter.

Honey pulled a face. 'I don't want my mother hurt, but you know how headstrong she can be. Warning her will do no good, so for now I think I'll let sleeping pigs lie — at least for the moment.'

'Don't you mean sleeping dogs?' asked Lindsey.

'No. The man's a pig. Sleeping pigs sounds about right.'

CHAPTER NINETEEN

A party of doctors from the city hospital had booked in with their wives for a birthday celebration. 'Work hard, play hard' was a saying they lived up to — and then some! By the time they'd been coaxed up to their rooms, they'd polished off far more than the weekly alcoholic limit per head as recommended by the National Health Service. Not bad for a four-hour session.

Giving a hand with the clearing up was more of a necessity than an option, mainly because someone had to be in charge of operations and those that should have been could not. Highly appreciative of the food, wine and service, the chef and head waiter had been invited to join the merry throng — one of whom was wearing his wife's high heels by the end of the evening. Hence, Smudger and Claus were sleeping it off on the settees in the bar, and the boss was left with debris, a mop and a bucket.

Those left exchanged their concerns about ever ending up in the operating theatre with one of that lot holding a scalpel.

'Might cut out the wrong thing,' said Doris, their casual and very plump breakfast cook who'd been called in as an extra pair of hands. 'I knows I got a lot of flesh, but I don't want to lose any by misadventure.'

It briefly crossed Honey's mind that Doris could do with a bit of flesh reduction. Couldn't say so, of course.

By one o'clock she was left to lay the tables for the morning. The hotel was quiet, the building creaking as the day's heat seeped from its walls.

She was lost in thought when someone banged on the bar door at around two.

'We're closed,' she called out once she'd settled back in her skin.

Whoever it was banged again.

In no mood to be pleasant, she adopted her *I'm going to punch your lights out* kind of voice.

'Go away! You'll wake my guests and I won't be happy. If you keep it up, I promise you, I'll call the police.'

No more knocking.

The mop and bucket were finally finished with. It was approaching three o'clock by the time she tumbled into bed, face unwashed, limbs aching with weariness and clothes thrown into a heap on the floor.

A church clock chimed three. As if she needed to be reminded. Instantly roused from a moment of truly deep sleep, she blinked her eyes open as the clock struck its last note. She frowned. Why had she woken up so abruptly? She was used to the clock. It didn't normally disturb her. It swiftly entered her head that she had heard something else. A tap, tap, tapping at her door.

Feeling puzzled rather than nervy, she got up on one elbow. 'Lindsey?'

Lindsey was sleeping over at a friend's place in Bradford on Avon, but it was possible that she'd changed her mind and come home.

Her tired brain slowly turned over. It couldn't be Lindsey. Lindsey would have answered.

She reached for her silk dressing gown then glanced down at herself. Naked. Silk dressing gown was not a good idea. She pulled on a scruffy pair of leggings and a 'comfort' sweater, big and baggy and hiding a multitude of sins.

Looking like an egg with legs, she crept out to the hallway, grabbing what she thought was a walking stick en route.

'Who's there?' Her voice wasn't much more than a loud whisper. 'This is my home. The hotel entrance is round at the front,' she said, suddenly deciding that it must be a hotel guest who'd gone astray, not beyond the bounds of possibility. Perhaps one of the surgeons had gone walkabout. Thinking about it, at this moment in time they'd be hard pressed to find their way back to the hospital unassisted.

This is my home! The thought was profound. An Englishman's — or Englishwoman's home was her castle. She had a right to protect it, though it helped if you were bigger than the other guy.

'I'm armed,' she said, a little too shakily. She raised the walking stick, which promptly attacked her. Her hair was caught on fine metal spokes. She'd picked up an umbrella by mistake.

Judging by the length of shadow falling through the glass half of the front door, this guy was big!

'Hello? Mrs Driver? I'm talking softly through your door so I don't wake your guests. It's Peter Jones, I got your messages.'

He was here? At gone three in the morning? What sort of excuse did he have? She asked him.

'I just flew into Gatwick at eight o'clock tonight. I had a modelling job in Dubai. Sorry I couldn't get in touch sooner, but things took longer than they should have. Good shoot though. Good money too.'

A good one, it turns out.

After disentangling herself from the umbrella spokes, she opened the door. Her hair stuck out at one side in a tangled mess. A good match with the outfit, she thought on catching a glimpse of her reflection.

As she opened the door, his smile shone in the darkness. 'Andrea said you wanted to speak to me.'

Once they were both cradling cups of coffee and sitting comfortably, she asked him what she wanted to know.

'Who hired you?'

'A chef.'

The most obvious contender — the one she knew best — immediately sprang to mind.

Her stomach cleaved to her spine. 'Do you know his name?'

'Sure I do. So do you.'

The worst-case scenario had reared its head. Smudger serving time in the modern-day equivalent to Devil's Island; hopefully he'd get an en suite room. He wasn't very sociable at the best of times, but terrible in confined spaces.

She heard herself asking for confirmation in a squeaky, unfamiliar and very nervous voice. 'Who?' and 'What was his name?' Her voice sounded far away.

Please don't let it be Smudger. Please, please, please!

Peter carried on, all youthful confidence and lust for living glowing in his big brown eyes. 'That young chef fellah — Richard. I wasn't going to do it at first. It was a bit too heavy to be a fun thing. But I could see he was suffering. That's what makes people do over-the-top things. Had no time for that boss of his, none at all.' Well, that was OK! As long as Smudger was out of the picture. Honey sighed with relief and felt her blood pressure take a nosedive. Great. She'd spotted a custard slice in the fridge back at the hotel. And a tub of Cornish clotted cream and a piece of over-ripe Stilton. This was cause for celebration. No need to advertise for a new chef.

'Very naughty all the same,' said Honey, shaking her head like a disapproving aged aunt.

'Well . . .' he looked contrite and made a 'so-so' movement with his hand. 'I just felt sorry for that guy. And he did pay well. Can't look a gift horse in the mouth.'

Peter grinned. 'Anyway,' he said, 'Richard just did it to wind her up and make her look bad. And I had a bit of a problem — let's just say I was in need of cash. It seemed a great idea at the time.' His wide mouth stopped smiling. He sucked in his bottom lip. 'Fact is, from what I've heard, Stella was a tart and her chef was a shit. They suited each other.'

He confirmed what she was thinking; yes, he had been telling the truth about the argument and Stella threatening to kill him.

'I think someone was hustling her for money,' said Peter. 'If you know what I mean.'

'Blackmail?'

'No. Sex. She paid him for it. That Oliver bloke. That's what Richard told me, and judging by that argument . . .'

Clocking Honey's dumbstruck expression, he proceeded to explain.

'It was like this,' he said, using his hands as an extension to his voice, waving them up and down in line with cadence. 'According to Richard she paid this guy Oliver Stafford far more than he was worth. Mind you, it's rumoured Oliver had a lot of stamina. Did you know him?'

His question took her unawares. 'Uh . . . no . . . no, I didn't.'

Honey was no longer concentrating on Peter's long, drawn-out explanation. At last they had a suspect. Richard Carmelli. Now, what had Stella and Oliver done to him to make him that mad? Mad enough to kill?

Deep in thought, she didn't immediately notice that Peter was eyeing her over the rim of his cup. Alarm bells rang.

'You're a nice-looking woman. Have you got a husband?' he asked.

'No. I'm a widow.'

'Do you want one?'

His brown eyes were full of innocent appeal, like a puppy dog looking for a home.

'No,' she said adamantly, shaking her head. 'I've got someone in mind.'

It was almost the truth; it was just that Steve was too tired to read the signals. But he would. In time he would.

* * *

The phone rang just as Richard Carmelli got out of the bath. Typical. Night off and someone couldn't wait until he'd finished. No matter.

He picked up the phone. 'Hi there.'

Nobody answered. His jaw tightened. 'I know it's you. Stop mucking about.'

Still no response, and yet he knew — *definitely* knew someone was there.

'Sod off!'

He slammed the phone down. His heart hammered in his chest. The game was over. He had to get away. He picked up the phone and dialled the only person he knew was truly innocent.

'Mark? I need to lie low for a while . . . Can you pick me up?'

CHAPTER TWENTY

This thing between her mother and Mead was annoying Honey no end. It bugged her when she was doing paperwork, it bugged her when she was at the hairdressers, and it bugged her now on her way to see Richard Carmelli. Was the randy butcher after her mother's body or the hotel's meat order? If the latter, would he drop her mother now she'd made it clear that her chef was in charge of ordering supplies?

She called round to her mother's flat on the pretext of delivering a slab of Smudger's home-made fruit cake and a box of Earl Grey. Her mother answered the door wearing a mud mask and a dressing gown. Her legs were smeared in something similar to the stuff on her face.

Honey eyed her up and down. 'This looks like a serious beauty treatment session.'

'It is. I've got a hot date tonight.' Her mother's lips stayed in a straight line. 'I can't move my lips too much. It'll crack the mask.'

'Right.' Honey followed her mother into the palatial flat with views across the city. 'Anyone I know?' It was a stupid question. Of course she knew.

Her mother stood in the middle of the room doing windmills with her arms.

'Roland, of course. Excuse me while I do my exercises. I can't sit down. I've got moisturiser on my legs. It's new stuff, guaranteed to exfoliate and moisturise all at the same time. You know how much I love labour-saving beauty products.'

'Don't tell me the price,' said Honey, waving one hand dismissively after putting the cake and tea out in the kitchen.

Slim hope! Gloria Cross set great store by big prices. She had to tell.

'Less than a hundred.'

Honey rolled her eyes and shook her head. A pot of Nivea cream was the closest she ever got to serious moisturising. Her mother was a sucker for brand names, preferably French.

Hair products, pedicures, manicures and shrink-wrap fat removal; her mother's annual expenditure on beauty treatments and clothes was mind-boggling. But today was not the time to be criticising her expenditure. Should she say what was on her mind, or not?

Despite the mud pack, the look on Gloria's face said it all. Her eyes sparkled. Romance wasn't dead. Yet.

She felt a bit schoolmarmish as she sat down, folding her hands and gathering her thoughts.

'Mother, I think we need to talk.'

'Hurry up, dear. These days it takes me a wee bit longer to achieve perfection. I don't want to keep my darling Roland waiting.'

Honey fixed her gaze on a gilt-framed still life hanging on the opposite wall; plums piled high and purple grapes falling from a silver salver. Right! Her mother was a plum ripe for the plucking, and Roland Mead was plum rotten — she knew it! She knew it in her bones, but how best to broach the subject?'

'I think Roland Mead is a creep!'

Hardly subtle. Not what she'd had in mind at all. It just fell off her tongue.

Her mother was surprisingly reticent. 'Now, now, dear. You're turning quite green.'

Honey was almost — though not quite — speechless. 'Jealous? Me?'

'Yes, dear. I'm seeing the green-eyed monster in you.'

'That's eye shadow, mother.'

Holding her face stiff for fear of cracking the chocolate-coloured mask, her mother eyed her sidelong. 'Get out of my space, Miss Busybody.'

Get out of my space?

Honey slapped her thighs as she got to her feet. 'OK! OK! I'm going. But don't say I didn't warn you.'

Cool as a cucumber, her mother began spreading scarlet varnish over her fingernails.

'No need to warn me, Hannah my darling. I know what he is.'

'You do?'

'Sure. He's a red-blooded man and after my body.'

Honey grimaced. 'He's also a wholesale butcher and just as likely to be after my meat order!'

Enough was enough. She took her leave and headed for sanity — if chasing after a disgruntled chef could be called that. Never mind. It beat being told she was jealous of her mother's love life.

A short time later, Honey swung into the car park of the Beau Brummell. The interim manager told her that Richard Carmelli hadn't been there for days and gave her his home address.

'If you find him, tell him he's fired.'

Fair enough!

She rang Casper to ask him if he knew of anyone in particular that Stella might have upset.

'I will have a list ready for you, though it may fall well short of the true total. Our darling deceased Stella made a habit of upsetting people.'

She scooted over to the other side of town, almost enjoying the ease with which the black Volkswagen Beetle nosed through the traffic. Not too much traffic at this time of day, and she found a parking space right outside the Old Dispensary.

Detached and elegantly imposing, the building had dispensed dubious cures for common and uncommon ailments in years gone by. Now converted for multiple occupation, it looked out on the A36 and Cleveland Bridge. Buses, cars and Lycra-clad cyclists brushed past the miniature Roman temples embellishing each end of the bridge. At least, they looked like Roman temples. In reality they were little more than toll booths with Roman-style pediments and Dorian columns, a product of early nineteenth-century imperial pretensions. The Romans hadn't had toll booths or a bridge here when they ruled the city. The original boundary was closer to the city centre and bounded by a cemetery. Some of the graves still remained.

One of the booths had a sign outside saying, 'Aromatherapy oils for sale'. The others looked to be craft shops this week. By next week they could be something entirely different. That was the way it was in Bath — 'for fun and profit'. Now, who was it that had said that? Probably Beau Brummell himself, that Regency rake with an eye for the main chance (and the ladies) and the ear of the Prince Regent. He was what would now be termed a 'fixer'. No change there, then.

'Whatever you want, sir, I will endeavour to get.'

And then some!

As she eyed the bridge, a head popped out between the Dorian columns and waved. She squinted. Clint had acquired another little sideline. She waved back. What was he selling? Artwork, herbal remedies or something questionably ethnic? She blanked the possibility that it might be something illegal. Clint was a dab hand with a scrubbing brush and the kitchen mop. She had to give him some slack.

She sent a text to Steve. *Richard Carmelli hired the cowboy. Am off to find him.* Well, that should make him shift his butt! There was no evidence to support Carmelli being the murderer, but she had to make a start with or without Doherty.

Richard Carmelli lived on the second floor of the Old Dispensary. His name was written in green felt tip beside his buzzer.

She pressed it once, twice, three times; there was no answer.

She pressed the one above that. A woman answered. 'Yes?'

'I'm looking for Richard Carmelli. I'm not getting any reply when I press his buzzer.'

'So?'

Not the helpful type.

'Has he gone away?'

'I hope so,' the voice snarled. 'And taken his bloody drum kit with him!'

No welcome mat outside *her* door, Honey imagined.

She pressed the one below. An old voice crackled in response.

Honey asked her about Richard Carmelli.

'Can you speak up a bit, dearie?'

She said it louder.

'Who?'

Louder again. A passer-by paid her undue attention. He was wearing a knitted hat in Rastafarian colours.

'You talkin' to me, honey?'

'Get lost.'

The young man put up his hands and inched away.

She strained to hear the old woman.

'Oh, you mean the young man from upstairs.'

'That's right. The one who played the drums.'

'Did he?'

So she was that deaf.

'Do you know anything about him?'

She was sure her voice was carrying to the other side of the road. Despite the traffic noise, more people were looking in her direction.

'Of course I do. Come on in. I'll make you a cup of tea.'

The kettle was already on by the time she was inside the entrance hall and heading into the ground-floor flat.

Miss Meadows was small and thin as a bird. The hands that poured hot water into the pot were like sparrow's claws, tiny and fine; they'd be feather-light in the hand, Honey guessed.

She was shown into a pale-green living room. The carpet was green, the furniture was green and the walls were that old Georgian green eggshell colour. Thankfully the ceiling was white, otherwise she would have felt she'd been swallowed by the Jolly Green Giant.

With a fragile, fluttering wave, Miss Meadows gestured that she sit down. She chose an old settee with squashy cushions, then wished she hadn't. The cushions almost swallowed her. She swapped to an upright chair.

White china cups decorated with ivy leaves — green, of course — sat on a silver tray. The teapot, sugar bowl and milk jug matched the cups and saucers. The tray was covered with a green tray cloth edged with a red cross-stitch design. Silver edging betrayed the tray's quality.

'He's gone away,' said Miss Meadows once she'd gone through her own version of the tea ceremony. This consisted of using a real tea strainer, real tea leaves, sugar dispensed with silver tongs and milk poured from a silver-lidded jug. Honey had to shake her head emphatically in order to emphasise that she did not want sugar. Miss Meadows was more than a bit deaf.

'When did he go?'

Her shout seemed to bounce off the high ceiling and come crashing down around them. Miss Meadows looked vague. 'What was that you said?'

'When did he go? Him from upstairs,' she shouted, pointing at the ceiling.

She could tell from the old dear's expression that she still hadn't heard what she'd said. She wondered if she could lip read.

She repeated herself, louder this time and exaggerated her lip movements, moving them like melting rubber.

'Hold on, dear,' said Miss Meadows.

A high-pitched squeal followed as Miss Meadows' fragile fingers fiddled with something in her pocket. A hearing aid.

‘That’s better,’ she said at last. ‘I try not to this thing too much to save batteries. But sometimes one needs to know what is being said.’

With what she considered the patience of a saint, Honey repeated the same question. ‘I was asking about Richard Carmelli.’

Miss Meadows winced and adjusted her hearing aid. ‘No need to shout, dear.’

That awful squeak again.

Honey took a sip of tea and counted to ten.

‘Such a nice young man,’ said Miss Meadows, her tiny head tilted to one side, peering at her like a short-sighted sparrow. ‘He played the drums, you know.’

‘Yes, I know.’ Honey curbed her impatience with another sip of tea. *It was me that told you that.*

‘Biscuit?’

Miss Meadows pushed forward a plate of Garibaldis.

‘No, thank you. I’m trying to lose weight.’

‘I’ve never had that problem,’ said Miss Meadows, and tucked in.

‘So he went away — Richard Carmelli, your neighbour.’

Miss Meadows nodded, swallowed her biscuit and took a loud slurp of tea.

‘Lovely biscuits.’ She picked up another one. ‘He left with a friend. I watched them from the window. He didn’t take much. Just one article of luggage. One of those soft things. Not a suitcase.’

‘A holdall?’

‘Is that what they call them?’

‘Yes. They fold up easily. What did the friend look like?’

Miss Meadows chewed and sucked on her biscuit. At the same time she looked up at the ceiling with her dark-brown eyes. In contrast, her hair was snowy white. In her youth she might have been pretty — like a dormouse, not taking up much room.

'Fair . . . ish. Corn colour, I think. About five-foot-ten and wearing a black leather jacket with a white line down each sleeve.'

Honey felt the colour draining from her face. She knew that jacket very well. Its owner worked for her. Mark 'Smudger' Smith!

'Are you sure about that?'

She nodded. 'Oh, yes.' And took another Garibaldi. 'His car was parked right outside. It was very small. No room for a drum kit.' She shook her head, as if small cars with no room for musical equipment were an affront to good taste.

The description of the car was going to confirm her worse fears. The jacket was bad enough. Her stomach muscles tightened. She knew, she just *knew* what Miss Meadows was going to say next.'

'The car was green with shiny wheels and a black hood. The hood was down, of course. The day was clement. They drove off. But they have been back, of course. To collect the post,' she explained in answer to Honey's questioning look. 'Sometimes it's that nice young Richard, and sometimes it's his friend, the nice young man who collected him that day. The girl used to come too, but not for a while.'

Honey remembered the one and only day off sick Smudger had taken. Paranoia swept in with a vengeance. What if he'd been really ill and couldn't work anymore? Or worse still, what if he'd really been for a job interview? Now she knew the truth and breathed a sigh of relief. He'd been lying. Phew!

Just at that moment, a four-wheel-drive Mercedes pulled out of one of the parking spaces outside. Another car rolling along with the morning traffic stopped, indicated and pulled into the empty space. A green sports car. The driver got out.

Honey stood up. 'Thank you for the tea, Miss Meadows.'

'Do come again. What did you say your name was?'

'Driver. Hannah Driver. My friends call me Honey.'

'How sweet.'

The door to the ground-floor flat shut behind her at the very same moment as Smudger turned the key to the front door. He stopped in his tracks when he saw her.

'I'm parked along the end,' she said. 'You didn't see me.'

'Christ!' he murmured and closed his eyes.

'I think you've got some explaining to do.'

He nodded. 'Yeah. I suppose so.'

'Where is he?'

Smudger grimaced. 'At my place.'

'I'll follow you.'

* * *

After they'd parked their respective vehicles, Honey made her way to Smudger's flat. He got there before her, had opened up but was now looking disconsolate, standing in the doorway.

'He's gone.'

'Are you lying?'

'Scout's honour.' He held up three fingers.

She pushed past him, her jaw grimly set for action — or at least a bloody good argument. 'I doubt you were ever a bloody scout.'

The living room was typically laddish. No pictures on the walls, no ornaments, just magazines and newspapers stacked in heaps. A few beer cans formed a tight pyramid in front of the large bay window.

'So where's he gone? In here?'

She peeked into the bedroom. Nothing more unnerving than a pile of dirty laundry and a hijacked road sign saying 'Access Only'. Next the bathroom. No one there either.

When she got back into the living room, Smudger was standing in front of the window, hands in pockets. He was staring at the road outside in that vague way that meant he was seeing nothing.

All of a sudden she was angry.

'What the bloody hell do you think you're playing at?'

Holding back a whole dictionary of insults and expletives, she stood with her fists on her hips like Widow Twanky in Aladdin — though not so ugly, she hoped.

'He's a mate. I had to help him out.'

'Mark, he could well be a murderer.'

It wasn't often she called him by his first name. It was usually either Smudger or Chef. But serious crime calls for serious measures.

Smudger stood looking his usual square-faced self — non-committal, convinced he was right.

'Well?'

Smudger gave her one of his challenging looks, the sort he used when they were having a tussle over whether to use mange tout or French beans.

'Fire me if you like!'

There it was — the first salvo in a battle of nerves.

Her blood ran cold. 'Do you think I'm going to fire you?'

She tried not to show just how much the comment unnerved her. There again, depending on what these two had been up to, she might lose her chef anyway. Nervous tension twisted her stomach, and she felt a half-inch of slack in her waistband.

It was no good. This was serious. A girl had to do what a girl had to do. 'I have to tell Steve Doherty. You know that, don't you?'

He shrugged and gestured with his hands. 'Yeah.'

Feeling like a fink but telling herself she had no choice, she pulled out her phone.

Steve answered on the third ring. 'Hi there, stranger!'

She explained about Richard Carmelli and the Grande Epicure.

'You'd better come into the station. And bring Smith with you.'

CHAPTER TWENTY-ONE

'Oliver Stafford deserved to die.'

Glancing at Smudger's expression, Honey could see that he meant it. 'I don't think you should say that in the vicinity of Manvers Street police station.'

The rain was belting down. Even the thrashing backwards and forwards of the windscreen wipers failed to make much impact. Visibility was poor and spasmodic. And she hadn't brought a coat.

She made a face at the rain. 'I'm not walking all the way from the car park.'

'Your choice.' Smudger offered up another of his 'not bothered' shrugs.

She threw him a withering look. 'We wouldn't be here at all if you'd told the truth from the start.'

'It's a grown man's prerogative.'

'Grown man? You're thirty-six going on ten years old.'

'This is the police car park,' he said, sounding surprised as the Volkswagen did a swift right and mounted the curb.

'Clever boy.'

'They won't like you parking here. See?' He pointed at a sign. '*Patrol vehicles and staff cars only.*'

'I'm almost staff.'

Smudger looked bemused. He snorted. 'In your dreams. That copper only tolerates you 'cos he wants to get 'is leg over.'

'Chef!' She felt herself blushing. 'That's no way to talk to your boss!'

He grinned. Smudger was a good chef and knew it. He was a loyal employee but he knew how to play her. Right now she found his mix of bluntness and insight incredibly refreshing.

She eased herself out of the car buttocks first and proceeded to strip the seat cover from off the driver's seat.

Smudger looked bemused. 'You don't need to vandalise your own car. Leave it in a side street long enough and someone will do it for you.'

She ignored him. 'This is an emergency. I paid good money for this hairdo.'

The seat cover was made of stretchy grey material trimmed with a red racing stripe. It wasn't much protection against the rain, but the head rest bit fitted neatly over her head, the rest did a little to shield her shoulders.

The rain began trickling down her neck almost immediately. So much for her makeshift raincoat. By the time they were inside, her hair was flat and sticking to her skull.

'I've just had this done,' Honey muttered. 'Now look!'

Her bouncy hairdo was plastered to her head like a shiny wimple. She tried dissecting it with her fingers, plumping it out so that it looked reasonably presentable.

Steve met them in the foyer. Sensibly, he was wearing a rain-proof jacket with a hood.

'We're going for coffee.'

'We can't. It's raining. Look at my hair.'

She could see he was looking, but not really *seeing* it.

'I thought the wet look was fashionable.'

'Only if you're a sea lion!'

He herded them out of the door and nodded at the desk sergeant on the way out.

He grabbed Smudger's shoulder. 'What the hell are you playing at? You've been mucking me around.'

Smudger was taller and heavier, so Honey's eyes boggled when Steve caught hold of his collar and spun him round so they were snarling into each other's faces.

'Where is he?'

As Smudger shook his head, the look in his eyes hardened and his hands clenched into sizeable fists. Honey held her breath. She could feel the hostility sizzling between them.

Recognising he was in a no-win situation, Smudger gave in. His voice was surprisingly even when he answered. 'I don't know. I honestly don't know.'

Something about his expression seemed to hit a chord with Doherty. His hands loosened.

'OK. OK. I'll believe you, but you have some explaining to do.'

Smudger nodded.

* * *

Charmy Down was deserted. No one disturbed the battered buildings or the weeds pushing through the concrete. Sometimes a heavy plant firm parked unused earthmovers. Otherwise, the place had a neglected air, and yet the old buildings were visible from the A46, stuck like a lighthouse at the top of an incline. The buildings had been built for the RAF back in the Second World War and as such were flat-roofed and uninteresting. Back then, practicality had been more important than aesthetics. There was a good view of the main road from one lot of windows and a good view of green fields falling away into the valley from the other side.

Richard Carmelli parked his car where it could not be seen from either the road or the fields, shielded by an old building on one side and a bulldozer on the other. He knew this place from the days when he'd come here camping with his stepfather. He knew how to light a fire without it being seen, how it felt to snuggle down inside a thick sleeping bag. Just like a boy scout, he'd come prepared. He was always prepared, always planning ahead for any eventuality.

He tipped the contents of his holdall onto the floor. Tinned beans, sausages, soups — he could survive for days on this. He'd also brought coronation chicken. A lot of coronation chicken.

He got out his phone and selected a familiar name from the phonebook. A female voice answered.

'It's me,' he said softly.

'Where are you?'

He smiled. 'I'm a fighter pilot.'

'I see.'

Of course she did. She knew this place as well as he did. They'd camped here when they were children and played among the tumbling ruins. That was in the days before the heavy plant was left here. It had been all wildflowers and tall grass back then, a fun place for kids with a view of the valley.

'Don't worry about me.'

'Richard, you don't need to do this. I'm fine. I'm happy.'

Her brother paused. 'Is Sylvester around?'

'He's in the kitchen. The police are going to ask him questions. You know that, don't you?'

'Yes. They're bound to. But it's not enough that Oliver's dead. I want his name slandered. I want people to know what he got involved in. Then I'll give myself up.'

'Richard, don't do it for my sake. Please don't.'

He grinned. 'I've got to get it out of my system. I'm rattling a few cages, that's for sure. Calling in favours too.' It was time to hang up. 'I'll be in touch.'

She didn't argue. He hadn't explained all his reasons for doing what he was doing. It was too complicated and much too dangerous. He hadn't even told Smudger everything he should have.

He felt bad letting Smudger down, but he'd had no choice. He hoped Smudger would understand. He had to hide until things calmed down. No one ever came here. No one else would know he was here.

CHAPTER TWENTY-TWO

Few and far between were the times when Honey had seen Smudger looking worried, but he was now.

She squeezed his arm affectionately. 'Don't worry. It's just questions.'

Over coffee Honey and Steve listened and learned about what had happened to make Richard plot revenge.

A subdued Smudger warmed his hands around the coffee mug as he swigged at it.

'It was three years ago in France at this competition — the Grande Epicure.' He raised his eyes to Honey's face. 'Before I worked for you. Young Ricky had already won God knows how many 'Young Chef of the Year' competitions. But this was the big banana and he was tipped to win. Richard's a great chef.'

'Greater than you?' Honey asked.

His expression darkened then lightened again. 'He had great potential.'

Honey took that as a yes.

'The competition consisted of three parts: starter, main course and dessert. Richard was good at all of it, but particularly at desserts. I won the starter course, Oliver second, Oliver won the main course, Richard second. Richard was expected to win the dessert course, but he didn't. Someone substituted salt for sugar. We all knew who.'

'So Oliver won?'

'Yep! Trouble was Richard was such a sensitive lad. He took it to heart. Took to drugs after that, so I hear. I didn't hear anything from him until he phoned me just after Oliver got well and truly roasted.'

Honey frowned as she thought things through. 'That's a bit strange, isn't it? I presume he hated Oliver, so why go to work with him at the Beau Brummell?'

A wicked grin lightened Smudger's face. 'To get his own back. Oliver hated practical jokes. It wound 'im right up.'

Steve had stepped into his ultra-serious mode. 'But why involve Stella Broadbent? We know Richard was responsible for the Peter-Jones-playing-a-cowboy debacle?'

'Come on. Out with it.'

Steve's look was steadfast, almost unblinking, loath to miss anything.

Smudger cleared his throat. 'This is what happened, right? Every Sunday, Oliver and Stella would go up to the honeymoon suite to "organise the weekly menu".'

A mental picture of Stella's office flashed into Honey's mind: large desk, thick carpet, comfortable chairs, ideal surroundings for office work. On the other hand, the honeymoon suite would no doubt have more varied and intimate prospects.

'They used to get in the bath together. Richard said he could hear them from outside.'

'Menus tend to go soggy in the bath,' said Honey. She shot a swift look at Steve. 'Not that I've had any experience of that.'

Smudger nodded. 'Correct. Richard used to go outside for a smoke behind the veg shed. They didn't know it, but he could hear them from there, splashing about and all that.'

Steve had let his coffee go cold. Honey could tell by his grim expression that he wasn't letting up on Smudger that easily. And she'd told Chef that everything would be OK.

'He didn't confront them?' Steve asked.

Smudger, who thankfully was far from being his volatile self, shook his head. 'Nope. Richard had a quirky sense of humour.'

'Hence the hunky cowboy act,' said Honey. 'It's a well-known fact that Stella got drunk as a skunk when she was letting her hair down. She wouldn't know whether she'd got married or flown to the moon as far as that goes.'

Smudger took on a bemused expression. 'Correct about the booze. But the cowboy strippergram? No.' He chuckled and shook his head emphatically.

Honey narrowed her eyes as a thought suddenly struck her. 'And it was expensive.'

Smudger grinned. 'No offence intended, but chefs ain't exactly overpaid — unless they end up with their own restaurant in the West End of London and their own TV show. Perhaps if I swore a lot more . . .'

'You swear plenty enough!'

Steve put on his serious hat. 'So where is he?'

Smudger was emphatic. 'I've already told you, I don't bloody know. He had a phone call and shot off, and before you ask, he didn't tell me who it was or where he was going. He should have been back by now.'

Steve's expression remained firm. 'And Brian Brodie. What's the connection?'

Smudger shrugged. 'No idea. All I know is that he was at the Grande Epicure at the same time as the rest of us.'

* * *

They finished up and dropped off Smudger at the Green River. Steve studied the floor as they walked into to reception.

'Do you think Carmelli did it?' she asked him.

'I don't know. He had a grievance and he had been playing silly devils. I can't stand practical jokes. They can backfire badly. A friend of mine told all his family and friends that he'd won the lottery. His wife took him at his word and said that the moment the money came in she would take her half and shove off with his brother. Apparently they'd been having an affair for years.'

They reached reception, both quiet, both thoughtful.

'So where do we go from here?'

Steve sighed. 'How about a walk?'

Things were quiet, so she chanced it. They walked down Great Pulteney Street towards the bridge, the abbey and the heart of the city. A guy dressed as a clown was handing out flyers for a new restaurant. Despite the clown make-up, the spider's cobweb tattoo and the nose rings gave Clint away.

She took one of his flyers. 'Clint. Nice day.'

She sensed the white face turning whiter. 'Crikey, Mrs Driver. I didn't recognise you.'

She thought about saying that *he* was the one in make-up.

'Clint, if you take on any more jobs the tax man's going to have a field day.'

Clint groaned. 'Don't say things like that, Mrs Driver. I won't be able to sleep at night.' He spotted Steve. 'Nice day, Mr Doherty, sir.'

He did a quick salute — two fingers at the side of the head — something between boy scout and downright rude. Then he was gone.

Steve smiled and shook his head in mock despair. 'I reckon I could arrest that bloke on a whole portfolio of charges.'

'He works hard.'

'Does he ever go to bed?' Honey shrugged. Clint was always working. Perhaps he was just naturally hyperactive, or perhaps it was something else.

One of Roland Mead's delivery vans drove past. Honey eyed it with contempt.

Steve seemed to read her mind. 'Mead's vans are everywhere.'

'He's courting my mother.'

'That's an old-fashioned term.'

'My mother's an old-fashioned girl.'

They were like two tourists out for a stroll. Honey was enjoying this; the day was warm, and a band across the road in Parade Gardens was playing everyone's favourite bit from Dvorak's *New World Symphony*. Never mind crime, never mind murder; something about designer stubble turned a girl on. She wondered whether the look was due to laziness or intentional. Or did he have a weak chin? She sneaked a quick glance. No. Strong chin. Strong jaw. Both prerequisites for Honey.

By the time they were strolling around Parade Gardens, their elbows were brushing. Funny how erotic that could be — just touching, just brushing.

'I've been thinking . . .' he said.

She tucked away her thoughts and adopted a deadpan expression, the one that said, *I'm in professional mode, wouldn't dream of being anything else. Where do we go next?*

'And?'

'I've been wondering when we're going to get round to going to bed together.'

The deadpan expression went down the toilet.

'Um . . . well . . . I've been kind of busy . . . and you have too . . . so . . .'

Her voice trailed away. There was no way she was going to admit to the floorshow he'd slept through or tell him that he'd missed his chance. What if he had been awake? Wow, we could be an item by now. Now, that was a Lindsey kind of statement. Her mother's generation called it courting, her daughter's called it being an item. The world was so confusing — or was it? She breathed in and held it; yes, he did smell nice, and that stubble would feel so . . . She drew back from going there. She hadn't answered his question.

They were still walking along, Steve looking unperturbed, almost as though all he'd made was a comment about the weather.

'It would have happened by now if we worked together more regularly. Why don't you join the police force? You'd look good in a uniform.'

His smile betrayed that he was really thinking of what lay *beneath* the uniform.

'I don't want to. I like what I do. I like meeting people.'

A crocodile of American tourists trooped by, led by a large woman holding aloft a pink umbrella. What was it about that colour and Americans? Mary Jane likewise floated around in a permanent pink haze.

'I meet people too,' said Steve. 'OK, I admit some of them are scum.'

Honey raised her eyebrows. 'In Bath? Don't let Casper hear you say that. He swears that this city is God's little acre.'

Steve grimaced. 'He's biased. Never mind that, you still haven't answered my question.'

She shook her head lazily. 'Well . . . you have to ask yourself whether getting close might have a detrimental impact on our professional relationship.'

He looked at her. 'Was that English?'

'Of course it was.'

Emptying her mind of what was possible between them left room for other thoughts to creep in.

'Stafford must have hired Peter Jones but through Carmelli. It was meant to embarrass her, to get her off his back.'

Steve raised his eyebrows. 'I suppose it's possible, though only Carmelli could confirm that.'

Honey nodded decisively. 'I'm sure of it.'

Falling into silent thinking, they walked on. Steve was first to break the silence, returning to the previous subject.

'I suppose it means that we should take a rain check.'

The word fell out of her mouth before she could stop it. 'Yes.'

She wanted to kick herself. Her mouth was not voicing what she really wanted to say. *OK, I want to jump your bones. Let's set a date.*

It was too late. She couldn't go back on it. She had her pride.

Steve did a kind of hunching thing with his shoulders — something between a reluctant shrug and a stretch.

'You're right, and I'm tired. No point in going off half-cock is there?'

She smiled. No point at all.

CHAPTER TWENTY-THREE

Steve Doherty sifted the pieces of paper on his desk, moving them around like so many playing cards. He told his team what Smudger Smith had told him about the cooking competition and Richard Carmelli. Honey had been invited to sit in. As she listened she took notes from which she could compile a report for Casper.

Steve was well into his stride. His voice was strong. He sounded committed.

'Richard Carmelli is the only person we've come across with a motive. Possibly strong enough to commit murder, but possibly not. Oliver Stafford was none too popular, but Carmelli had been playing practical jokes on him for weeks knowing full well that he hated them.'

A detective interrupted. 'What sort of jokes, boss?'

Steve looked to Honey to fill in the details.

'Misdirected post, calls from girlfriends being redirected to his wife at home, and a so-called pregnant woman turning up at his workplace. She actually had a pillow stuffed up her dress.'

The pregnant woman had been a friend of Richard's and hadn't charged for her services. The cowboy had cost good money.

Steve thanked her and carried on. 'There's a few questions we still need to ask — when we find him.'

So far Steve had been looking down at the pieces of paper. Everyone in the room was slouching, taking it in but leisurely. Steve flicked his gaze from the desk to the detectives sprawled and slouched in front of him. One or two had one eye on him and one on their computer. No doubt they were playing Spider Solitaire. In the past he'd done the same when he was bored, frustrated or both. Well, he'd soon put pay to that.

It came full pelt from his diaphragm. 'Wake up, people!'

There followed a general readjustment of bodies and eyes.

Steve's eyes flitted between each face in turn, adding a little warning: *Don't go to sleep on me. Listen to what I am saying.*

'There has to be a link between Oliver Stafford and Brian Brodie besides this cooking contest they entered in France.

'Apparently, Richard Carmelli only had it in for Oliver Stafford, so why Brian Brodie?'

Honey frowned. 'Why Stella?'

A mix of admiring and hostile eyes turned in her direction. The men were admiring. The women looked as though they would execute her on the spot. Steve brought out the beast in uniformed women.

Steve's frown matched hers. 'Maybe this isn't about the chefs. Maybe this is about her.'

'Another question,' said Honey, attracting silent glares from the girls in blue. 'What about the marks around Stella's throat?'

Steve threw her a grateful nod. 'That's a good point. Pathology confirms that these were inflicted prior to her demise and that the car crash killed her. However, we have to ask ourselves, did someone frighten Stella Broadbent, bearing in mind that she was already drunk? A lethal cocktail, fear and alcohol. If one doesn't get you, the other will.'

CHAPTER TWENTY-FOUR

It had been a pleasant day before her mother and Roland turned up. The moment her mother was out of earshot, Roland Mead leaped forward, his breath falling over her.

'You'll regret not doing business with me. No one can touch me for price.'

'The Davis brothers supply quality.'

'Profit!' said Roland. 'That's what this game's all about, lass. Profit. You can stuff quality up your shirt!'

Not for the first time she wondered what it was her mother saw in the man. She managed to mutter, 'Up *your* shirt' before her mother came back.

Honey's dislike for Roland Mead seemed to grow with every meeting. He'd tried currying favour with Chef, now he was trying it on with her — again.

Her mother had brought him in for coffee and ordered a tray with three cups. 'Hannah, darling, do join us. We'd love you to, wouldn't we Roland?'

Roland said something in agreement.

'I'm too busy, Mother.'

'Don't disappoint us,' Gloria mewed. She adopted the classic cocker spaniel look; no other dog could look so mournful. She looked up into Roland's reddish face. 'This is the problem when you get older, Roland. The young are too busy to bother with you.'

Roland turned all bluff and hearty. He patted the empty space in the chair immediately opposite him. 'Come on, girl. Take the weight of your feet.'

She glanced back at the reception desk. Mary Jane was standing there, a splash of colour in a psychedelic pink and pistachio kaftan with matching trousers.

'I'm sorry, Mother. Mary Jane is waiting at reception.'

Ever helpful, Mary Jane overheard and decided to help out. She'd taken to helping out waitressing on tables since she'd moved into the hotel lock, stock and barrel. Her assistance was mostly confined to clearing the dishes. No one had objected. Most restaurant diners and hotel guests had been shocked into silence. Black and white was the usual uniform for waitresses, most of whom were young and agile. Mary Jane, at six feet tall and wearing pink, took some getting used to.

'I only want brochures. I know where they're kept,' Mary Jane called out. Ignoring the notice banning guests from going behind the reception desk, she did just that and helped herself. The phone began to ring while she was there. Honey got up.

Mary Jane got there first. 'I got it. You stay there with your mother and enjoy your coffee.'

'There you are,' said her mother. 'Sit down.'

'Now you and I should get to know each other better,' said Roland, his smile as watery as his eyes.

Honey kept one ear on Mary Jane.

'You're calling from La Jolla? Hey, that's where I'm from.'

Honey groaned. Whoever was phoning merely wanted to book a room and would want to know the price. By the time they got off the line from Mary Jane, their phone bill would pay for three nights' accommodation.

She told Roland the same as she had before: her chef chose suppliers and so far she'd not found any reason not to continue that policy.

Her mother passed her a coffee. She put it down on the table. Mary Jane was in full flow.

'Well, honey, if you're coming to England, then you have to visit Bath, and if you're coming to Bath there's nowhere else better to say than the Green River Hotel. Would you believe it's even got a resident ghost? Not that he'll bother you, unless you're a relative. Sir Cedric and I are intimately acquainted 'cos, do you know what? I *am* a relative!'

Honey groaned inwardly. Now the caller would think that everyone at the hotel — and possibly in the whole city of Bath — was as batty as Mary Jane.

* * *

By mid-morning Honey had it in her mind to go for a drive.

The edge of the reception desk was digging into her behind and her arms were folded. Lindsey was sitting in front of the computer screen.

'I need to talk to Sylvester Pardoe,' she said thoughtfully.

'Haven't the police spoken to him?'

Honey shook her head. 'He's too lightweight a contender to figure in their enquiries. But I've got a feeling in my water . . .'

'Then go for it — but plan things, Mother. I know you like to fly by the seat of your pants, but let's take this one step at a time.'

Feeling suitably chastised, Honey raised questioning eyebrows. 'Lead on, Sherlock. What do I do?'

Lindsey tapped a few keys. 'Bullet-point the reasons you need to speak to him.'

Honey paused, her emotion stirred by the sight of her daughter's face bathed in computer-generated light.

'Right! Number one. He attended the Grande Epicure in France three years ago along with the two dead chefs and our own, dear Smudge.'

'OK.' More tapping of keys. 'And what's the significance of that?'

'I don't know. I think the dead men did. It's just finding someone they might have mentioned it to.'

They both fell to silence as their eyes met. This was telepathy of the mundane variety.

'Oliver never mentioned it to me,' said Lindsey, and flushing slightly, looked away.

Honey forced herself back on track. 'Right. Number two, he opted out of judging the competition at the last minute. Why was that?'

Lindsey typed it in. 'Did you think of phoning him again?'

'He won't speak to me. I'll have to go up there.'

Lindsey sat back in her chair. She had a mature look about her that's rarely found on people under forty.

'You know Smudge had an affair with Oliver's wife?'

'Yes, I know. I just don't understand why he didn't tell me.'

Lindsey pulled a face. 'Because he'd seen your reaction to my fall from grace. Oliver Stafford had a very open view of marriage. He expected his wife to have the same. Smudger said she found it hard to exercise her carte blanche. Said it made her feel sick.'

'But he still went ahead?' Honey couldn't believe it.

'Not so much sexually as supportive. I think things got quite serious, almost to the stage of setting up home together.'

'So why didn't they go through with it?'

'Oliver got murdered. She's free now.'

Honey threw back her head as the truth hit her like a stone-age cudgel.

'Oh my God. No wonder he's been so offhand. He got involved and got dumped. She used him as a crutch.'

'Cow,' muttered Lindsey. 'Poor Smudge.'

* * *

Leaving with a list of questions, Honey retrieved her car from the underground car park where it usually sat and gunned it for the A46 and Oxford.

Green, yellow and corn-gold fields fell like blankets to either side of the road. Once past Westonbirt Arboretum, honey-coloured cottages clustered around village greens and village pubs. Grander houses became more frequent, the latter glowing with Virginia creeper showing signs of changing to red.

Judging by its exterior of mullion windows and iron tie rods shaped like horseshoes, the Haywain was once just an ordinary pub. Long before Chelsea tractors and Mercedes sports cars, drovers on their way to market and ploughmen had congregated beneath its smoke-blackened beams to drink cider and eat their bread and cheese.

Now the building boasted two Michelin stars. In years long past, the cost of just one item from its menu would have kept a ploughman or drover for nigh on a year.

The slate floor was grey and shiny, the oak beams ancient and wide. Suffused with the vision of how many people had passed under its mass, Honey reached up and touched it.

'It's real. Not plastic,' said an attractive young waiter, white cloth over his arm, silver tray clutched like a breastplate to his body. He had an honest face and a keen smile.

'I'd like to speak to Sylvester Pardoe.'

'And the name of your company?'

She couldn't believe her luck. The waiter had assumed she was a sales rep. It was on the tip of her tongue to set the guy right, but her crafty side kicked in. Telling the truth would probably result in her being shown the door.

'Liaisons L'Escargots,' she said. Heaven knows where the name came from, but it sounded good. 'Fat little snails from the best fields in the West Country.'

She flashed him a confident smile. 'Better than the French produce,' she added.

He asked her if she had a card. She acted out the pretence of looking for one.

'No,' she said, shaking her head sadly. She went on to explain that she'd had her handbag stolen the day before and was waiting for a new batch.

'That's a shame,' said the waiter. 'Never mind. What did you say your name was?'

'Mary Jane Jefferies!'

The tall American's name was once again the first that came into her head. It was something to do with the paranormal bit — as though her spirit was whispering in her ear.

The waiter went off. She watched his tight rear and tighter trousers walk away, then had a look round while she waited.

Glasses were being collected. The last of the lunchtime diners were paying their bills and sauntering off to the cloakrooms before leaving.

The walls were painted off-white; the mullion windows were intact and tapestries rather than modern artwork complemented furnishings that could have been made just after Cromwell had hacked off the head of King Charles I. The oak furniture and old-style artefacts pleased her. To his credit, Sylvester Pardoe had resisted the urge to follow fashion trends and make the old place plain and modern.

A young couple came in making enquiries about a wedding. 'I think you need to see Mr Pardoe himself,' she told them. 'We could be going in the same direction.'

The waiter came back. This time it was his face that was tight. She had a feeling what was coming.

'He says you should have made an appointment first, but that he can spare you five minutes.'

'Thanks for your efforts. I appreciate it.'

He shrugged and managed a nervous smile. 'It was nothing.'

She guessed it was far from nothing. If she guessed right, his ear had been well and truly chewed if Pardoe's attitude on the phone was anything to go by.

Mentally girding up her loins, she followed where he led.

She heard Pardoe before she saw him and winced at the bad language. She reminded herself that he was a chef, not just a restaurant owner.

Another F-word rocked the eardrums of everyone within shouting distance. My word, Smudger's vocabulary was reserved compared to this!

Pardoe was verbally wiping the floor with a diminutive commis chef. It was something to do with making coq au vin with red wine instead of white. The words he used to describe what he'd do if it ever happened again were unrepeatable.

'Now get out of here!'

The poor creature, head bowed, scurried off like a hamster in search of a wheel.

The man with the ponytail and the heavy fringe falling over his face swivelled round to face her.

Unsmiling, he glanced at his watch.

'You've got five minutes.'

Pardoe was not immediately aware of the young couple following Honey.

'I'm not selling snails. I've come to talk about murder. These people behind me have come to talk about a wedding. Perhaps you'd like to deal with them first.'

For a moment Pardoe looked shell-shocked, his expression flitting from arrogance to discomfort and closely followed by gushing familiarity.

Teeth flashing, he addressed the young couple. 'My profound apologies. Mr Greg and Miss Sommer?'

He arranged for them to have coffee and a complimentary glass of champagne in the lounge while perusing menus and table arrangements.

'I'll be right with you after I've dealt with this lady,' he said, his smile not quite reaching his eyes.

Mr Happy closed the door. Mr Furious turned to face her. 'What the bloody hell—'

'Don't shout at me, Mr Pardoe!'

He couldn't have looked more surprised if she'd slapped him in the face with a pound of cod.

She took the initiative. 'I'm Hannah Driver, crime liaison officer.' She swiftly flashed her wallet, showing him her Bath Library card, complete with officious-looking picture.

'I work with the police on behalf of Bath Hotels Association regarding the murder of Oliver Stafford and Brian Brodie. I need to ask you some questions.'

She groped in her bag for a notebook and a pen. The former came to hand. The latter did not. Deeper and deeper she went. Pens always seemed to worm their way to the bottom.

The tips of her fingers touched one. At the same time her sleeve snagged on something. When she pulled her arm out the 'something' came too.

'Bugger,' she said, her face already reddening at the sight of the outsize bra dangling from her wrist. 'They built them to last back then,' she said apologetically as she tried to untangle herself from the metal fasteners. Why did it always happen to her? And why now, just when she was trying to adopt a tone of authority?

She looked at Pardoe. His jaw was slack and his mouth wide open. She actually saw a twinkle in his eyes. Well, that was a turn up!

First the corners of his mouth twitched. The twitch ultimately grew into a wide grin.

'What the f . . . ?'

Honey regained her composure. 'I beg your pardon!'

She sensed Sylvester Pardoe didn't pardon himself for anyone, however.

'I am of the opinion that bad language is a last resort of a moron,' she added, pushing the offending item back into her bag. 'Now. Shall we make a start?'

'Crack on,' he said, a half-smile wavering on his face as he settled himself into a chair.

Honey did the same, pulling a chair forward so she could rest her notepad on the corner of the very trendy, blue metal desk. In her mind she thanked herself for shoving the giant undergarment into her bag. Pardoe's mood might never have lifted but for them.

'Right. First off—'

'Hold it right there. I'll tell you what I do know — that bloody witch Broadbent was screwing her chef. Mind you, he'd screw anything, depending on the stakes. This could be about sex or it could be about money.'

Honey pounced on the money angle. 'You mean he wanted a cut of the action?'

He dropped his head in a curt nod. 'And before you ask — no, I don't know what kind of wedge we're talking about here. Something valuable. Something that would keep *my old friend* Oliver in the lifestyle he was accustomed to.'

'Why did you opt out of judging the Bath International Taste Competition?'

'Simple. I hated him.'

'And what about Brian Brodie? Were he and Oliver close?'

'In a way. Brian limped along in his shadow.'

She frowned. 'I understand you met Stafford and Brodie at the Grande Epicure some time ago. Did they do something there that irked you?'

'That's my business.'

Honey eyed the hard features, the firm chin, the lips set in a straight thin line. The soft look in his eyes was at odds with all that. Sylvester Pardoe was burning inside, but why?

She sensed he wasn't going to give up any more, unless perhaps she came at him on a more personal level?

'My chef, Mark Smith, attended the Grande Epicure. Did you hate him too?'

She held her breath as she awaited his answer.

Sylvester Pardoe shook his head and smiled sadly. 'Poor Smudger. He's a good egg and a good chef, but when he gets on the beer . . .'

Smiling, Honey nodded her head knowingly. Four pints and her chef was a handful. Any more than that and he was comatose. 'Vulnerable to pressure,' she said winningly.

'Aren't we all?'

'I find family pressures are worse than business pressures,' she said without thinking, without expecting Pardoe's reaction.

He didn't meet her look, so didn't see her watching his knuckles turning white. He was clenching his fists fit to burst. Sylvester Pardoe was quick-tempered, arrogant and a damn sight more. But there was something else beneath the surface, something she couldn't quite put her finger on . . .

Suddenly the door opened. 'Sylvester, Mr Greg and Miss . . . Oh, hello.' The woman who had entered the room was slim and dark. She had a winning smile and a beautiful face — or at least half of one. Her right cheek was badly scarred, as if it had once been scalded.

She turned to Pardoe. 'I'm sorry, Sylvester. I didn't know you were busy.'

Pardoe got to his feet. 'She's just leaving.'

Honey was being shown the door. The interview was at an end.

The lovely young woman looked a little disconcerted, arching one eyebrow at Pardoe as though she required an explanation. None was forthcoming.

Honey blurted out, 'I was trying to sell your husband some snails.' A split second later it came to her what she'd just said. She'd assumed that this woman was Sylvester Pardoe's wife. Judging by the young woman's response, the smile and the arched eyebrow levelling out, she was right.

'We use local ones. Are yours local?' asked Mrs Pardoe.

'Yes. Sort of. From Cornwall.'

Mrs Pardoe nodded. 'I see.'

Sylvester Pardoe came out from behind his desk. 'I'll see you out,' he said to Honey, then turned to his wife. 'Tell the young couple I'll be with them shortly.' All trace of the loudmouthed lout was gone. This, she guessed, was the better half that hovered beneath the surface.

Honey allowed him to cup her elbow and escort her out.

'Thank you for that,' he said once they were outside.

'For owning up to being a snail salesman? I quite like snails.'

'They're OK,' he said.

Again there was that look in his eyes, a mix of tenderness and concern.

'I didn't want her to know why you were here.'

'May I ask you why?'

'No.'

She turned away from him, wresting her elbow out of his grasp. 'Do I have to go back in and ask your wife?'

He caught her elbow.

'No! Please.' He looked pained. He sounded pleading.

She wondered how many times in a day, in a week, in his whole life he had used the word 'please'.

Folding her arms, she stood in front of him, looking grimly and directly into his face. She saw his discomfort. There was no need to ask questions now. He had to tell it as it was. He had no choice.

He looked away towards the road, gathered his thoughts and looked back at her.

'You saw her face?'

She had a horrible feeling where this was going to go. 'She was scalded?'

'Yes. Hot fat.'

The day was cool, and yet in that instance, imagining how it had felt, the air turned warm, then hot.

She didn't ask because she knew he preferred to tell. And he did.

'My wife is also a chef. She too had been entered for the Grande Epicure. That's where we met. We clicked straightaway. Stafford was jealous. He wanted what I had. Gina didn't want to know, and I thought we were safe. We weren't. Stafford made advances. She refused them, made a fool of him in front of everyone when she accused him of stealing pasta she'd made herself that morning. He denied it. She proved it. The bowl she'd stored it in was marked on the bottom. He was furious. The scene with the fat happened when no one was around. He said it was an accident.'

Not once had he looked at her as he related this. He paused now and seemed deep in thought.

She dug her hands in her pockets and waited. The hot feeling had passed over her. A cold chill remained.

He took a deep breath. 'I wanted to kill him.'

'Did you?'

Eyeing her sidelong, he shook his head slowly and methodically, almost as though he was measuring the distance between his own thoughts and wondering what her response might be.

The softness in his eyes was obliterated with outright hatred.

'Gina is Italian?'

He nodded and looked away. She studied his profile, thinking what a fine Heathcliff he made to Gina's Cathy. Her pulse began to race. She'd seen those features, that profile before.

'What was your wife's maiden name?'

She waited impatiently, wondering if he would answer and confirm her suspicion, or lie and leave her to check at the records office.

'She was Gina Carmelli before we were married.'

And then she knew and was suddenly overcome with a great feeling of foreboding. Richard Carmelli had had more than one axe to grind.

CHAPTER TWENTY-FIVE

Before starting the car, she phoned the hotel and asked for Lindsey. Mary Jane answered.

'Hi there. This is the Green River Hotel. What can we do for you?'

Honey frowned. 'Where's Lindsey?'

'A nice young man phoned. He wanted to speak to you, but Lindsey told him you weren't here. He said it was vital he talked to someone and that he had information about the murders.'

Richard Carmelli! 'So, what did he tell her?'

'No idea. He hasn't told her yet. At least I don't think so. She only left ten minutes ago.'

Talking to Mary Jane was sometimes like pushing a large jelly bean uphill; it didn't go straight and kept rolling in odd directions.

'So, she isn't there.'

'No. She's gone out. The young guy insisted. She's quite safe, Smudger says; he knows the guy and swears he's trustworthy.'

'Let me speak to Smudger.'

'Hold on. I'll just press this here button . . .'

The line went dead. Honey shouted down the phone. No response. The line was dead. She dialled again.

'Is that you, Honey?'

Honey rolled her eyes. 'You should have said this is the Green River Hotel. It might not have been me.'

'Of course it was you. I knew it was you.'

Communicating with older folk was often difficult, something to do with the different plains of life. With Mary Jane it was like dealing with life on another planet.

There again, perhaps she *had* known it was her. After all, this was a doctor of the paranormal.

Smudger came on the line. ''Lo.' Amazing how he could shorten 'hello' to one syllable.

'You didn't say that Sylvester Pardoe was married to Richard Carmelli's sister.'

'Hmm.'

'Stop grunting. Grunts are not words. Why didn't you tell me?'

'You're the private dick. Work it out for yourself.'

Honey sighed and rolled her eyes. 'He has a motive.' *But does Richard Carmelli have an alibi?* she asked herself. *Come to that, how about Sylvester Pardoe?*

'My daughter's gone to meet a possible murderer. Why is that?'

'Ask Mary Jane. She took the message. Must say I was surprised, though. Why would he ask Lindsey to meet him? Why not you?' Smudger sounded puzzled, as though he really couldn't understand it himself.

A cold chill made Honey chant her fears. 'Oliver Stafford and Brian Brodie were responsible for Gina's disfigurement. Stella was having an affair with Oliver. Perhaps our murderer is out of control and out to kill anyone who had anything to do with Oliver.'

'He wouldn't do that. Not to Lindsey.' He didn't sound totally convinced.

'Where were they meeting?' Honey asked, her throat suddenly dry.

'I don't know. Mary Jane took the call and passed on the details.'

'Put me on to her. Now!'

He didn't waste a minute.

'Hi there, Honey!'

Judging by Mary Jane's chirpy voice, she had no idea of what she'd done.

It was difficult, but Honey forced herself to moderate her tone, telling herself it was just an age thing and she too would be old one day.

'Now think carefully, Mary Jane. Where did the young man ask Lindsey to meet him?'

'The young man?'

'The young man who phoned. You passed the message on to Lindsey.'

'Oh.' There followed a pause. Honey imagined her with one finger on her cheek, her misty eyes studying the ceiling. 'Yes. He said to meet him at . . . Oh my! Now, where was it?'

'Mary Jane! Think! For goodness' sake, *think*!' Honey's moderate tone slipped a bit. 'Come on, come on, come on,' she muttered under her breath.

Whether any of her urgings were doing any good was another matter. Mary Jane was on planet Zarcon nine-tenths of the time. She even drifted away when you were speaking to her. Like now.

Fearing for her daughter's safety, Honey hit the panic button and the moderation went flying out of the window. 'Mary Jane, *think*!'

She heard a whine of worry on the other end of the line. 'Oh dear. I don't remember,' said Mary Jane.

Honey closed her eyes, tried deep breathing and counted to ten. Nothing alleviated her concern for Lindsey's safety.

'Put Smudger back on,' she managed to say, still taking deep breaths, still trying to squash the panic making her blood race.

She explained the situation. 'Mary Jane hasn't a clue where Lindsey's got to. I'm afraid for her, Smudge. Richard may be your mate, but he's got an axe to grind and he may not have finished grinding it yet. Get onto Steve. Ask him to keep a lookout for her.'

After she'd said it, she realised how worthless it was. How could Steve keep a lookout? No one knew where Lindsey was.

She punched in Lindsey's number on her mobile. '*The person you have contacted is not available . . .*'

She threw her phone down, turned the key and gunned the engine.

The journey from Oxford to Bath passed in a blur. Never mind the speed limit. Each mile seemed four times as long as it should be. Not until she hit junction 18 on the M4 did she finally take the pressure off the accelerator.

Damn the yellow lines, damn the traffic wardens, she parked where she could, promising herself she wouldn't be a minute, just long enough to check with Steve.

He was on his way out. They bumped into one another in the foyer.

'Easy,' he said, grabbing hold of her arms.

'I'm not flapping,' she said, giving an impatient shrug. 'I promise I'm not flapping.'

He gave her a sidelong, dubious look.

'Have you found her?'

'Let me get you home.' He began guiding her towards the car.

She shrugged his hands off her arms. 'Don't patronise me. I asked if you'd found her.'

Bad temper had no effect on either his manner or the firmness of the hands that pushed her into the front passenger seat. He pulled up outside the Green River. 'You go in. I'll park it for you.'

She didn't need him to say it twice. Like a greyhound she sprang out of the car and through the hotel doors.

Anna was on reception. Mary Jane was nowhere to be seen.

Honey glanced at an incredibly beautiful floral display that hadn't been there when she'd left that morning. If she'd had time she would have questioned where they'd come from. As it was, blooming bouquets were the last thing on her mind.

Anna smiled. 'Mrs Driver. Good evening.'

'Any news?'

Anna frowned. 'Of what, Mrs Driver?'

'Lindsey. My daughter.'

The corners of Anna's wide mouth stiffened as she frowned. 'Lindsey? Lindsey is in the conservatory with a nice-looking man.'

Honey stared at her. Was it possible that Richard Carmelli was actually here?

She headed through the lounge and into the conservatory, a light and airy place of woven rattan with pale-coloured upholstery. Overhead fans provided the air conditioning and tall palms in terracotta pots provided the shade.

Lindsey looked up when she saw her. 'My mother,' Honey heard her say.

The man sitting opposite her pushed back his chair, stood up and held out his hand.

He was slim, about forty, with light-coloured hair and hazel eyes. The colour of his eyes matched his suit.

The first thought that crossed her mind was that this was not the sort of guy Lindsey usually went for. He was too neat, too conservative. Ragged jeans and carelessly buttoned designer shirts were more her cup of tea. The second thought was that it thankfully wasn't Richard Carmelli.

'Slade,' said the man offering his hand. 'Wayne Slade.'

They shook hands. Honey tried to work out where she'd seen him before.

'I'm sorry. I've a terrible memory for names, but I feel I should know you.'

Lindsey was doing charades behind his back and silently mouthing the clues.

Charades had never been Honey's favourite party game. Postman's knock had been her game of choice. Much more fun. No guessing, just kissing and minor fumbling — usually in a broom cupboard.

'I was staying here a while back.' A red blush exploded over his cheeks. 'I was a wee bit naughty. Got my fingers burned. But you and your daughter were very discreet. I brought these back.'

He indicated the shoes and clothes neatly stacked on a spare chair. A chef's hat sat beside it all.

'The hat was your daughter's idea,' he said as if reading her mind. 'I told my mother that I'd been to a fancy-dress party dressed as a chef.'

'Of course!' She remembered the naked man tied to the bed. Overwhelmed by the relief of finding Lindsey safe, she made the most brazen faux pas. 'I'm sorry,' she said in an exuberant rush, 'but I didn't recognise you with your clothes on.'

Lindsey pulled a face.

Richard Slade stammered, 'Um . . . yes . . . um . . .'

Swift action was called for.

Honey took a deep breath. 'That's marvellous! That's really marvellous and I'm so glad to see you. To see you both,' she exclaimed, hugging each of them in turn, saving the tightest hug for Lindsey, of course.

Richard Slade's blush intensified. 'I brought you flowers,' he said. 'As a thank you.'

Honey nodded profusely. 'I saw them. They're lovely. And you're lovely.'

'That's very kind of you.'

She sensed his acute embarrassment 'It's not often we're thanked so wonderfully. So really, really wonderfully.'

She couldn't help the wide, stupid smile or the gushing oratory. She couldn't help sounding as though the return of a chef's outfit was the most wonderful thing in the world. She didn't care how she sounded or how she looked. Lindsey was safe and Richard Carmelli was nowhere in sight.

Honey breathed a sigh of relief.

CHAPTER TWENTY-SIX

Under cover of darkness, Richard Carmelli made his way through Larkhall to the lock-up garage where he kept his motorcycle. He reasoned that a motorcycle could give him a better edge than the car.

A streetlight behind him glinted on the black fairing and chrome bodywork. He checked the fuel tank. Plenty. Got his helmet from where he usually left it, on the workbench at the rear of the garage, and put it on.

Once he'd donned his leather gloves, he rolled the bike out, sat astride and turned the key. The powerful Kawasaki engine purred into life. Sliding his visor down over his eyes, he turned the throttle. The sound changed from a purr to a roar. He set off back the way he came, speeding along the M4 then branching off onto the M5 and finally the Avonmouth turnoff.

During the day the motorways were chock-a-block with traffic. At this time in the morning his route was unobstructed. The wheels ate up the empty miles. Flat-roofed units dealing in car tyres, hydraulic hoses and second-hand office furniture lined St Andrew's Way. Only the watered-down orange streetlights lit his progress, punctuated by the lights of twenty-four-hour garage forecourts, lighthouses in a sleeping city.

He took a turning off towards the docks and passed blank metal walls of prefabricated warehouses. There was a truck ahead of him with a Czechoslovakian number plate. He glanced up, even though he guessed what it was carrying and where it was going — the same place as he.

There had to be somewhere to hide his bike. To his right was a privet hedge and tough railings around an electrical substation. To his left was an empty yard in front of a darkened building — empty, that is, except for two waste skips. The property, like most of those on the industrial estate, had been built in the sixties or early seventies and was being renovated.

Sliding off to his left, he drove in between the two metal skips. The haulage truck had swung across the road, its unit nosing into the gate of the next property, its rig running at a right angle.

Keeping low, Richard crept towards the side wall of the warehouse. Like others around, it was constructed of metal sheets, a modern building designed to be maintenance free. The sound of the truck braking and stopping mixed with that of the cooling units above his head.

Still keeping low, he squeezed through a gap in the railings. The truck cab was only feet away. He saw the driver get out of the left-hand door. Not a British truck, where the steering wheel is on the right.

He got out his phone and took a quick shot of the printing on the side of the truck. It said, *R. W. Mead, International Meatpackers and Warehousing*. He added the text, 'Check this out,' and sent it to Smudger. He trusted the chef to understand its significance, then asked himself why he'd done it. Why couldn't he check it out himself?

Creeping along with the railings against his back, he kept low and listened. Two men came out of the warehouse. There was conversation going back and forth, mostly in English. He strained to hear what was being said and chanced getting closer.

Not looking where he was going, he stepped on a sheet of bent iron. The upright end clanged against the railings.

A voice rang out. 'Who's there?'

Richard fled, squeezing himself back through the gap in the fence. He heard running feet, the sound of a car starting up. He ran faster, sliding to a halt next to the waste skips. He considered lying low. No. Not a good idea, he decided. He leaped onto the saddle. The motorcycle burst into life and he was gone.

Empty roads meant he could build up speed, but then so could the car that was following him.

He sped back towards the motorway, frequently glancing over his shoulder. There were headlights. No details. He didn't have time for details.

There was some traffic on the motorway. Weaving his way through, he kept up the pressure until junction 18 and the A46, accelerating the last two hundred feet to the slip road before dropping the revs. The speed dropped with it.

The traffic lights at the exit stayed green until the very last moment, flashing amber as he passed through. He almost whooped with joy. The lights had changed to red. Whoever was pursuing him would have to stop.

He didn't bother to take the Kawasaki back to the garage in Larkhall but headed for Charmy Down. It was where he felt safe.

Relieved to be back, he took off his helmet and wiped his sweating brow. Carefully, he peered out at the road from between the two bulldozers. Nothing. Not a car in sight. He smiled. Thank God for the traffic lights.

Letting out a whoop of joy, he headed inside for his sleeping bag and the comparative safety of his tumbledown haven.

Ripping off his crash helmet, he sighed with relief and wiped the sweat from his forehead. His stomach chose that moment to rumble. He was hungry. Perhaps there were a few crumbs of coronation chicken left in the plastic box. He grinned. Coronation chicken. That was a laugh. Chicken it most certainly was not.

* * *

It had been a helter-skelter of a ride. He'd driven pretty fast the whole way and had to jump a red light, but now he'd slowed down, having spotted the rear light of a motorbike reflecting off the back of a bulldozer, parked just off the road in the abandoned RAF base. Now he stopped and spoke into his phone.

'Boss? I know where he is.'

CHAPTER TWENTY-SEVEN

Mary Jane kept a low profile until the time came when she'd forgotten that she'd muddled up a message and sent Honey diving into despair. A few hours later she was practising her tai chi movements out in the garden.

On coming back from parking the car, Steve had been amused at Warren Slade's plight but relieved for Honey that Lindsey was safe.

'He asked me out,' said Lindsey, referring to Warren Slade. A wicked smile played around her mouth.

Honey thought twice about asking the obvious question, but couldn't help herself.

'Tell me you turned him down.' She felt her temperature plummet as she said it. The fact that she'd seen Slade in the nude would wash over her — as long as Lindsey didn't date him.

'He's interested in medieval tapestries.'

This was bad.

'But I turned him down. I told him I've got an allergy to dust mites.'

Honey breathed a sigh of relief.

She invited Steve down to the coach house to discuss progress in the case. 'I need to relax,' she said by way of an excuse. 'Is that OK with you, Lindsey? Can you cope?'

Lindsey was still smiling, amused that she'd managed to wind her mother up, but her face softened. 'You don't need my approval. Hurry along there, Mother dear, or I might take him there myself!'

Steve grinned. 'Thanks Lindsey. It's nice for an old man to feel wanted.'

Once in her private accommodation, she poured them a glass of chilled Chardonnay, sat herself down and kicked off her shoes.

'I never want another day like today.' She swigged at the glass and raised it. 'Here's to Warren Slade and his leather jock-strap. Far preferable to Richard Carmelli and his kitchen knife!'

'We're still looking for him,' he said. 'No luck so far.'

'Have you asked Mrs Pardoe? She's his sister. It's all to do with her — more so her than anything else, I think. So it stands to reason they're close,' said Honey, looking worriedly up into his face.

Sighing, he plunged his finger into his wine and began swirling it around.

'We've asked her. She says she doesn't know. I'm not sure that she's telling the truth, but her husband sticks around. I get the impression he doesn't want her to trip over her words and tell us something that would crack this case.'

Cradling her drink with both hands, Honey nodded. 'Her husband is extra protective.'

'You can say that again.'

They both fell to silence, absorbed in their thoughts.

Honey began voicing hers. 'Judging by attitude alone, Pardoe is as much a suspect as Carmelli. Remember, Stafford and Pardoe had a fight — according to Eric.'

'I take it you mean your man in the tri-corner hat and satin britches.'

'The sedan chair bearer.'

He smirked. 'Strikes me there's too many people wearing fancy dress in this city.' He swigged back his drink. 'We need a break. We need something to happen that might point us in the right direction. Time I was going.' He got to his feet.

'Can't you stay a bit longer?'

There it was, her neediness burst out of her mouth before she could put the brakes on.

'Duty calls,' he said, setting his glass back down on the table.

'Oh well.'

She swooped on the empty glasses and headed for the kitchen. Steve followed her.

'Can I have a kiss goodbye?'

She put the glasses down, turned and looked at him. The kitchen counter dug into her back, but she didn't care, and who gave a toss about dirty dishes in the sink? They could wait. Steve Doherty was here and close and about to give her the snog of her life.

It all went according to plan — hot lips, hot bodies, her breasts pressing against his chest. They were as close as they could get, her rear flattened against the kitchen sink and everything else flattened by him.

'That was good,' he said breathlessly as they came apart.

Honey took a big gulp of air. 'One more,' she said, diving forward again. Unfortunately, they collided with each other, nose to nose. On impact they both sprang back, and the pocket of Honey's jeans caught on a drawer handle. The stitching parted with the cloth, and there was a loud ripping sound.

'Did I do that?' he said, his palm lingering over the ripped pocket and the rounded flesh beneath it.

'I'll wear it with pride,' she said.

He smiled. 'I'd better go before I'm tempted to carry out an in-depth inspection.'

'I'll keep them just as they are. You can do one another time.'

CHAPTER TWENTY-EIGHT

'Hannah, darling, I need to get over to Roland's place.'

Honey ground her teeth in response. Up until now Roland had picked up her mother from her flat in Cavendish Crescent and driven her everywhere in his Rolls Royce. But her mother had a habit of finding her things to do. Just because she had the full responsibility of running a hotel, didn't mean she couldn't find a minute to ferry her mother around. That was her mother's opinion. Honey merely boiled with resentment and kept her opinion to herself.

'Mother, I *am* busy.'

Gloria's sigh sounded down the phone like a small hurricane. 'It's not often I ask you for favours, darling.'

Honey's stomach threatened to throw up on the carpet. Her mother was so good at stirring up feelings of guilt.

Lindsey distracted her, choosing that moment to wander by, a picture dressed in a white tracksuit trimmed with pink.

'Perhaps Lindsey . . .'

Her daughter's alarm was instantly written all over her face. 'I'm off to the gym. I'm meeting people.'

Honey thought about using the old guilt trick on her own daughter. No. Certain things in one's genes were best bred out of existence.

'So, where are you?' she asked her mother after wishing her a daughter a good time.

'Here. Look.' She was on the other side of the reception doors waving her mobile phone in the air. 'I've got myself a new phone. A load of different coloured covers came with it, so I can coordinate with my outfit.'

The main door swung open. If *Vogue* ever did a style mag for the over-sixty-fives, then her mother would have been the cover girl. Colour coordination figured high on her mother's agenda. Even her dusters and dishcloths were colour-coordinated — not that she used them. She had a 'daily' who came in to indulge in domestic tasks.

Mary Jane was 'helping out' again. Honey had asked her to replenish the brochure rack and generally tidy it up. It kept her out of the restaurant and from hogging the phone.

Honey smoothed down her skirt and straightened her blouse. Her mother had that effect on her. She noticed a smear of something prawn coloured on her sleeve. She swivelled it around so that it didn't show.

'So where's Prince Charming?' she asked her mother.

'His Roller's in the garage having something done to its big end or something — something mechanical anyway,' she said, dismissively waving her hands. 'So we decided to have a night off.' Gloria's eyes twinkled, and her lips, presently coloured with 'Perfect Peach' lipstick and liner, spread in a conspiratorial smile. 'But I thought I would go over anyway and surprise him. Look, I'm all prepared.' She brought out a bottle of champagne, a tin of caviar and a packet of luxury crackers from a carrier bag. 'Aren't Marks and Spencer wonderful?'

Honey wasn't thinking of the contents of the carrier bag. Alarm bells were ringing.

'Mother, do you want to reconsider that idea?'

Her face, carefully made up with top-flight foundation, crumpled and a suspicious look came to her eyes.

'Why?'

She couldn't bring herself to say what she was thinking, that perhaps Roland was trying to let her down gently.

Perhaps Lindsey was right and he'd really been after the meat order. Butchering was literally a cut-throat business. But it was no good. She couldn't bring herself to say that.

She shrugged. 'Well, Roland might want a night off. You know, to wash his hair or something.'

Honey cringed. It was a pretty lame excuse. Especially since the man wore a toupee.

'I'll wash it for him. I like toying with men's hair.' She winked and made a little clicking sound at the side of her mouth.

The permutations of that particular comment were endless. Honey resigned herself to the fact that her mother's hormones were still raging. There was no getting out of this.

'OK. I'll get Anna to take over reception.'

Mary Jane, who had finished sorting out the brochure racks and was listening in, collared her before she could escape.

'I've got a table-tapping session with the Psychic Development lot down at the college. Can I cadge a lift?'

'How can I refuse?'

As she drove, the two senior citizens chatted in the back, mostly about men, although true to form Mary Jane did bring the less physical sort into the conversation.

'I expect Sir Cedric and your darling departed have made acquaintance on the other side,' said Mary Jane. 'I expect they're meeting on common ground.'

Gloria fixed her with a jaundiced eye. 'Common tarts, more like! That's how my ex-husband died — on top of a tart.'

'Mother, he married her,' Honey reminded her.

'You always defend him,' Gloria snarled, accusation burning in her eyes.

'He was my father. And she *was* his wife — eventually.'

'Yeah. *Eventually* is the word! There she was all in white when he'd been bonking her for months. Trooping down the aisle like a born-again virgin.'

Mary Jane patted Gloria's hand as she got out. 'Life's too short to be bitter, Gloria. You must have cared for the man once.'

Her mother made her angry bulldog sound.

Undeterred, Mary Jane patted her shoulder. 'Never mind, gal. What say you I try to get Herman to rock my table? What would you like me to tell him?'

Gloria's scowl was as dark as Bodmin Moor. 'Tell him that rocking your table is about as close as he's ever got to making the earth move for me.'

* * *

Gloria's mood had lightened the moment there was no one to remind her that her husband had walked out for a bimbo with a Barbie doll figure. The past was dead and buried. Her mother was not.

'Roland will be surprised,' she said as they headed up towards the Royal Crescent. Lowering her head, she peered out and up at the elegant facades of the perfect houses set in a perfect crescent. Even a one-bedroom flat here could cost half a million or more. To own a whole house would cost a fortune. 'I wonder whether he's furnished his place with antiques,' she said.

Honey sensed refurbishment plans were being made, though something else was more pertinent. 'So you've never been inside his place?'

Her mother smirked in a manner far too salacious for a woman of her age. 'Not yet. We're kinda building up to it. There's a great deal of mutual respect between us. We're not the kind that jump in the sack and jump out again. We're looking at long-term commitment here. And once I'm married and happy as Larry—' she patted her daughter's arm — 'then I can get our home the way I want it, and turn my attention back to finding a nice man for you.'

Honey suppressed a shiver. 'Don't rush into things, Mother. There's a lot to be said for a long engagement.' She felt like a coward and a killjoy, but mostly she was a woman who wanted to run her own life.

The sun was setting in a rosy glow and throwing long shadows. During the day the crescent had soaked up the sun. Now at sunset those same stones released the trapped warmth. It made you want to cuddle up and lay your cheek against the warm stone.

Overall there was grandeur. To Honey's mind, Bath's Royal Crescent resembled a grand tiara, raised as it was slightly above the city. For the most part, traffic was banned from trundling over the cobbled road. She spotted Harold and Eric's blue sedan at one end of the crescent. Aubrey and Bert, their business rivals who ran a green sedan, were at the other end.

Honey drove around the back and found a parking space. 'Do you know which number it is?'

Her mother angled her slim legs out of the car. 'Of course I do.' This evening she'd donned the little black dress, real pearl earrings, a matching necklace and bracelet. She wore high heels, and Honey noticed fishnet stockings and red shoes.

Her mother straightened her skirt and lifted her head. 'Do I look good?'

Fishnet stockings and red shoes might have screamed, 'I'm a tart and I'm dirt cheap' on some women. On her mother they looked fabulous. Age had nothing to do with it; she had the knack of throwing the right things together.

'You look great.' Honey meant it. There were times when her mother made her feel proud. There were other times she shrank to two inches and wanted to drown herself in a puddle.

Her mother smiled then looked her up and down. 'We'll have to do something about those jeans, Hannah. They've seen better days.'

Honey was back in the puddle. She managed a tight smile. 'Yeah.'

She didn't go into detail about them having seen some action and Steve Doherty ripping them. Things would get too complicated.

Honey handed her mother the carrier bag of goodies. 'Do you want me to come with you?'

Her mother glared. 'Certainly not. This party's strictly for grown-ups.'

Her mother tottered off. She lingered, strolling into the crescent and heading for Harold and Eric.

'How's business?'

Harold tried to put on a happy face. 'OK.'

Eric, on the other hand, had the expression of a squashed walnut. 'Foul. There's nothing but couples.'

The solution seemed simple. 'Why don't you team up with Aubrey and Bert? They can take one, and you can take one. That makes two.'

'We can count,' said Eric, his dour manner unchanged. 'It's a matter of principle. We started first, and they copied us.'

'Does that matter? I mean, if my place is full and I've got people wanting rooms, I send them on to other hotels. It works both ways. When they're full, they send them on to me.' Honey thought she sounded pretty eloquent, even wise. What she said was quite true. Hoteliers were basically generous people. Except for Stella Broadbent. That cow wouldn't pass anything on except perhaps a cold or a severe case of influenza.

She smiled sweetly. 'So how about you guys burying the hatchet and forming a cooperative? United we stand. Strength in numbers and all that.'

The reasoning seemed to work — at least with one half of the business.

Harold jerked up his britches and looked at Eric. 'I reckon we should try and come to some arrangement.'

Eric glared at him. 'Traitor.'

Harold sighed and shook his head. 'Eric, I've got to earn some money.' He paused as if churning things over in his mind. 'If we don't earn anything, then I'm going to have to give this up and get a proper job.'

Eric's head swivelled round in double-quick time. 'You wouldn't!'

'I've got no choice.' There was nothing threatening in Harold's tone; he laid it on the line flat and without embellishment.

Eric's expression turned from downright stubbornness to outright shock. Laid-back Harold stood his ground.

'Well,' said Eric. 'Well . . .'

It might have been fun to see how it played out now their crisis meeting was over, but hers was about to begin.

Heels tip-tapping like an out-of-control metronome, her mother was heading her way apace, far quicker than when she'd been going in the other direction. Humiliation coloured her Estée Lauder foundation. Something was wrong! Badly wrong.

Her mother came to a halt. Her face was like stone. Her bottom lip trembled. He told me it was his house. He told me he lived there alone.'

Guessing the problem, Honey peered into her mother's face with what she thought was a sympathetic expression.

'Isn't he there?'

'There's someone else there.'

'Who's there?'

'A woman.'

'Are you sure?'

Her mother turned angry eyes on her. 'I'm not that senile!'

She took hold of her mother's arm. 'Let's go for a coffee.'

Her mother shook her off. 'Don't patronise me.'

'I'm sorry.'

Honey looked over her mother's head to Harold and Eric. They looked concerned.

'Is there a problem?' asked Harold.

'My mother was calling on a friend. It doesn't look as though he's at home.'

In all honesty, she didn't know whether she'd got the wrong end of the stick, but her mother wasn't being very forthcoming. She looked shell-shocked; she looked small.

'A woman answered the door,' growled Gloria. She looked up suddenly. Honey's gaze travelled in the same direction.

A tall woman in her late forties with Mediterranean looks and a swaying derriere was striding towards them. A black patent belt cinched in the waistline of a red, wrapa-round dress. If sex really did come on legs, then she was it.

She came level, an amused smile playing around her lips. She stopped but wasn't completely still. *Undulating*, thought Honey. Her curves just wouldn't stay still. Except that they didn't wobble. Ouch! How did she do that? One slinky leg rested provocatively against the other in a classic seductive pose.

'My apologies, *Signora*. Are you all right?'

Gloria's red lips compressed in a tight straight line. She nodded brusquely.

'If I offended you in any way . . .' The woman's voice was as languorous as her looks.

Jaw stiff as iron, her mother nodded again, mouth tightly buttoned.

Honey said nothing as she attempted to size the situation up.

The glamour-puss departed with a final bright-red smile and a huskily whispered, '*Ciao*.'

The eyes of the sedan chair bearers followed the rolling rump until it was out of sight.

Honey waited for an explanation. It was slow in coming and hissed through tightly clenched teeth. 'She thought I was Roland's mother.'

'And I don't suppose she was the housekeeper.'

Her mother scowled. 'Depends what you mean by keeping house.'

'That woman had the same effect on me last time,' said Eric, pushing his hat further back so he could mop the sweat that had broken out on his brow.

There was something about his tone of voice that made Honey curious.

'Do you see her often?'

He smirked and winked at her. 'Not as often as I'd like. That one's as fiery as they come. Hot-blooded, like — you know, in the right department. Though there's something about someone shouting and swearing at you in a foreign language. Know what I mean?'

Honey's curiosity intensified. The instinct of a hotelier is sharper than that of lesser mortals; it has to be. Judging a book by its cover isn't enough. You have to be able to get to the first page, if nothing else.

'Must have been some scene.'

'That it was. She's a passionate one.'

Her mother was almost spinning on the spot, wanting to go. 'Passionate? Fishwife, more like!'

Honey bit her lip. The woman was far from being a fishwife — too glittery, too gorgeous. Her mother wouldn't thank her for showing any signs of pity. But she did. She couldn't help it.

Eric made a clicking noise at the side of his mouth. 'That chef went knocking at her door. Gave 'im 'ell, she did.'

'That chef?'

'One of them I 'ad fighting in my pub.'

'Pardoe?'

He nodded. 'That's right. Sylvester Pardoe.'

CHAPTER TWENTY-NINE

It was dark out, but cosy and warm inside the old building at Charmy Down. Richard Carmelli spread his last portion of coronation chicken onto a hunk of wholemeal bread. He eyed it cautiously before spreading it, telling himself that he should make it last and not eat this much all at once. He washed it down with a can of 7up.

A wind got up. The trees on the other side of the fence began to rustle and creak. Most of the glass was missing from the windows and the doors were ill-fitting. Richard tucked himself into his sleeping bag. No point in staying up. No point in sitting and freezing his butt off.

He dozed off.

He didn't know how long he'd slept, but he woke up aware that the walls around him were shaking. Bits of loose plaster trembled and fell to the floor. Even the floor itself was vibrating beneath him.

The wall at his head shook as something clanged against it. He blinked himself to wakefulness. His logic kicked in. Someone had started up one of the machines outside. Kids probably, joy riders wanting a change from nicking motors; heavy plant was far more exciting. You could knock a building down with one of the buckets on those machines.

'Oi!'

He shouted as he struggled out of his sleeping bag. Clang! Another hit. Old bricks were dislodged and old plaster crumbled to dust.

He struggled to his feet, aware he wanted to pee but having no time.

He dragged open the old door and swore beneath his breath. The bucket of the earthmoving machine was hanging in mid-air. The air was thick with diesel fumes.

He shouted and waved at the windscreen of the cab. Someone had to be in there, but he couldn't see them. Again the bucket hit the side of the building.

'Oi! Knock it off! D'you hear me? Knock it off!'

The bucket seemed to tremble. The engine accelerated. The air was filled with exhaust fumes, stinging his eyes, filling his lungs.

There was barely time to see the bucket swing, barely time to get out of its way.

Accompanied by a cloud of diesel smoke, it swung again, stopped above him, then dropped.

* * *

Ernie Kemp rented a transport yard down near the motorway interchange, where the passing traffic sounded like a rushing wind and the hedgerows were thick with dirt and discarded crisp bags. The yard was surrounded by tall wire fences and filled with oily black puddles. Steep-sided tipper trucks — great big ones with 'Motorway Maintenance' written across the back, were parked side by side like a load of snuggling triceratops. But there were some trucks he didn't have room for; that was why today he was off up Charmy Down to make room for one that wasn't being used at present. It just meant moving the other truck already up there. He muttered under his breath as he drove over the rutted track leading to the old RAF yard.

'Fred Foster, can't you park your bloody plant a bit bloody better than that?'

'Bloody' was his favourite swear word; it had been ever since he'd married Pauline and she'd balked at his vast itinerary of unmentionable words that rough men in rough company tended to use. And he needed to use rough words; Fred Foster never parked any of his machines very tidily.

Ernie came to a stop, shut off the engine of his sleek, silver Mercedes and got out. He frowned when he saw the car parked between the buildings.

'Fred?' he shouted.

He looked at the car again. No! An old Ford? Fred was careful, but not that careful. He did like a bit of something decent around him. A Ford, yes, but not an old one, and he'd definitely choose top of the range if he did. And whose motorbike was that? Surely something way beyond old Fred's capabilities?

He called out again. A few rooks took off from the nearby trees. The sound of a tractor filtered up from the valley. A host of squalling seagulls followed the machine as it trekked backwards and forwards.

He headed for the nearest machine. Its tail end was sticking out into the yard. Its heavy metal bucket was lowered between the two buildings.

What he saw next made him stop in his tracks. Two legs — two human legs — plus the lower part of a torso stuck out from beneath the bucket.

Shaking from his head to his boots, he pulled out a small container of tablets from his pocket. His heart was hammering against his rib cage, his blood rushing into his ears.

Poor old Fred. He should have been more careful. I told him to be more careful.

And then he heard a car, turned and saw the familiar black Land Rover Discovery pull into the yard.

He recognised the face behind the wheel.

'Fred!' he shouted, running forward on shaking legs. 'Fred! Call the police! And an ambulance, and . . . everybody!'

CHAPTER THIRTY

'I like scraping Jersey Royals,' said Honey in answer to her chef's searching look. She'd phoned Steve telling him about Sylvester Pardoe's visit to the address in the Royal Crescent. Roland Mead's address. Why had he gone there?

Steve had said he would investigate. Once that was done she'd headed for the relative safety of the kitchen. Her mother had stayed overnight, in too much of a state to go back to her own place. Murder most foul was on the menu. Gloria Cross was vengeful and didn't care who knew it.

The potatoes were small, covered in flaky skins and a devil to scrape, but she had to take her annoyance out on something — or somebody.

Smudger Smith was having none of it. He stood looking at her, waiting for the rest of the reason.

'And I'm out here avoiding my mother.'

He nodded in mute understanding and got on with what he was doing.

The woman scorned had nothing on her mother. When treated kindly she could sometimes be a pain in the neck. Make her look a fool and things could get deadly.

Mary Jane, bless her, was doing her best to make her mother feel better. 'Now come on, Gloria honey, pull yourself together.'

Mary Jane had managed to persuade her to have a tarot reading. Her mood hadn't improved much, even when Mary Jane had explained that the fool suspended upside down didn't mean what she thought it did. There was no placating her.

'I know,' said Mary Jane. 'Take a snifter of my tonic. I guarantee it'll make you feel better.'

The last Honey had seen of the pair of them was her mother taking more than a snifter of Mary Jane's tonic and Mary Jane telling her that she had plenty.

She'd whispered her thanks to Mary Jane before scooting away.

'You carry on, Honey,' said Mary Jane. 'Me and your mother will be just fine.'

'I wouldn't touch that stuff,' said Smudger when she told him.

Honey attacked a potato. 'It looked like syrup of figs. Smelled like rubber sports shoes.'

Smudger dipped his finger into the roux he was making. 'Hmm. Not quite haute cuisine, then?'

'No. More like eye of newt and leg of frog . . . Still, if it does the trick. I don't want her to go on until her dying day about what she'd like to do to Roland Mead. I warned her, didn't I?'

Smudger grimaced. 'The bloke's on a roll. He thinks he can do as he likes.'

Honey nodded and attacked a particularly evasive blemish in a small potato. 'I won't hear the last of this for a while. She's sworn revenge — breach of promise, even.'

'Breach of what?'

'It's an old law. I told her it was no longer on the statutes, but she didn't care. She wants his ass!'

Chuckles and sly grins ran around the kitchen, but didn't last. Today was a very important day. Everyone fell to silence and carried on with the tasks allotted to them.

Honey adjusted her pristine hat and brushed an imagined smut from her perfectly white overall.

She glanced up at the clock.

'He's late.'

Smudger threw his head back and closed his eyes. 'Prolonging the agony. Typical!'

The phone burbled.

Like a pack of wary meerkats, everyone turned to face it. No one rushed to pick it up until Smudger made a dash, sliding the last few feet.

'OK.' He looked at Honey. 'Mr Westlake's here. Look busy,' he barked at the kitchen staff. Heads down, they laboured on with their work as though the environmental health officer was no big deal. If only!

Adopting her best welcoming smile, Honey met him at the door. 'Mr Westlake, how nice to see you. Do come in.'

Mr Westlake had never shown any signs of having a nervous disposition — until now. There was a haunted look in his eyes, and he seemed almost relieved when the kitchen door was safely closed behind him.

'Right. Shall we start?' said Honey in the most sugary tone she could muster.

His hands shook as he arranged the official forms on his clipboard. His pen was fastened by Velcro to the clipboard, but still he managed to drop it.

'I'm retiring, you know.' He said it vaguely, as though the fact had suddenly hit him and come as a great surprise. 'I think it's time,' he added, his bald pate gleaming like a freckled bowling ball beneath the stark lighting.

Face full of concern, Honey asked him if he was all right.

He looked back at her blankly. 'You're not usually in the kitchen when I call.'

He said it in a strangely searching way, as though he were seeking a kindred spirit who was also suffering the same kind of haunting he was suffering himself.

She couldn't admit that she was hiding away from her mother, so she began fabricating a convincing lie. 'I just thought I'd help out—'

'Your mother's been telling me about some problems she's been having,' he interrupted, his voice shaking.

The truth was out. She did her best to paper over the cracks.

'Well, she is going through a bit of a crisis.'

'With a man,' said Mr Westlake. 'She told me all about it.'

Honey groaned. Smudger rolled his eyes. The rest of the kitchen did their level best to stifle their giggles, though Gayle, the young commis chef, laughed so much she had to run for the ladies room. The kitchen porter hid his head inside the dishwasher, his shoulders shaking with mirth.

Honey apologised. Mr Westlake, who was usually such a stickler for getting stuck into the job of rooting out unsafe hygiene procedures, appeared severely unsettled at having landed the job of agony aunt.

Honey broke the cardinal rule and offered him a cup of tea. Mr Westlake broke his own cardinal rule and accepted.

Fearing he might collapse then and there, she offered to accompany him out into the courtyard, where he could sit in the sun. He accepted her offer.

She looked askance at her head chef. He looked askance right back. Was it really possible that her mother wittering on about her love life had worn down the contrary environmental health officer? If the skill could be bottled, the catering industry would be queuing up to buy it!

They sat down on the comfortable wooden benches set beside a neat wooden table.

'Nice,' he said, looking around him.

'Yes. Nice.'

As trite as it was, at this moment in time Honey was feeling nice. Nice seemed a . . . well . . . *nice* word. Usually she was on edge when Mr Westlake called. Today, well . . .

Perhaps it was the calming surroundings, perhaps the cup of tea, perhaps the home-made oat biscuits with real almonds, or perhaps having escaped her mother's brow-beating oratory, but whatever it was due to, Mr Westlake began to unwind.

'I retire at the end of this week, and when one is retiring, dear lady, one tends to better evaluate good kitchen practice.'

Her heart sank. He wasn't going to give her kitchen a good going over once he'd drunk his tea, was he? She closed her eyes and prayed. Mr Westlake carried on with his assessment of the rules and regulations, especially with regard to meat.

'I particularly condone separate fridges for cooked and uncooked meats, and in the case of uncooked, I would even go so far as to divide meat further: poultry in one, pork in another, beef another, and so on.'

She wondered about game, but wasn't going to ask. He carried on.

'Ground meat is a problem. Ground pork and ground chicken look very much the same. Tons of cheap ground meat is coming in from Europe. Unfortunately, it is not always quite what it seems. Chicken and pork all ground up together. Very worrying if you happen to be Jewish or of the Islamic faith. Are you of either of those?' he asked suddenly.

'No.'

He picked up his clipboard, nervous fingers fiddling with the pen.

'That's good.'

She glimpsed the reflection of her face in the window opposite. Flummoxed was the only word to describe it. What did any of this have to do with his inspection?

'I'd better carry on.'

He got to his feet and tottered back into the kitchen. His inspection was fast and furious. She could barely keep up with him. At the end of it, everything was in order.

Unseen by Mr Westlake, Smudger did a silent 'Phew' and swiped the back of his hand across his forehead.

'Just one thing, dear lady,' said Mr Westlake as she guided him towards the door. 'Is there a rear entrance I can use?'

She smiled. 'Of course there is. Follow me.'

She'd fully expected the whole of the catering team to be clapping wildly when she went back in. Instead Smudger was looking grim.

'Don't tell me my mother's made it up with Roland?'

Her head chef was standing with his hands on his hips. He looked down at the floor when he shook his head.

'Steve Doherty wants to see us. Richard Carmelli is dead. And it weren't an accident.'

CHAPTER THIRTY-ONE

The bar door was closed to the public, making it a good place to talk. The lights were off. It was a cool, green place that had a hollow emptiness about it when it was cleared of paying guests. Staff wouldn't come in until it was open and neither would her mother. Gloria Cross didn't approve of drinking. Her third husband had — too much, as it turned out.

Steve and a uniformed colleague were swift in movement, sweeping into the bar, declining to sit down and looking impatient to go.

Honey noticed he was having trouble meeting her eyes. His questioning was directed at her head chef.

'We're busying ourselves questioning suspects and witnesses. You're one of them. Tell us all you know about Richard Carmelli. Where you met, what form the relationship took and whether you wanted to kill him.'

Smudger was unruffled. 'He was a mate. Mates don't kill each other.'

Honey held her breath.

'Depends on whether one of them has a bit of a temper.'

Gone was the sexy Steve of the other evening. This was serious.

Honey felt her mouth growing dry. 'He couldn't have done it. He was here when it happened,' she blurted.

'When what happened?'

'When everything happened.'

Steve's serious expression stayed in situ, though his eyes twinkled when he looked at her. There were a few interesting observations in that look, and none of them had anything to do with crime. He turned back to Smudger. 'We'll need to take samples from your hands and beneath your fingernails. Do you know how to drive an excavator or any other item of heavy plant?'

'I could learn,' he said with a grin.

'This isn't a joke.' Steve's look hardened.

Honey noticed.

Smudger noticed too. His attitude shifted ninety degrees. 'No. Never needed to. There's not much of a call for driving heavy plant in a hotel kitchen.' He frowned. 'How did Richard die?'

Steve stated the facts without too much description of the gore. 'Someone brought a half-ton bucket down on his head up at the old RAF place at Charmy Down.'

Honey felt the blood drain from her face and pool somewhere around knee level.

The gathering fell to silence, their faces bathed in reflected thoughts. Even Smudger's country boy cheeks paled to rice pudding white.

Each was picturing Richard Carmelli's demise: legs sticking out from beneath an iron bucket, head smashed like an overripe strawberry.

The situation called for an inappropriate intrusion — someone to say or do something smart or funny, anything to break the stony silence.

Can anyone do cartwheels? Honey wondered. They were all on pause and needing to move on.

Suddenly there was a sound. Someone was mumbling. They all looked at each other.

'I didn't catch that,' Steve said to her.

'I didn't say anything.'

She looked at Smudger. He shrugged. 'Not me.'

'The bum! The low-down, snake-in-the-grass, rat-assed bum!' The voice was slurred, but still recognisable.

Honey felt her face reddening and saw amusement trickling across Steve Doherty's face.

Fingers thick with diamond rings appeared on the bar top — first one hand, then the other.

All eyes were on the bar, except for Smudger, who was still distracted, still in shock. He was shaking his head. 'Whoever did it is a low-down . . .'

'Bum!'

Steve gave a nod of acknowledgement. 'I couldn't have put it better myself.'

'Roland Mead is a bum!'

Gloria Cross's blurry vision travelled around the room. Recognising a captive audience when she saw it, she smiled.

Honey sensed a performance coming on, groaned and hid her face in her hands.

Without looking at her, she knew that her mother's face was lighting up. First there'd be a joke in the worst possible taste.

'Bum!' Gloria's reverberant voice rang around the dimly lit bar. 'What do you call a dwarf with short legs? A LOW-DOWN BUM!'

Honey peered through her fingers. Steve's serious expression had fractured into a wide grin. 'Your mother isn't too hot on political correctness.'

Honey reeled off a number of pathetic excuses. 'She doesn't know the meaning of the term. She's old! And she's not usually in the bar. She doesn't drink.'

His grin widened. 'She does now.'

Her mother's shoulders came into view, then her chest.

Oh Christ!

The room went goggle-eyed. Steve Doherty's jaw dropped. His uniformed colleague sniggered but was silenced with a warning glare from his boss.

Honey groaned. Lindsey must have put the big pink brassiere behind the bar. Gloria had evidently found it and tried it on. As for the alcohol . . .?

Her mother's face was blearily happy, soft like kiddies' building clay. 'Mary Jane gave me a strong tonic.' She hiccupped. 'It was *very* strong, but it's done me the power of good.' Wobbling slightly, she looked down at her chest with a slightly surprised but accepting look. 'My! I was always a 36B. Do you think the tonic did that?'

CHAPTER THIRTY-TWO

Two days later, Steve dropped in for coffee and brought her the result of his enquiries regarding Sylvester Pardoe.

'He's well covered with alibis,' he said, resting his elbows on his knees as he ran his fingers through his hair.

Honey could feel his frustration.

'But why did he call on Roland Mead?'

'He said it was a while ago. He was looking for Stafford.'

She was about to ask him why Pardoe would ask Mead for the chef's whereabouts, but Steve pre-empted her question.

'He said he'd come down to look up old pals, and Carmelli pointed him in that direction.'

Honey frowned. 'Friends? So that was just an amiable fisticuff in Eric's pub?' She shook her head. 'No. Don't believe it. Friends don't try to punch each other's lights out.'

Steve sighed and rubbed at the corners of his eyes with two fingers.

'I've just told you, he's got an alibi for each of the murders. He was shocked at the last murder, though.'

'He would be. Richard Carmelli was his brother-in-law. Did anyone question Gina Carmelli?'

Steve sighed again, though deeper this time. 'She confirmed her husband's story — or stories.' He lay back against the soft comfort of the creamy-coloured Knole settee — an expensive little number she'd picked up at auction and had reupholstered at even more expense. 'Christ, I'm knackered,' he muttered, closing his eyes.

'You could do with going to bed.'

One eye reopened and eyed her with expectant hope. 'Are you offering?'

She slapped his shoulder. 'I thought you were tired. You need some time off.'

He mumbled an agreement and yawned. 'How about dinner tomorrow night? My place.' He smiled seductively, his eyelids as heavy with innuendo as they were with tiredness.

She smiled right back. 'That's nice. It'll be the first time.' She said it meaningfully.

His eyebrows arched. 'Really?'

She shook her head. 'The first time I've been invited to your place, Steve. My God, you are tired.'

He drained his coffee and offered his cup. 'Another, please. I've got to keep going. I'm under too much pressure. I've got a chief constable giving me hassle.'

Honey pulled a face. 'It could be worse. I've got a broken-hearted senior citizen being a continual pain in the backside.'

A smile hovered around his mouth. 'Point taken. How is your mother?'

'In purdah. She's telling everyone that she's had a virus and is out of circulation until she gets over it. Perhaps in a day or two she'll make her golf morning or her duties at Secondhand Rose — it's a dress shop,' she added in response to his questioning look.

He put down his empty coffee cup. 'Tomato juice, egg yolk and plain flour.'

She got his drift. 'Yes, if it was just a hangover. Useless if you've just been jilted.'

Steve twisted around so he could watch her retreat into the kitchen. When she came back in his chin was resting on his hands, his eyes following her all the way. His eyes looked up at her in that certain way, making her feel . . . well . . . sexy.

'Your mother needs to get out and about to get over it.'

Honey sat herself down beside him, arm sprawled languorously along the back of the settee.

'I suggested it. She nearly bit my head off. Told me not to tell her that there were plenty more fish in the sea because men her age were mostly dead in the water.'

Steve held his hands up in mute surrender. 'What do I know about women? What do I know about men, for that matter?'

Honey poured herself fresh coffee. 'Too early for booze,' she said in answer to his raised eyebrows.

'Has Lothario tried to get in contact?'

She nodded. 'She refused to take the call. Lindsey spoke to him. He told her he was in London.'

'Just as well. It's ended and that's that.'

'No. Not with my mother, it isn't.' She tried to call him back.

Sighing, he began searching in his right-hand pocket. 'I've got the pathology report on Carmelli.'

Honey sipped and watched him closely as he unfolded a piece of paper torn from a notepad. The way he moved and did things had a masculine surety about it. Positive. Full thrust on the throttle. Her complexion turned pink.

She put her cup down. 'The coffee's hot,' she said, wafting her hand in front of her face. 'It needs to cool down.'

Liar!

Dark-fringed and true-blue, his eyes flickered between her and the scrap of paper. 'Not the official report, of course. I just wrote down what was relevant.' He smiled a little wearily, as though she'd teased him into being a little more upbeat.

That smile. *Will you please stop that!*

His eyes dropped to the paper. 'I think massive contusion to the head is a bit of an understatement, and I won't go into detail on that score. He hadn't long eaten; cooked meat and curry mixture mixed with mayonnaise in a sandwich. The bread was from half a loaf we found on site and the sandwich filling came from a sealed plastic container.'

Honey frowned. 'Coronation chicken. A dish invented at the time of the Queen's coronation. Quite standard.'

'Not if the main ingredient is supposed to be chicken. Says here it contained a mixture of ground meat.'

'Let me see that.' She grabbed it, her face darkening the more she read. 'Richard had quite a lot of this. He had some in the fridge at his flat, and I was in the kitchen at the Beau Brummell when he was making a batch. He gave me some. All the plastic containers were labelled coronation chicken. Definitely.'

Steve looked thoughtful. 'What does it signify?'

Honey shrugged and shook her head. 'Nothing if you're dead. But if that's the case, then Roland Mead is breaking the law, besides a host of hygiene and quality control issues. And I've got the evidence sitting in my freezer.'

'We need to test it.'

She nodded, understanding his implications. 'You can have it.'

Shortly after Steve left, she phoned Mr Westlake, referring him to their previous conversation.

'You were talking about the trade in ground meat coming into this country from Europe. Is it illegal?'

'Most definitely! Firstly, there's the Trade Description Act, then there's falsification of country of origin — in some cases it's a case of throw everything from all over into one big mincer and grind it up. Not too dangerous if it's all fresh, but the bulk of it is not. A lot of it is past its sell-by date, some fit only for pet food, some not even fit for that.'

'Have you ever found any of this stuff in Bath?'

He gave a short cough. 'Ahem! I would be breaching protocol if I told you that. Of course, should you ever have information that could help us prosecute, we would treat such information in the strictest confidence . . .'

'Not yet. But I'll keep you informed.'

'Uh . . . yes. By phone for preference. No need for me to come round.'

Honey smiled as she disconnected and couldn't help feeling an overwhelming surge of affection for her mother, so overwhelming that she just had to snatch her from Mary Jane's clutches and offer her tea and sympathy.

* * *

Romantic breakdowns are as much torture for friends and relatives as they are for the injured party. Honey was at breaking point herself. Her mother was flitting between periods of stony silence and outbursts of red-hot anger.

Lindsey, being young, was used to having friends of her own age sobbing on her shoulder. Having her grandmother doing the same was something different. She tried making useful suggestions — just as she did to her friends.

'How about taking up a hobby?'

Her grandmother had fixed her with a jaundiced eye. 'Like what?'

Lindsey had wracked her brains. Advising friends to take up paragliding or rock climbing was one thing. Telling her grandmother to do that was downright dangerous! Now, what hobbies did older people go in for?

'How about something artistic like silk painting or antique restoration?'

The implications were obvious. The jaundiced look turned swiftly into the evil eye.

'I'm not geriatric, you know!'

Lindsey back-pedalled on a bicycle of excuses.

'Of course not, Grandma . . .'

'And don't call me that. Call me Gloria. I want everyone to call me Gloria, not Grandma, not ever again,' she snapped.

Everyone spent the rest of the day treading on eggshells each time they ran into her. A sigh of relief reverberated through the building once she'd departed for her own place.

'I feel so guilty,' Lindsey said later to her mother after she'd repeated the conversation. They were making the bed in room sixteen. The couple had been on honeymoon and overslept their checkout time. Well, that was what they said, though judging by the moans of delight coming from beyond the 'Do Not Disturb' sign, sleeping was not to blame.

Honey shook her head and buried a few punches into the pillow on her side of the bed.

'No need. Just look at it this way: it could have been worse. You could have suggested she join the Darby and Joan Club and taken up knitting.'

Lindsey stopped smoothing the sheet down on her side and looked tellingly at her mother.

Honey met her guilty expression with one of shock-horror. 'You didn't!'

'No, I didn't. Not in so many words.'

Honey adopted the saintly pose, hands together, eyes raised to the ceiling. 'Thank Heaven for small mercies!'

* * *

It would have been easy to forget Roland Mead and let bygones be bygones, except for one thing: Gloria Cross was not one to let sleeping dogs lie. Her dark periods brought her hotfoot from her flat to the hotel. For the fifth, tenth, twentieth time, family, hotel guests, the dishwasher, the greengrocer and the man who collected the laundry were treated to the details of what had happened and what she would say or do when she saw him again.

'I've tried phoning him, but am not getting a reply. I tried his office, but they told me he's gone abroad. Blast,' she said, after giving the home number another go.

Honey took the phone from her. 'Let me have a go.'

She rang. No reply.

She then rang the office and got the same answer as her mother had. 'He's out of the country, apparently.'

Her mother frowned. 'Are you sure?'

'I'm sure.'

Gloria pouted. 'It's annoying, but I do love men of international standing. He did mention Budapest and Prague a few times.'

Honey frowned. 'Did he really? Does he buy meat from there? Bit strange if he does seeing as he boasts that all his meat is British. Purely a sales pitch I suppose. Hotel meat orders are very lucrative along with school meals, etc. But I have seen his trucks. International is painted along the side in very large letters.'

'He goes over there a lot.'

Honey's thoughts were in overdrive. Mead was a braggart and yet he kept quiet about the international side of his business. 'I wonder why,' she mused.

Her mother was wearing a growly look. 'I'm out for his blood. Roland Mead doesn't make a fool of me and get away with it. I'm onto him. Just you wait and see.'

CHAPTER THIRTY-THREE

Steve's place, eight o'clock, come prepared. That was how Honey presented the occasion to her mature but still active hormones.

Dressed to knock Steve Doherty out of his socks, she was poised on the curb like a ballet dancer about to leap into action. The pavements were still wet but the rain had stopped. Cue right: a big car going too fast and heading her way. The wheels hit a pothole full of water; the water hit Honey.

'Thanks.'

She stood there drenched in water. It trickled from her hair and through her make-up, leaving sooty streaks down her face. Her pressed, fresh clothes were soaked and limp. And why had she brought her day bag? It was big and tan and not at all suitable for an evening out. She undid the zipper and peered inside. She groaned. The big pink brassiere was taking up most of the room. She'd shoved it in there after taking it from her mother and forgotten it was there. It just had to go.

Tomorrow, she determined, they were off back to auction.

She rolled her eyes. What sort of night was this going to be?

She considered calling the whole thing off. Her right foot moved to go home, her left stayed put. Half of her wanted Steve Doherty, the other half wanted to leave well alone. Her track record with men influenced the latter response, but what was left of her hormones were willing and able.

So she stayed. And waited.

Steve drove up carefully, avoiding the small lake in the road. He wound down his window and peered out, briefly surveying her from top to toe. 'Is the wet look in just now?'

She jerked the car door open and got in. 'Drive.'

'OK.'

She sat silently and sullenly. Seductive was no longer a word anyone could use to describe the way she looked. Steaming might be better — steaming temper, steaming clothes, *and* she was steaming up the windows. Steve adjusted the air conditioning so that it blew directly onto the windscreen.

Steve did a circuit of the inner city — over Pulteney Bridge, past the old Admiralty building now turned into luxury apartments, over the river, back over the river turning back into the city.

Once she had noticed that they were going around in a circle, Honey frowned. 'Where are you going?'

'You tell me. You phoned me. Told me we had to call in on someone before we went to dinner. You didn't say who.'

Honey apologised. 'My mother wants to unburden herself. *Again.*' She said it with a groan. She was so looking forward to an evening with Steve at his place. Her mother's phone call had scuppered that.

Steve made a face.

'In order to get him out of her system, she's going to pick Roland Mead to pieces.'

'Like a vulture?'

Honey grimaced. 'Hell hath no fury like a woman scorned.'

Steve shivered. 'Sheesh!'

Her mother's flat had cost around the same as a detached farmhouse with forty acres. Not that her mother would have ever considered living in a farmhouse, surrounded by all that grass and mud. She was more a kitten-heel type than green wellington boots.

They heard her just as they were approaching the front door. She was looking down at them from her balcony. Built in the early nineteenth century, the balcony was constructed of wrought iron. It had a Napoleonic look about it, a bit like those found in the French Quarter of New Orleans, and was crammed with flowers.

'About time. I've poured three sherries.'

'I hate sherry,' Steve murmured.

'Humour her,' muttered Honey from the corner of her mouth.

Honey stepped back so she could see better. Her mother's face was framed by pink geraniums and purple petunias.

She did her bit on dishy Doherty's behalf. 'Steve's driving, so no sherry for him.'

Her mother's head bobbed in acknowledgement before disappearing.

'Thanks,' said Steve, as Honey punched in the security number.

'No great shakes, except that I'll probably end up swilling yours back as well. Not good. I hate the stuff.'

As usual, her mother was impeccably dressed in a navy-and-white top trimmed with red buttons on the sleeves and in a diagonal line across her chest. Her trousers were red and matched her toenails and her lipstick.

Eyes outlined with Estée Lauder's best gave Honey the once over. 'You look terrible.'

Honey bit her tongue. 'It wasn't intentional. I looked good when I started out.'

Her mother's look of horror was undiminished. 'Who did it?'

'A car went through a puddle.'

Her mother handed her a schooner of sherry. Wanting to get it over with, she downed it in one. Like Steve, she found it too sweet and too rich. Her mother knew this. She'd told her enough times. Cod liver oil came in the same category; her mother considered it good for her. Normally she was totally opposed to alcohol, but for some reason sherry and port wine were exempt — or had been. Things had changed recently thanks to Roland Mead.

'You could do with another.'

Dark liquid glugged like oil into the glass.

'Drink it.'

Holding back a grimace, Honey gave in, this time sipping, making it last in case she got poured a third.

Steve sipped at his orange juice. She envied him.

Her mother turned silent, her eyes downcast and her lips pressed tightly together.

'Aren't you having one?' Honey asked her.

'Certainly!' Snapping out of her reverie, she reached for the decanter.

'Allow me,' said Steve.

Her mother raised her finely plucked eyebrows, looking surprised that someone who disliked shaving could be such a gentleman.

'Say when,' he said.

'When' didn't happen until the dark-red liquid was a hair's breadth from the rim of the glass.

Her mother tilted the glass and drank the lot, and Honey exchanged a surprised look with Steve. Roland Mead had replaced her mother with an alcoholic alien.

'Right!' said Gloria Cross, firmly setting the glass back on the tray. 'Now let's dish the dirt! I'll teach you to cross me, Roland Mead!' She held her daughter's eyes and shook her head. 'I knew I should never have trusted a man with tattoos.' She narrowed her eyes. 'My own mother told me never to trust a man with tattoos, especially when they were hidden from view.'

Honey felt a deep warmth creep up her neck. Was her mother saying what she thought she was saying? Come to think of it, she'd never noticed tattoos on any *exposed* surface of Roland Mead's body.

She and Steve exchanged looks of surprise. They were reaching the same conclusion.

Her mother leaned close — surprisingly close — to Steve, the man who didn't shave enough for her liking. Her eyes narrowed.

'I phoned his office and became such a nuisance they passed me onto one department after another. I ended up talking to somebody in the warehouse. He sounded discontented with his job. People fed up with their jobs are always glad of bending somebody's ear. Cyril, that was his name, has worked there for years and can't wait to retire. He loved talking to me, telling me all that was wrong and how Roland takes advantage of his good nature. Went on to say how often he's out of the country and gets phone calls at all hours from people in Eastern Europe. Reckons there's more going on than bringing in meat. That's what he told me. In his opinion Roland has too much to do with foreigners. In and out with their vans and their trucks down at that new frozen place of his in Avonmouth. I took a drive down there thinking I might collar him, but he wasn't around. My, you ought to see that place. It must have cost him a small fortune. He's always on about it. And all those vans he has. According to Cyril, he bought twelve new ones this year alone. Can you imagine that?'

Steve frowned. 'I don't quite get the gist of what you're saying.'

'It's obvious,' said Gloria, shooting him an elderly citizen's *I know better than you* look. 'He's overstretched himself and he's cutting corners to keep the bank manager happy. That's why he's importing from over the water. It's cheap and he can sell it dear. But he keeps pretty hush hush about it. But I worked it out. I put two and two together.'

'Where do the trucks come from?'

Her mother thought about it. 'I think he said from all over Europe; a lot from Eastern Europe. He's got a plant there, you see — what they call a processing plant.' She nodded emphatically and a hard gleam came into her eyes. 'I saw cash change hands. A driver was mouthing off. He was speaking foreign, but I caught the English words. Roland didn't know I overheard. I was supposed to stay in the car.'

Steve rested his elbows on his knees, clasped his hands beneath his chin and fixed his eyes on her mother's face. Steve could do wonders with his eyes. 'So what was said exactly?'

A conclusion came creeping into Honey's mind. Was it a wild guess, or was she finally on the right track? One person might be able to help her. While Steve and her mother continued to talk, she rang Casper. Neville, his receptionist, answered at first.

'He's in the bath.'

What is it with that man?

'He'll wash all his natural oils away.'

'I don't think that will cut much ice,' murmured Neville. 'He does a lot of thinking in the bath.'

'It can't be helped. I have to interrupt his train of thought. Ask him to put down his loofah and talk to me.'

'Not possible,' he replied in a superior tone. 'Ask me and I'll ask him.' Neville gave the impression of being a bulldog, guarding his master's territory — in this case the bathroom. In actuality he was a dab hand at flower arranging and interior design.

Honey sighed. 'Can you ask him whether he was first choice to head the judges at the Bath International Taste Extravaganza, the one Oliver Stafford won, or whether he was called in as second choice?'

Neville coughed nervously. 'I don't think that is *quite* the way to put it.'

Bullseye. 'Was he?'

Neville lowered his voice. 'Well . . . he was . . . in a way. There were some who said he had far too *distinguished* a palate for such a commercial venture. You know of course that our chef, Jean Pierre, did not enter?'

She knew, of course. Jean Pierre was of the opinion that any chef who wasn't French was just a cook. Entering competitions was not part of his remit.

'So who was supposed to be chair?' Again, Honey knew the answer. But she wanted to hear it from him.

Neville's deep sigh of relief reverberated out of the receiver. 'Sylvester Pardoe. He has his own restaurant and hotel in Oxford. At the last minute someone pointed out that he knew too many of the contestants to be impartial, so Casper took charge. Is that all you wanted to know, or do you still need to disturb Casper?'

'Can you tell me who pointed out the fact?'

'No. No idea. Someone with a vested interest?'

Carmelli — or Smudger?

After thanking him, she switched off her phone. She knew her eyes were shining. She could see the fact just by looking at Steve. His were shining too, reflecting hers because he knew she'd learned something important.

Steve's happy look of impending enlightenment disappeared, replaced by a questioning look. 'And?'

'Just a minute.'

She pressed a familiar key on her phone. Smudger answered.

'What sort of dish was Oliver Stafford cooking up at the contest?'

'Something with chicken, same as the rest of us.'

'Cut up or whole chicken breasts?'

'Um.' Smudger thought about it. 'His dish consisted of cutting up the breasts. I think it was some kind of variation on chicken à la king, though not so mundane as that. Mundane enough, though,' he added with waspish disdain.

Steve was eyeing her expectantly. 'Well?'

Although a bit squiffy, her mother was eyeing her expectantly too, though through a sherry-induced haze. 'Well, Hannah, darling? Spill the beans!'

'The meat. That's what this was all about.' She turned to Steve. 'You found ground mixed meat in Richard Carmelli's stomach. I know for a fact that his last meal was coronation chicken. I saw him ladling the portions into cartons, and he told me himself that he was having some for lunch. He said he had loads of it to get rid of and was taking some home with him. And before he shot off to Charmy Down, he cleared his fridge out. There was nothing in it when we checked.'

Steve looked incredulous. 'And someone killed him for taking his work home? I can't see it. Stealing, yes, but nicking a chicken is pretty low in the crime pecking order.'

He grinned and tugged at the lock of hair falling over his forehead.

Honey fixed him with narrowed eyes that dared him to continue joking. 'Very droll. But that was it. It wasn't chicken; it was a mixture of ground-up chicken and pork. It's cheap and comes in from Eastern Europe. My EHO told me all about it.'

Visits from environmental health officers were never welcome. A prerequisite for the job was the ability to get chefs' and hoteliers' backs up. Mr Westlake was retiring, and perhaps it was out of a sense of remorse that he'd accepted a cup of Earl Grey and talked of the derring-do going on in the industry.

Carried away with this train of thought, Honey failed to control the right hand that reached for the sherry and topped her glass up. She was on a roll.

'The meat comes in from Eastern Europe,' she was saying. 'Mead has a processing plant there. Standards are not as high as here. To save time and money, some white meats like poultry and pork are shoved in together, especially when it comes to ground meats used in pies and curry-type dishes. No one can really tell the difference — which is why Smudger was right in saying that Oliver Stafford had stolen our chicken breasts. Oliver and Stella had found out that Casper had replaced Sylvester Pardoe at the last minute and Casper would taste the difference! Casper St John Gervais is the most fastidious, discerning epicurean I know.'

Steve looked at her blankly.

She explained. 'An epicurean has a very discerning palette. It's Roman. A god of food or something — I think.'

He nodded good-naturedly. 'I can live with that. And the murderer is?'

Honey didn't answer. Steve followed her sidelong gaze to her mother.

'I wouldn't put anything past that man,' her mother snarled before sliding back onto the settee, her head sinking into a plush velvet cushion.

There was no point in waking her up. Dinner was still on and gooseberries were not welcome.

CHAPTER THIRTY-FOUR

Tired of living in a city flat, Steve had purchased a small cottage on the Wellsway, the main road connecting Bath with the ancient city of Wells. Both cities vied for trade in the tourist market, Bath boasting its Roman Baths and Wells its thousand-year-old cathedral.

A continuous stream of traffic passed the front of the property during daylight hours, quelled at around six thirty and spasmed for the rest of the night.

It boasted a rear entrance with convenient private parking. Steve drove round the back and nosed the car against his garden wall. A dozen stone steps descended into a small but pretty garden.

Two more steps took them into an octagonal conservatory; two steps more and they were standing in the kitchen-diner.

Honey eyed her surroundings with interest. She'd expected a muddled, masculine interior with no thought given to design or tidiness — somewhere to sleep and unwind. It wasn't like that. Spotlights had been set into the floor and ceiling, their focused beams the only barrier between the cooking and eating area. The sitting room was forward of that.

He told her it had two bedrooms and a bathroom upstairs. 'You can try them later.'

That cheeky grin again.

This was the point at which a woman of mature years and rounded body got cold feet. Cover of darkness was best before she considered taking a bedroom test.

Perhaps her nervousness showed, or perhaps he was nervous too. She wasn't just one of his colleagues. They had a relationship going on here — both working and otherwise.

Talking about work formed the breathing space for both of them.

As Honey washed and prepped the lettuce, Steve added olive oil to the pasta and a dash of Valpolicella to the sauce.

'We'll drink the rest,' he said, filling two glasses to the brim.

Honey eyed the generous measures. 'Well, they're certainly more than the advised daily measure.'

Steve handed her a glass. 'You can cope. You can cope with more than you think you can. Cheers.'

Their eyes met as they took the first sip. The wine tasted warm and rounded as it rolled around her tongue. They were so close. Too close. Her nerves were in knots. Just a little more time . . . Like a tennis pro at Wimbledon, she took the initiative and batted a safe return.

'So! Was there anything on the security tape?'

'From the Beau Brummell?' He looked away. 'No. The tapes weren't running during the early hours of the morning.'

Honey frowned. Her nervousness dissipated. 'Are you sure?'

'Definitely. The tapes are run every night and kept for a week. But there were none — none at all for that week between the hours of one and six in the morning. They were switched off.'

The pillow and a rolled-up sleeping bag popped into her mind. 'The security guard was asleep in the rear bathroom.' She explained about washing her injured hand on the day he'd interviewed Stella Broadbent and seeing them there.

'But Peter says that when he crept back, there *was* a security guard on duty.'

Steve offered her a taster of sauce from the wooden stirring spoon.

'Which means that he'd either forgotten to switch it on . . .'

'Or,' said Honey sucking back the hot sauce. She frowned. 'Was there only one security guard? I mean, did they work in shifts? One on, one off? Which security guard did the bedroll belong to? The one Peter saw on duty or the one due to come on?'

'That's the way it usually works.' Steve drank more wine then frowned as well. 'There are too many people in fancy dress around here.'

Honey nodded. 'And pork pretending to be chicken.'

'What?'

'And foreign truck drivers . . .'

Honey's voice trailed off into nothing. Her thoughts were going full pelt. 'What was that my mother said?'

Steve too was looking thoughtful. Honey guessed that his thoughts were racing along the same track as her own.

'Money changing hands at a meat warehouse,' he said in a low voice. 'And who was SAP?' Steve added.

Honey frowned. 'SAP?'

'It was written in a notebook we found with Richard Carmelli's things.'

Suddenly all thoughts of going to bed with him flew out of the window. This was all wrong. It should never have happened.

'You didn't tell me that.'

'Didn't I?'

'I thought we were supposed to be sharing information.' She felt quite hurt.

'We thought it was something to do with Pardoe. Except that he doesn't have a second name.'

'It's not a name. It's computer software!' Honey put down her glass, picked up the phone and called the hotel.

Mary Jane answered. Honey made impatient sounds and insisted on speaking to Lindsey.

'What's the name of the software big companies use on their computers?'

'Are you talking multi-platform?'

'You tell me.'

'SAP.'

'Can we get into that and find out something about a company's dealings?'

'We don't have SAP on our system. Like I've just said, it's multi-platform — human resources, building maintenance, supplies, tax and so on. We're not big enough. What are you up to?'

'Is there any way we can get into someone else's system and find out their international dealings?'

'You mean is there any way yours truly can do that?'

'You've got it.'

'No.'

'Drat!'

'But I know a man who can. Whose system are we hacking into?'

'R. W. Mead, International Meatpackers and Warehousing.'

'Sounds about the right size and type of operation. I'll get back to you.'

Steve looked puzzled. 'What are you up to?'

'As my beloved daughter has just pointed out, SAP is a multi-platform computer system used by large companies.'

'You sound very informed.'

Honey made a face. 'I'm only repeating what I've been told.' Her thoughts began having their own Derby Day, racing around her mind. This time Steve's thoughts weren't with her but on a track of their own.

He stroked a lock of hair back from her forehead. 'Look, let's enjoy tonight and get back to work in the morning. What do you say? Hmm?'

His touch made her tingle, but the thought that he'd kept something so vital from her left her feeling annoyed.

'While we're waiting for a result, I think we should take a look at Roland Mead's warehouse in Avonmouth,' she said. She watched closely for his reaction.

'Christ!' He brushed his hand over his eyes. 'Look, Honey . . .'

She pressed on. 'My mother said he has deliveries once a week, and one's due tonight. Don't you think it would be a good idea to get over there and check it out?'

Steve sighed and looked her up and down. 'I could think of other things I'd prefer to check out, but . . .' He shook his head disconsolately. 'I take your point.' Sighing again, he turned off the glow beneath the sauce and the pasta and set down his spoon. He then proceeded to make a big show of tidying things up. He was neat, but she guessed he wasn't always *that* neat.

She knew he would question going at all. And why not? After all, she was mostly going on gut instinct. He'd have to dig for her Achilles heel to dissuade her. But first he'd have to find it.

Knowing how much she liked her food, he gave it one more try. 'I take it dinner can wait?'

Honey grimaced. She hadn't expected him to home in that accurately, but prided herself on swift counteraction. 'My waistline can go without.'

Unfortunately, her stomach was not in unison with her waistline and wouldn't stop rumbling on the journey from Bath to the Severnside port of Avonmouth. She considered getting a Mars bar in a service station on the main road close to the port. Sheer willpower and pride held her off. Steve would say, 'We should have had dinner and let this be until tomorrow.'

As it was, he'd hardly spoken a word since they'd got into the car. He stared grimly over the steering wheel at the pitch-black night and the dour surroundings.

Transport depots, warehousing and industrial units, some new and some square and flat and dating from the sixties, lined each side of the road. The main gates were open.

Steve's gaze searched the perimeter. 'There's bound to be a security guard.'

Just at that moment an articulated truck with foreign number plates rolled in through the gate. The name *R. W. Mead, International Meatpackers and Warehousing* was emblazoned along the side.

A truck brandishing foreign number plates had just pulled in. The stench of hot diesel fumes fell over them.

Four men stepped forward expectantly, their figures silhouetted against the bright light from within. The driver jumped down from the long-distance sleeping cab and joined them.

Steve crept further forward. Honey followed him to cower behind a dusty bush next to a gap in the railings. As he stepped out of the brightness, she recognised Roland Mead. He was smiling and slapping the men on the back. He shook hands with the driver. Something was said, but she couldn't hear what it was.

He wound an arm around the shoulders of a man wearing a black T-shirt and blue jeans. Roland's head was bent close to the other man's, as though he didn't want anyone else hearing what was said.

Honey strained to hear. Something about 'doing a good job of that one'.

Roland Mead slapped the man on the back again then disappeared behind the truck. An engine fired up. Headlights burst into life. The white Rolls Royce glided slowly out of the compound gates.

The man he'd been speaking to was now making his way back to the other men and facing them.

Honey saw his face. Her heart skipped a beat. She knew him. She felt Steve tensing beside her. He'd recognised him too. This was the security guard from the Beau Brummell Hotel. The *first* security guard, the one who'd lifted the wooden barrier. The second guard they'd come across, the one that should have been on duty, had been asleep. No wonder he'd been flustered.

The men laughed and joked, their voices the only sound on the deserted estate except for the distant hum of heavy traffic on the motorway.

Two of the men did something between the cab of the truck and its trailer where the air and fuel hoses clipped onto the brakes and the diesel tank.

'Two tanks,' whispered Doherty.

Honey said nothing, but guessed that had some significance.

The high-pitched sound of a forklift preceded its appearance. It drove up to the area between the truck and the trailer, to the exact spot where the men had been unclipping hoses and other connections. Accompanied by shouted instructions, the forklift edged away from the truck, the large fuel tank resting on its metal prongs.

One of the men raised his hand and called a halt. Honey and Doherty watched in amazement as the top of the supposed fuel tank was lifted like the lid of a suitcase.

Honey looked at Steve and read his expression. Fuel tanks didn't have hinges. They only had a hole where the fuel went in. One tank still remained.

Satisfied by the contents of the tank, the men followed the forklift into the warehouse.

She whispered to Steve. 'That's not a fuel tank is it?'

'Clever. Long-distance trucks travelling all over Europe often have two fuel tanks. That one possibly has one and a half. To avoid suspicion, fuel can still be pumped into it, but only fills the bottom half. The rest is courier space. And we can guess what that is, can't we?'

Steve dug into his pocket. 'Damn.'

'What is it?' said Honey.

'I need to call for backup.'

'Where's your phone?'

'I left it in a drawer at home, so it wouldn't disturb our night together. Can I borrow yours?'

Honey looked sheepish. 'I did the same thing.'

Steve groaned.

She felt stupid, but there was nothing to be done. They'd both been of the same mind.

Slinging her big bag more securely behind her, Honey eased her way through the fence. Doherty followed, swearing under his breath. Honey imagined the police trained their officers not to do hare-brained things like this. She just flew by the seat of her pants. They had to take a look, to confirm their suspicions. Nailing Mead for food description violations was one thing. Nailing him for drug running was quite another. No wonder he could afford a house in the Royal Crescent.

The light pooling outwards from the wide, truck-size entrance was suddenly dimmed.

Honey paused, narrowing her eyes so she could see better now the glare had subsided.

Steve signalled that they should move to the right.

Honey pointed at the tops of two, perhaps three heads she could see through a glass partition in a brightly lit office. Hopefully all four men were inside. If Doherty was having the same thoughts, he gave no sign of it. They eased away following the rubber trail markings of the forklift.

A sign just ahead said 'Cold Store'. Without saying a word to each other, they headed in that direction.

Other signs saying 'Wash your hands before handling meat products,' proliferated around a set of double doors. There were glass windows at eye level. On the other side, Honey could see carcass after carcass hanging from metal hooks. To their right the hooks and a row of stainless-steel shelving stood empty, no doubt awaiting the delivery standing outside and the morning shift that would unload that particular consignment.

The forklift stood abandoned in front of the shelving, its arms still holding its load.

Carried away by thoughts of glory, Doherty slid up the safety bar that held the doors closed.

The two of them stepped inside, and Honey's breath caught in her throat as the chill hit her.

Steve's face was flushed with excitement. 'Look at this!'

He eased his fingertips beneath what looked like a lip running around the tank.

Even before he heaved it open, Honey guessed what they would see.

Metal scraped against metal as he pushed open the lid.

Silence reigned.

Shivering now, Honey wrapped her arms around herself. 'I take it that's not self-raising flour.'

Doherty shook his head. 'No. That stuff's much more dangerous to your health.'

'Don't you have to taste it like they do on TV cop shows?'

He shook his head.

Something made Honey turn round. A pair of eyes looked back at her through the window.

'Steve!'

He turned and saw them too.

'Hey!'

He sprinted and fell shoulder first against the door. It didn't budge. Wrinkles appeared at the sides of the eyes looking in from the other side. Honey guessed the guy was laughing.

'Let us out!' Steve shouted, beating his fists against the door.

Something appeared in front of the pair of eyes. Honey recognised what it was.

'That's a thermal switch. It alters temperature by remote control.'

The needle was presently pointing at the palest band of blue, but even as they watched, it began to move towards a deeper, more dangerous shade.

CHAPTER THIRTY-FIVE

'We have to keep warm. Keep talking. Tell me about your job with the Probation Service.'

She looked at him. 'While I'm jumping up and down?'

'Keep jumping. You must keep jumping.'

The cold was intense. The fact that they were surrounded by frozen-solid sides of cow didn't help.

'So. Go on. Tell me.'

'I worked in IT, and I don't mean computers. Perish the thought. I started in Probation typing out social enquiry reports, and then I got promoted to senior clerical officer in Intermediate Treatment.'

'What does that mean when it's at home?'

Honey continued to jump up and down and flap her arms. Her breath was still white. Her fingers felt numb. 'Well, we used to take young offenders camping, rock climbing, orienteering, sailing — Duke of Edinburgh Award type stuff, things to inspire young minds and divert them from their criminal ways.'

'Sounds . . . more like . . . days out . . . on jollies . . . to me,' said Steve, his words expelled between vigorous arm waving and bouts of jumping.

'It's termed *therapy*,' said Honey, stopping to catch her breath.

Steve stopped too. Usually he'd have made some disbelieving comment. But not here. He shivered.

'Scientists reckon that we lose more heat out of the top of our heads than anywhere else.' He rubbed at his ears and did his best to pull his collar up higher. 'Wish I had a hat. A balaclava would be nice. I hate having cold ears.' He was right to be worried. His ears were turning blue. He rubbed them again.

Honey had a brainwave. She unzipped her big brown bag, searching for the unmistakable stitching of 'Big Bertha'.

'Madonna, eat your heart out,' she muttered, grabbing the strap and pulling it out.

Steve was slapping his arms around himself to keep warm. He stopped when he saw the mighty J-cups.

'Are they human?'

'Made for a very large woman. And now we're going to wear them. Don't worry,' she said in response to the nervous look in his eyes. 'You don't have to take anything off. You can wear it on your head.'

He looked at her in horror. 'Will I hell!'

'Think of your ears, Steve.'

'I'll risk it.'

'Look,' she said, spreading the brassiere out so he could better understand the possibilities. 'We'll both use it. You have one cup on your head, I'll have the other. And we can cuddle up together to keep warm. Even jump up and down a bit.'

The last bit seemed to sway him. He didn't even struggle when she placed one of the supersized cups on his head and the other on hers. The side panels were left dangling over their ears. Steve had the hooked side, and she had the eyes. She thought about tying them together. Steve had the same thought. 'That's better,' he said.

Like conjoined twins, they were closer than close, the bra cups fitting them like caps.

Honey glanced at their blurred reflection in the stainless steel. 'We look like a couple of mushrooms.'

Steve made a shuddering sound with his lips. 'Brrrr. I know I wanted to get into your underwear, but this isn't quite what I had in mind.'

* * *

'I wanted to speak to your mother before she goes to bed.'

It was one o'clock in the morning and Lindsey had been clearing down when her grandmother phoned.

'She's not home.'

'I was worried she was thinking about spending the night with that Doherty character, the cop who can't afford the price of a razor. But I phoned her and she didn't answer. And then I phoned the police station and asked them to phone him, but they got no answer either. OK, I understand your mother not answering her phone, but a cop would. I'm certain he would.'

It almost choked Lindsey to admit she might be right, but she did have a point. Like a novice trapeze act, her mother and Doherty swung to and fro as though timing the right moment to jump. Up until now they hadn't quite made it, but perhaps her grandmother was right. It could finally have happened, but Steve Doherty wouldn't want to miss out on any police action.

Gloria went on to relate what had gone on earlier that evening before they'd dashed off. 'Roland Mead is a scumbag. I think they've gone off to prove it.'

'Perhaps you're right.'

'Of course I'm right.'

Lindsey promised she would check and call her grandmother back. The first thing she did was to phone the police and ask for Steve Doherty.

'He's not here. Can you call back later?'

'Do you happen to know where he is?'

The female voice hesitated as though in two minds about whether she wanted to know where Doherty was. Good practice won over jealousy. 'I'll check.'

After a few muted mutterings she came back on the line. 'No one's seen him. We've been trying to get hold of him, but he's not answering his home or personal phone.'

That said it all as far as Lindsey was concerned. As she replaced the phone, her eyes caught sight of something on her mother's scribble pad. The 'chicken' in 'coronation chicken' was underlined. So was the word 'pork'. Beside it were the initials 'RC'. Her heart skipped a beat. Richard Carmelli. Chicken and pork. Her thoughts did cartwheels as her concern for her mother increased. Everyone had assumed the killing of these chefs was about rivalry and something that had happened three years before. But was it really about butchers and the Trade Description Act, or was she jumping the gun?

Then she picked up her phone and read a text from Warren Slade regarding details from Roland Mead's computer system. She rang her grandmother and explained what was afoot.

'There's big money involved and the sums don't add up. Have you any idea where my mother could be?'

CHAPTER THIRTY-SIX

Gloria Cross insisted on accompanying her granddaughter to Avonmouth. Lindsey had tried getting the police to keep a look out for her mother's car, but no one seemed that interested. Obviously Steve Doherty's reputation had a lot to do with it. Shrinking wallflower he was not! And they certainly weren't interested in checking Roland Mead's cold store at Avonmouth.

'I'll speak to DI Doherty as soon as he gets back tomorrow,' said the spokesperson at the other end of the phone.

They checked Doherty's place before leaving. His car was gone and he'd left a table lamp on in the front room, easily seen when Lindsey had peered through a window.

Lindsey floored it to Avonmouth with her grandmother navigating. Gloria Cross narrowed her eyes as she peered into the darkness. 'I don't remember this many trees.'

Lindsey rolled her eyes and pulled into the curb. 'So, where is his place?'

Her grandmother pointed towards the trees. 'On the other side of them, I think. There's a lane through there, see?'

Normally Lindsey didn't like walking down unlit lanes at night, but Avonmouth was like a ghost town after dark. Rapists and murderers were likely to be thin on the ground.

The only criminals around would be more interested in pinching tyres or car parts from one of the many outlets lining the roads.

Lindsey looked round as they crossed the road. There was no sign of her mother's car. Maybe it was hidden, either by her mother or someone else. It was very likely she was with Steve in his car. Either way she was out and about somewhere.

The night was warm, but the sudden profusion of worrying thoughts made her shiver. The trees rustled in a warm breeze as they found their way over the soft ground. The lane was a forgotten place, something left behind when the prefabricated warehouses had been built. It led to a mound of earth left by the contractors. Over time it had become covered in grass and foliage. At its summit was a concrete wall.

'I'm going up here,' said Lindsey, her feet slipping on the damp grass.

'Wait for me. I've got my trainers on. They're blue and silver. Designer, of course. Do you like them?'

'Not now, Grandma.'

'Gloria!'

'I am not calling you 'Gloria', Grandma!'

She clambered up the slope, presuming her grandmother was incapable of following her. She was quickly proved wrong. Red talons grabbed the hem of her jersey and hung onto it.

'Where are we?' asked her grandmother, hardly breathless from her climb.

'There,' said Lindsey. She pointed upwards. Gloria looked up at a huge sign saying, 'R. W. Mead, International Meat Packers and Warehousing'.

She spit into the grass. 'That man is too big for his boots!'

The concrete wall in front of them proved to be a parapet. Lindsey kept low, kneeling and showing just her head above the wall. She saw a door in the back of the building, but no security cameras. That didn't mean there were none, just that they were hidden from view. 'Should we be creeping around like this?'

Gloria stuck her head up over the parapet. 'Why not?'

Lindsey placed a hand over her head and pressed her back down.

'There could be cameras.'

'I'm in no mood to be put off by cameras or criminals. Anyway, are we one-hundred-per cent sure your mother's in there?'

'It seems that way.'

Gloria tutted. 'I can't believe Roland's taken your mother prisoner. Why would he do that?' She took a deep breath. 'Oh my God. Do you think it's a kinky sex thing?'

Lindsey threw her grandmother a look of pure, jaw-dropping shock. Grandmothers aren't supposed to know about that kind of stuff!

'What do you know about it?'

'One of those Xcite books sneaked into my Mills and Boon collection,' Gloria replied with a contemptuous sniff.

Lindsey shook away the shock and concentrated on what she was here to do. Taking big strides she began edging along the wall, searching for a way down to the rear door. Sure enough, a gap had been left at the very end where the back wall met that belonging to the property next door. Although only narrow, she was sure she could get through.

'Stay here,' she hissed to her grandmother.

'Like hell I will!'

Gloria eased through the wall after her, picking her way down over the tumbled hardcore and slick clay. Nails scratched on the side wall as they felt their way to the flat ground. Lindsey heard her grandmother cursing as a false fingernail popped off into the night.

The two women sprinted across to the door, Gloria remarking on how much she loved trainers and how she'd buy more now that she knew designer labels were available.

'There's bound to be an alarm,' said Lindsey, grateful for her grandmother's casual indifference to the danger they were in. Her heart was playing leapfrog. The sudden sound of voices sent them scurrying behind two huge waste bins, one labelled 'Meat Waste', the other 'Cardboard/Recyclables'.

A man emerged, whistling as he lifted the lid of the meat waste bin. A hoard of angry bluebottles rose in a buzzing mass. The lid slammed down and then he was gone.

'No alarm,' whispered Lindsey, greatly relieved. If people were working inside then no alarm would be on.

She felt the door handle, trying not to rattle it too much. It didn't budge.

'Locked. Now what?'

'We use a key.' Gloria bubbled with excitement. She was obviously enjoying this.

Lindsey was taken by surprise as a whole bunch of keys appeared, as likely to rattle as the door. Lindsey grabbed them. 'Where did you get these?'

'I stole them from Roland,' said her grandmother. 'I was going to throw them in the river just to inconvenience him, but I figured they might come in handy. I was right too.'

Pulse racing and hands sweaty with fear, Lindsey studied each key. Some were of the Yale type, made for a slim, round lock. The exterior light above the door picked out the most likely in the bunch. One by one she tried the longer, old-fashioned variety, getting lucky with the fourth one on the ring. Heart racing, Lindsey pulled the door slowly open, praying it wouldn't rattle or that some big galoot was standing on the inside waiting to grab them.

Inside was dimly lit. Offices behind glass partitions clung to the grey walls. A blank wall ran along their left-hand side. Above them, banks of compressors hummed in unison, working to keep the cold store down to temperature.

Lindsey was amazed when her grandmother pushed past her, keeping low and padding ahead like a preying panther in tracksuit and trainers.

'Grandma! Stop!' Lindsey rasped. This was foolhardy. If she went too far forward without checking, someone was bound to see her.

She stopped dead, turned and loped back. 'You're right. Softly, softly. It's these shoes. They keep running away with me.'

Gloria's behaviour was beginning to unsettle Lindsey. She tried a few deep breaths before continuing, grabbing her grandmother's arm just in case she felt the urge to sprint across to the other side. She nudged her and put a finger to her lips, indicating she remain silent.

'I didn't say a word,' hissed an indignant Gloria.

Lindsey clapped a hand over her parted lips and pointed to a shadow emerging into the open space.

At the other side of the empty space, a man dressed in a black T-shirt and jeans walked over to a set of double doors, emitting twin circles of light. For a moment his head obscured one of the windows. An ash-grey darkness gave objects shape but not outline.

He fiddled with something in his hands and said something she couldn't make out. Whatever he said ended in a chuckle; not a jolly chuckle, more a menacing one, the sort mad scientists sport as part of their stock in trade.

As he moved away the light fell out of the porthole again. He disappeared to their left, his lengthy shadow diminishing with each echoing step.

With the beating of her heart pounding in her ears, Lindsey counted the passing seconds. Thirty, sixty, ninety . . . He had to be gone by now?

'They've got to be over there,' whispered Gloria.

Lindsey nodded and whispered a quick response.

Running fast and low, they gained the other side of the storage area and the big double doors.

Lindsey peered in through the porthole on her door. Her jaw dropped.

Her grandmother was shorter so had to stand on tiptoe. 'Wish I'd worn heels,' she muttered before her jaw dropped like an elevator to basement level. 'Is that some kind of fashion statement?' She sounded intrigued rather than surprised.

Honey and Steve were standing together in the next room with what appeared to be a large bra over their heads.

'It's practical,' said Lindsey.

This was a very special moment. She hadn't told her mother in so many words, but she'd felt ashamed about getting involved with Oliver Stafford. She'd always prided herself on being a pretty good judge of character. Obviously she was not. It hurt and embarrassed her. Rescuing her mother and DI Doherty would help make things right.

Using both hands, she struggled to heave up the lever locking the door. While doing so, her mind leaped to the next logical step. 'Call for help, but do it outside in case someone hears you.'

'Will do.' Her grandmother grabbed the phone swinging from a chain around her neck and loped back the way they'd came.

Hearing footsteps again, she ducked back behind the waste bin. Her breathing sounded too loud even to her own ears. Could anyone else hear?

She heard footsteps come towards her hiding place, pause then retreat in another direction. Closing her eyes, she counted the seconds again. Ten, twenty, thirty . . .

Emerging from behind the bin, she made her way back to the freezer door, peered in and waved. Two faces as pale as frosted icing looked back at her and managed to return a hesitant, chilly wave of their own.

Wrapping both hands around the lever, she pushed it upwards. The lever made a clunking sound. A sliver of escaping air sighed as the seal was broken. Honey and Steve slid out right behind it, jumping up and down, teeth chattering and arms flapping in an effort to get warm.

Lindsey jumped with them. She'd done it. Suddenly someone touched her shoulder. If there'd been a high-jumping competition, she would have won it.

'I did it,' said her grandmother, looking mighty pleased with herself.

'I need to phone for backup,' said Steve his teeth chattering like castanets.

'Already done,' said Grandma.

'Not that I doubt you, but if you don't mind, a squad car will get here more quickly if I phone . . .' Shivering, Steve took her phone and went back inside the cold room so as not to be heard.

'That's a good idea,' whispered Gloria, a telling look in her eyes. 'The police should be informed.'

Honey noticed that look and it worried her. 'Who did you ring, mother?'

The whispering continued. 'Someone good at sorting out crooked butchers.'

On coming out from the cold room, Steve declared they had to lie low until they heard the wail of police sirens. 'Once we know we've got back-up, we can break cover. But not until then, otherwise we might all end up hung on meathooks.'

He ordered them to go back behind the wheelie bins.

Honey started to go with Lindsey and her mother, but Steve was off in the other direction. 'What about you?'

'I need to tackle them,' he whispered back.

'Alone?' Her eyes widened at the thought. Her fear wound like barbed wire around her belly. 'And you're unarmed. Come with us.'

His eyes twinkled and he shook his head. 'I'm going to start the ball rolling. I have to. And I do have a weapon — of sorts.'

He held up the brassiere; the ends were tied round his hands in garrotting mode. The steel wire between the cups would fit neatly against a windpipe.

Honey attached herself to his side. 'I'm coming with you.'

'No . . .'

'Yes. I need the action. I need to get my circulation going.'

'So do we,' said Lindsey and her grandmother.

Honey saw the mix of emotions flash through his eyes. Steve Doherty, roughie-toughie police officer, knew when he was beaten. Criminals were one thing; three generations of related females were something else.

They crept along behind him, making for where the security guard had disappeared. They found him and his cohorts in a small office at the end of the corridor. Three of them were sitting around a table drinking beer. The other, identifiable as the driver of the truck, was sound asleep on a scruffy sofa, his snores resonating out into the corridor.

'Do we wait?' whispered Honey.

He was about to shake his head, when Honey's mother had caught a fine, long fingernail on the frame surrounding the window.

'Drat! I paid good money for that!'

The men heard and sprang to their feet. The snoring evaporated.

Doherty looked anxious. He swore under his breath. They had no option but to act.

Kicking open the door, he barged in, his female support crowding in behind him. 'Halt! I'm a police officer.'

He fumbled to get out his warrant card, his 'weapon' still wound around his fingers. The men stared. For a moment they were dumbstruck.

What would have happened then was anybody's guess, except that the sirens started, screaming like banshees as they hurtled down St Andrew's Road and took the route to the R. W. Mead warehouses.

Mead's men ran but were pursued. In his haste to escape, the truck driver tripped over a roll of meat muslin and fell headlong into an empty waste drum lying on its side. Honey and Lindsey took advantage of the situation and upended it, trapping the man head down, his legs waving in the air.

Uniformed officers spilled through the door, grabbing the would-be escapees as Doherty directed.

'Him,' said Honey softly, her eyes alighting on the man in the black T-shirt. 'He's the one.'

'Chester,' said her mother. 'He's Roland Mead's chauffeur and does other stuff. Like Odd Job in that James Bond movie. He does everything for Roland, that dirty, stinking . . . That guy's got a whole load of different uniforms.'

'That figures.' Honey dragged her mother to one side. 'Leave it to Steve Doherty. This is his baby now. He'll have Roland arrested.'

Her mother nodded. 'Quite so. Good job he rang the police when he did.'

Lindsey was frowning and eyeing her grandmother suspiciously. 'I thought you rang them.'

Her mother looked sheepish. 'Not exactly. I was bursting to get Roland well and truly sorted.'

A nerve twitched beneath Honey's left eye. She had the feeling she wasn't going to like the answer, but the question had to be asked. 'So who did you phone to sort out your ex?'

'Won't tell you. Not until you tell me who got into Roland's computer system and found that secret file.'

Honey looked at each of them in turn, wondering what the hell they were talking about. Lindsey explained about the SAP system and hacking into Mead's computer system. 'Warren Slade, he that was indisposed in room twenty. He found the secret bills of lading for meat and the fuel bills and decided it didn't add up. There were journeys not accounted for, and the sizes of the fuel tanks didn't check out with the amount of fuel purchased. Warren Slade has a highly developed mathematical mind. It's all to do with probabilities and possibilities — at least, I think it is.' She looked at her mother and shrugged. 'You can't blame him for wanting some fun and getting left indisposed. He's a very intense sort of bloke, almost to the point of obsession.'

Her grandmother looked amused. 'So's the friend I rang to sort out Roland. He's got a thing about bad butchers and crap meat.'

Lindsey looked puzzled.

Honey burst out laughing. 'Haven't you guessed?' she said to her daughter.

CHAPTER THIRTY-SEVEN

That morning, Rozellia — her of the glorious black hair and swaying hips — was woken by a loud hammering at the front door. 'Do you hear that?'

Roland Mead stirred beside her, but did nothing about it. He mumbled something incoherent and snuggled down against the cool cotton pillow.

Rozellia swore in Italian. There was no other option but to slide her naked arms into a silk kimono. Padding down the stairs, she pondered on her reasons for staying with Roland. He was rich, but ignorant. Why hadn't she found herself a titled man, perhaps a count or a lord? A Swiss banker would have been equally acceptable, his wealth making up for lack of title. She could have stayed in Palermo, she mused, then frowned. Not Palermo. Much too provincial. Perhaps Rome.

On the plus side, he was so conceited about his sexual prowess, his power over women, that he didn't notice her penchant for young lovers; variety, in Rozellia's opinion, was definitely the spice of life. It suited her to be with him, at least for now.

The hammering continued. Rozellia's face clouded. The corners of her pouting mouth turned further downwards. Whoever was at the door was going to get a tongue-lashing.

She glanced at her watch. It had to be Chester. Convinced she was right, she released the security chain.

As Smudger swept in, both her and the door swung back and smacked against the wall. She was knocked to the ground. Smudger jerked her to her feet, his big hands holding tightly to her arms.

'Where is he?'

Her big eyes got bigger. 'Who are you?'

'I'm me. Where's the gaffer?'

Shocked to the core, she pointed in a vague way at the stairs.

Smudger grimaced. 'I'll find 'im!' he shouted, and bolted out of the hallway.

Rozellia, feeling somewhat dazed, slid down to the floor.

* * *

Smudger took the stairs two at a time. There were many doors along the landing, but one was showing a gap of some fifteen inches. He kicked that open with as much finesse as he had the front door.

'*You!*' he said.

If the man had been wearing pyjamas he would have grabbed his jacket collar and dragged him from the bed. As it was, Mead was naked — not a pretty sight in Smudger's opinion. Luckily the man had a hairy chest. Clutching great handfuls of chest hair, Smudger dragged Roland Mead from his bed and threw him across the room. His toupee, the glue a little tacky from wearing it in bed, fell off and stuck to the carpet.

'Get dressed,' Smudger said with a ruthless glower. 'The game's up.'

Mead's first reaction was to go on the defence. 'I've eaten little pricks like you for lunch,' he snarled, his hands tightening into fists. 'Come on. Take a poke at me. Go on,' he said, dancing around and grinning as though he were Mohammed Ali. In fact, he looked like an overweight dancing bear.

Smudger fixed his thoughts on those Mead had wanted dead, his emotions turning to blubber when he thought of what had happened. He tried to focus on something less emotional, but something he nonetheless cared about. He thought of rubbish steaks — those with too much fat, those cut too thin, those with too little marbling. It worked. His fingers curled into his palms. His knuckles rose to the challenge. One left hook and it was all over.

* * *

Later, the police didn't question Roland Mead's bruised jaw. Smudger told them that Roland had fallen down the stairs. They'd nodded in mute understanding, having used the same excuse themselves on occasion.

'She's nothing to do with it,' he added when they attempted to take Rozellia. 'I'll take care of her.'

He smiled at her.

Rozellia smiled right back. This was such fun! She liked the thought of a younger, more virile man taking care of her. OK, he wasn't rich, just one plaything of many, but things were coming on top with regard to Roland. She'd heard rumours.

Now she had a role to fill, as a witness testifying against her former lover. She'd known of the comings and goings at all hours of the day and night. She could give times and details. And of course, a large reward was in the offing. A little money to please herself was exactly what she needed. Enough to buy a ticket to Rio.

CHAPTER THIRTY-EIGHT

They had a party to celebrate solving the case. Shattered from the ordeal in the freezer, Honey left Lindsey to make the arrangements. The list of guests pleased her; there they all were enjoying themselves in *her* bar, eating and drinking and laughing together. Even Mr Westlake, the environmental health officer, popped in.

'I don't really have the time,' he said. 'Though I am retired.' His worried eyes swiftly surveyed the room. 'Your mother's not around, is she?'

'Not yet,' said Honey. Westlake drank the last of his tonic water and bid a dignified though speedy retreat.

Before leaving to take some well-earned sleep, Steve laid out the whys and wherefores of what had happened. It turned out that Oliver Stafford had been getting a cut from the meat racket, but had stumbled onto Mead's other business. He'd been getting his cut of that too but had been angling for more. Stella had been in on the cheap meat deal, but got stroppy when Oliver dropped her.

'And Brodie?' Honey asked Steve.

'He was in financial difficulties, heard what was going on from a drunken Stella and tried to cut himself in. Stella was the loose link in the chain. She had a drink problem and couldn't help sounding off. The meat scam could lead to the drug scam. The gang controlling the deal couldn't chance a big bust. It was through Stella's drinking that Richard Carmelli found out. Once the people Mead worked for heard the bad news, they were all dead meat, so to speak. Mead had no choice. He was in deep with some very heavy dealers. Chester was one of them, a mover and shaker rather than an odd-job man. Mead was scared of him.'

'And my mother?'

'Two-pronged attack. Yes, I suppose he was after your meat order, but he knew of your position between the police and the Hotels Association. He had orders to keep a tab on things.'

Honey couldn't resist stroking his tired-looking head. 'Are you going to bed now?'

He smiled. 'Are you?'

Lindsey chose that moment to interrupt. 'What shall I do with this?' She held up the unwanted item Honey had won at auction.

It was on Honey's tongue to tell her to throw the thing away, but somehow she couldn't do that. It had come in useful during the proceedings. Chucking it was like discarding a lucky charm.

'Hide it away somewhere. I'll think on it.'

Steve made arrangements to see Honey the following night. There were a lot of things to catch up on that had nothing whatsoever to do with police work, but he needed to rest before expending more energy.

She'd never expected to get rid of the awful underwear, but the phone call from Andrea Andover came from out of the blue.

'I hear you've got something that I could make use of.'

Honey tried to think what on earth she had that the large stunt woman could possibly find a use for. Not a clue!

'I'm doing a part as a Valkyrie type for a Hollywood special — stunting for an actress who isn't up to doing anything more energetic than waddling into McDonalds.'

Honey was drawing a blank. She asked Andrea to elucidate.

'There's a little item I believe you can help me with. I'm willing to pay. Alistair at Bonhams mentioned you bought it by mistake, and in his opinion they're exactly what I'm looking for.'

Realisation, like a strip of elastic, went *ping* in Honey's brain. Did she mean the mountainous mammary hammock?

'As I said,' Andrea went on. 'It's a Valkyrie type of part — you know, metal corset and boob defenders the size of pan lids. I could do with a bit of softness to protect my natural padding, if you get my drift.'

'You can have the brazier — brassiere,' she corrected herself.

A price was negotiated. Delivery details were arranged. Honey couldn't help the self-satisfied smile as she ended the call.

'You look pleased with yourself,' said Lindsey, just back from running her grandmother home. 'Anything to do with me?'

'I've got rid of something I really had no use for.'

Lindsey slid behind the reception desk and checked the computer over her mother's shoulder. 'You sound like one of my girlfriends when they've dumped a guy.'

Honey eyed her daughter's face in the glow of the screen and felt suddenly guilty. 'I'm sorry about my reaction to the Oliver Stafford thingy. I must resolve not to make mountains out of molehills,' she said, turning back to the job in hand, stuffing the large bra into an equally large envelope.

'You're making a good start,' said Lindsey, nodding casually at the envelope. 'You were never going to grow into them.'

'Thankfully,' said Honey.

'Are you seeing Steve later after the party?'

Honey smiled. Her thoughts reverted to that slinky black dress with the buttons, her mother's fishnet stockings and the high-heeled red shoes. They were exactly what was needed.

'Tomorrow night. Once he's had a chance to catch up on his sleep.'

THE END

ALSO BY JEAN G. GOODHIND

HONEY DRIVER MYSTERY SERIES
Book 1: MURDER, BED & BREAKFAST
Book 2: MENU FOR MURDER

Thank you for reading this book.

If you enjoyed it please leave feedback on Amazon or Goodreads, and if there is anything we missed or you have a question about, then please get in touch. We appreciate you choosing our book.

Founded in 2014 in Shoreditch, London, we at Joffe Books pride ourselves on our history of innovative publishing. We were thrilled to be shortlisted for Independent Publisher of the Year at the British Book Awards.

www.joffebooks.com

We're very grateful to eagle-eyed readers who take the time to contact us. Please send any errors you find to corrections@joffebooks.com. We'll get them fixed ASAP.

Printed in Great Britain
by Amazon

87769165R00153